DEATH COMES TO THE VILLAGE

CATHERINE LLOYD

KENSINGTON BOOKS
www.kensingtonbooks.com

KENSINGTON BOOKS are published by

Kensington Publishing Corp.
119 West 40th Street
New York, NY 10018

All Kensington titles, imprints, and distributed lines are available at special quantity discounts for bulk purchases for sales promotion, premiums, fund-raising, and educational or institutional use.

Special book excerpts or customized printings can also be created to fit specific needs. For details, write or phone the office of the Kensington Special Sales Manager: Kensington Publishing Corp., 119 West 40th Street, New York, NY 10018. Attn. Special Sales Department. Phone: 1-800-221-2647.

Kensington and the K logo Reg. U.S. Pat. & TM Off.

ISBN-13: 978-0-7582-8733-5
ISBN-10: 0-7582-8733-X
First Kensington Trade Paperback Printing: December 2013

eISBN-13: 978-0-7582-8734-2
eISBN-10: 0-7582-8734-8
First Kensington Electronic Edition: December 2013

10 9 8 7 6 5 4 3 2 1

Printed in the United States of America

*This is for my Mum, Pat, because she can finally put
this one out on her coffee table without blushing.
Love you, Mum XX*

Chapter 1

February 1816
Kurland St. Mary, England

"Damnation!"

Major Robert Kurland jerked awake from his uneasy half-sleep to the hoot of a barn owl and glared out into the darkness, his breathing uneven, his mouth dry.

When he was able to walk, he was going to take a gun out to the woods and slaughter every nocturnal creature that had disturbed his sleep for the past few months. Selfish, perhaps, but when sleep was as precious to him as water to a dying man, completely justified.

He levered himself upright against his pillows, aware of a fresh pain pounding in his head and the now familiar dragging ache of his broken leg. Foolishly, he'd instructed his valet to leave the curtains open, and now the entire landscape beyond his windows was bathed in moonlight. His gaze turned to the black bottle of laudanum and glass of water on his nightstand. He could dose himself, slide back down into the warmth of his bed, and sink into oblivion. . . .

It was tempting. But despite his doctor's advice, Robert

was reluctant to take too much of the opiate. Its siren call dulled his senses and made him forgetful and quite unlike himself. Resolutely, he turned his attention to the problem at hand. He would never get back to sleep unless he closed the curtains. The old clock on the mantelpiece wheezed and struck twice. If he rang the bell, Bookman would come, but it seemed wrong to disturb the other man's rest. He would simply have to manage for himself.

Robert drew back the covers and studied his bandaged and splinted left leg. If he'd been a horse, they would have shot him, rather than painstakingly trying to reset his shattered bones. Sometimes during the last hellish months, he wondered if that would've been for the best. Even after all this time, his leg was still pretty damn useless. He used his upper body strength to pivot and placed both his feet on the floor. Even such a small effort made him sweat and curse like the lowest class of soldier he'd commanded.

He grabbed hold of the dresser next to his bed and lifted himself upright, carefully placing the majority of his weight over his right side. It wasn't that far to the windows, and there were plenty of objects he could use to support himself along the way. Part of him was revolted by the spectacle he made, dragging his wounded body around. The rest of him refused to give up. If he stayed in bed, he was afraid he would eventually lose the will to rise again.

He staggered from the dresser to the wing chair by the fireside and sat long enough to regain his breath and determination. In the distance, the squat tower of the Norman church that divided his property from the village proper stood stark against the night sky. There was a path from the side of Kurland Hall that led directly to the church and the boxed pew his family had occupied for Sunday worship for generations. Not that he believed in God anymore, but appearances had to be maintained.

When he recovered, he would certainly take his seat in his appointed place at the front of the church. He'd learned the value of setting a good example, first from his father and then from the army.

If he recovered . . .

Robert set his teeth and stood up again, his attention fixed on the large bay windows. Three more lurching steps brought him up against a small desk that creaked rather ominously when he rested his weight against it. His chest was heaving as if he'd run a race, and his heart pounded so loudly he could hear it over the ticking of the clock. A shadow flickered over the full moon, and Robert saw the soaring outline of one of the owls.

He transferred his gaze to the heavy silk embroidered curtains. If he leaned forward, could he at least draw one of them closed? He reached out his hand, overbalanced, and had to rock back on his heels, sending an excruciating stab of pain up his left leg. The desk swayed along with him on its equally spindly legs. He propped himself up against the wall to regroup. Sweat ran down his face and his vision blurred.

He focused on the reassuring bulk of the church until his breathing steadied. He could do this. He *had* to do this. The ability to close his own damned curtains was a symbol of all his frustrations over the past few months. There was another chair close to the center of the two windows. If he could just reach that, he would achieve his aim. He stumbled forward and clutched at the back of the dainty chair, half-bent over it. As he straightened, his attention was caught by another shadow flitting across the park below.

He frowned. Not *flitting*. Whatever was out there was moving rather slowly, as if overburdened. Robert squinted and realized he wasn't looking at an animal, but at a person carrying something heavy, either in his arms, or over his shoulder. The unknown being continued toward the church, his shadow thrown up against the old flint wall into gigantic proportions.

"What the devil is going on?" Robert wondered aloud, as he craned his neck to get a better look. The chair tipped and he fell, his hands grabbing uselessly for purchase. Like a wounded animal, he turned, so that his right side hit the floor first and absorbed the sudden impact that made him want to puke up his guts. He came to rest on his back staring up at the white stucco ceiling. Considering the noise he'd made, he expected half his household to come tearing into his bedroom.

All remained quiet apart from the derisive hooting of the owls.

Robert wanted to laugh. He'd reached his goal, but he still hadn't managed to draw the curtains, and he was destined for an incredibly uncomfortable night on the floor. So much for the gallant major. He threw his forearm over his eyes and pressed hard. He hadn't cried since he was seven and been sent away to boarding school. Dignity be damned. He'd crawl back to bed.

"Now, don't forget to visit Major Kurland today, Lucy."

Lucy Harrington glanced at her father as he sat serenely drinking tea and eating boiled ham at the head of the table. Breakfast at the rectory was always a noisy affair, and this fine spring morning was no exception. Anna and Anthony were arguing about the weather, and the twins were throwing crusts of bread at each other. Sunlight gleamed through the bow windows, glancing off the silver coffeepot and the blond hair of the rector's two youngest children. Not that anything could make the twins look angelic. Before she could frame an appropriate answer, she coaxed the dripping honey-covered spoon from young Michael's fierce grip and endeavored to wipe his sticky face.

"Did you hear me, Lucy?"

"Yes, Papa, I did." She patted her youngest brother on the head, and poured him some more milk. "Are you not able to attend the major yourself?"

He frowned at her over the top of his spectacles. "I have to go to the horse fair at Saffron Walden. I need a new hunter."

Of course, her father's passion for horseflesh would always trump his other duties. Lucy nodded at the twins, and they hurriedly got down from the table and disappeared through the door. Moments later, Lucy heard their nurse calling them and the clatter of two sets of boots stealing down the back stairs. She supposed she should go and find the boys before they escaped into the woods, but her father gazed at her as though he expected an answer.

"I don't think Major Kurland enjoys my company, Papa." She placed her knife on her plate. "He much prefers to converse with you."

"Nonsense, my dear." The rector rose to his feet and surveyed the ruins of the breakfast table. "It is your duty to succor the sick and the poor, regardless of your own selfish desires."

Lucy raised her chin. "It is wash day. Who will supervise the staff if I am off visiting the sick?"

"You will contrive, Lucy. You always do." The rector folded his newspaper and laid it on the linen tablecloth. "I have the latest London papers in my study. Perhaps you might take them to Major Kurland and amuse him by reading the court scandal. It cannot be easy for a man of action such as our esteemed major to be laid up."

"I'm sure it isn't, Papa, but—"

The rector pushed in his chair. "I will be back for dinner, my dear. Please tell Cook that I cannot stomach any more mutton."

"I'll take out a line and fish for our dinner if you like," Anthony cut in with a wink at Lucy.

The rector paused to look down his long, aristocratic nose at his son. "You, sir, will be studying with Mr. Galton for your entrance exams for Cambridge."

"Not all day. I'll find time to fish. That is, if Lucy doesn't make me do the laundry."

Lucy smiled at her brother. "I wouldn't dare take you away from your studies."

Anthony grinned and returned his attention to his plate. Like most young men, his appetite was inexhaustible and quite indifferent to the ebb and flow of emotion around the rectory table.

"Well, whatever you put in front of me tonight, it had better not be mutton." The rector placed his spectacles in his waistcoat pocket. "I'll take Harris with me. You don't need him, do you?"

"No, Papa." Lucy started gathering up the dishes the twins had abandoned. "And I'll make sure Cook understands about your requirements for dinner."

Her father paused to kiss the top of her head before departing for the stables. His loud, cheerful voice boomed through the hallways, calling for Harris to bring his horse around. Lucy rested her chin on her hand and stared down at the crumbled remains of her toast and marmalade.

"It's all right, sis. I'll find time to go and fish whatever Father says."

She looked up at Anthony. "I'd appreciate it if you did. Unfortunately, unless you catch a whale, the rest of us will still be eating mutton. Cook has a whole side to get rid of."

Anthony groaned. "Can't you give *that* to the poor? I'm sure Major Kurland would love a bowl of mutton stew."

"He'd probably throw it at my head." Lucy put the lid on the butter dish. "A more ill-tempered man I have never met."

"But Lucy!" exclaimed her sister Anna. "He was wounded

fighting for his king and country at Waterloo. You can hardly expect him to be *pleasant*."

"He was pleasant enough when I first visited him with Father. It is only since I've taken up the burden of visiting him alone that he appears to think he owes me no courtesy whatsoever."

Anna reached across to squeeze Lucy's hand. At twenty, she was the acknowledged beauty of the family and only five years younger than Lucy. Her temperament was sunny and obliging and, unlike Lucy, she always saw the good in everyone. She was fair like the twins, whereas Lucy and her brother favored their dark-haired father.

"He can't *help* being difficult. Have you tried to cheer him up?"

"Of course I haven't. I sit there and sob into my handkerchief and bemoan his wounds."

"There is no need to be flippant." Anna glanced across at Anthony. "I just wondered if perhaps you were a little 'sharp' with him."

"As I am with my family?" Lucy raised her eyebrows. "Anna, if you want to visit the man in my stead, please, be my guest."

A delicate flush blossomed on Anna's cheeks. "Oh no, I'm sure he wouldn't want to see *me*."

"Fancy yourself lady of the manor, do you, Anna?" Anthony nudged his sister. "Even when you were a little girl, you always idolized Major Kurland."

Lucy sat back to survey her blushing sister. "That's true. I'd forgotten. You used to follow him around like an acolyte."

Anna sipped at her tea and kept her gaze demurely downcast. "Despite the great disparity in our ages, he was always very kind to me."

Lucy finished her toast. "Then perhaps you *should* go. I'll wager he won't snap at you for trying to make conversation."

"So that she can swoon over him?" Anthony snorted. "He's fifteen years older than her."

"So? Father was fifteen years older than Mother. It's quite common for a husband to be older than a wife."

"And yet she died before him because she had too many children." Anna's smile disappeared. "She was simply worn out with it."

Lucy reached for Anna's hand. "That might be true, but as Father will no doubt remind you, that is a woman's lot in life."

Anna snatched her hand free. "That doesn't make it any better, though, does it?"

Lucy could only agree. The loss of their mother in childbed almost seven years ago had devastated their family and left nineteen-year-old Lucy in charge of two squalling infants. As her mother became a distant memory, Lucy sometimes felt as if the twins *were* her children. They certainly treated her as their mother. She would be devastated when they were sent away to school in the autumn.

Lucy rose to her feet. There was no point sitting around moping. She'd learned long ago that achieved nothing. "Anna, if you don't wish to visit Major Kurland, you will have to supervise Betty and Mary while they do the laundry."

She tried not to look hopeful. Perhaps that would make Anna change her mind and take on her least favorite obligation of the day. To her disappointment, her sister merely nodded.

"Of course, I'll help. Shall I ring for Betty to clear the table?"

"No, I'll do it myself." Lucy glanced out the window at the bright sky. "Betty is already stripping the beds, and I don't want to disturb her. Best to start on the washing before this fine weather disappears."

"I'll help, too," Anthony offered. "Mr. Galton won't be here for another hour."

"But aren't you supposed to be aiding Edward in the church?"

Anthony's charming smile flashed out, reminding Lucy of her father. "Oh, Edward will manage. He doesn't like my assistance anyway. He worries that Father might give me his job." He snorted. "As if I would want to be a poor curate in a village like this."

"Hush, Anthony," Lucy admonished her brother. "Edward can hardly help his circumstances, can he? And if it weren't for him, Father couldn't avoid all the more onerous duties of being the rector of several small parishes."

"He likes the income, though, doesn't he?" Anthony finished his tea in one gulp.

"That's none of our business," Lucy said severely. "Despite his private income, Papa also has a large family to provide for. How do you think he pays for your tutor?"

Anthony's mouth settled into a sulky line. "He pays more for his horses than he does for my education, and he barely pays his curate a pittance."

The curate, Edward Calthrope, was a worthy man of about Lucy's age who lived with them at the rectory. He performed all the mundane tasks associated with the parish of Kurland St. Mary and the adjoining parishes of Lower Kurland and Kurland St. Anne that the rector was supposed to spiritually mentor, but preferred to avoid. Lucy wasn't quite sure of Edward's background as he rarely spoke about his family. How he had found his way to Kurland was something of a mystery.

"You should go and help Edward," Lucy admonished her brother. "He works far too hard."

"And I don't?" Anthony yawned, stretched out his legs, and looked down at his top boots. "I *am* cramming for Cambridge, you know."

Lucy picked up the nearest pile of plates and headed for the door. "And I have to visit Major Kurland. As Papa said, we all have to do things we'd rather not." She studied her brother. "You might not be so tired if you slept at night. I heard you creeping up the stairs at dawn this morning."

"Spying on me, Lucy? I didn't think it of you."

"Not spying, I was just getting up." She paused, but Anthony made no effort to explain where he'd been, and why should he? As a young man he was perfectly entitled to disappear when it suited him.

Anthony picked up his cup and plate. "All right, my dearest sister. I'm off to the church to scrape off candle wax and reset the mousetraps."

"Thank you." Lucy paused to smile at him. Despite his exasperating male habits, he was a remarkably good brother. She'd be losing him, too, if he passed his examinations and went up to Cambridge. That wasn't as worrying as the thought of losing the twins, but it still meant that her family was moving forward with their lives while she . . .

"Oh Miss Lucy!"

She turned to find the twins' nurse running down the main staircase of the house, her cap askew and her skirts held up to her knees.

"What is it, Jane?"

"Them two young heathens have run off, again! Whatever am I to do with them?"

"Let them be for the moment. They'll have to stop running wild soon enough."

Jane mopped her brow with the corner of her apron. "That's true enough, miss, although how they will get on at school, I cannot imagine."

Unfortunately, Lucy already knew from Anthony's experiences that life at boarding school would soon beat any willfulness out of the twins. She hated the very thought, but there was nothing she could do about it. Her father insisted they needed to become English gentlemen, and apparently, a *gentleman* had to withstand anything his enemies cared to throw at him without flinching. Despite her father reading passages to her about how the English school system mimicked the finer points of the Spartan *agoge,* Lucy was still not convinced it was the best way to bring up a child.

"They'll come back when they are hungry. Now, why don't you help me clear the table and get Miss Anna started on that huge laundry pile?"

It wasn't until much later that she remembered to search her father's study for the latest London newspapers to bring for the edification of Major Kurland. Not that he would appreciate the gesture. If he wanted to know all the latest gossip from Town, he could certainly afford to have his own newspapers delivered. His father had married an heiress from the industrial north, and unlike many aristocratic estates, Kurland was thriving.

Lucy chided herself for her unchristian thoughts and gathered up the printed sheets. The study smelled of brandy, saddle leather, and the bay rum her father's valet used after he shaved him. She glanced at the rows of books and imagined herself in Anthony's place being tutored for Cambridge. Her father always said she was far too intelligent for a girl, but he'd never stopped her from reading any of the books she requested, even the slightly scandalous ones. She replaced the stopper in the inkwell. Perhaps with Anthony and the twins leaving, she might finally be able to talk to her father about her plans for the future.

After checking that her basket held everything she needed for her various visits in the village, Lucy set out. She kept a wary eye on the weather, which was still quite unpredictable and veered from sunshine to clouds within moments. She tied the ribbons of her plain straw bonnet firmly under her chin, and buttoned up her blue wool pelisse. She might look like the spinster aunt she was surely destined to become, but at least she was warm.

Along the driveway that led up to the rectory, some straggling spring flowers raised their heads toward the bright sunlight. In a few weeks the rest would follow and the flower beds would be a sea of yellow and purple. About ten years previously, her father had rebuilt the rectory in a soft yellow stone that reminded Lucy of the houses in Bath. It was a square and symmetrical building with four rectangular windows to each side of the white front door, very much in the classical style of Robert Adam, whom he had greatly admired.

The rector had given up trying to repair the two-hundred-year-old house that stood there previously, and had it demolished. Lucy still fondly remembered the older rectory with its diamond-paned windows, wooden beams, sloping ceilings, and winding staircases. As a child, it had felt like living in a fairy-tale castle. She was practical enough to admit that it must have been difficult to maintain for a man with a young and ever-increasing family. The new house still seemed a little ill at ease and out of place, the scars of its construction evident in the hard edges of the new pathways and the lack of large trees.

Lucy did appreciate that the roof no longer leaked, and that the kitchen had both a proper chimney and a closed stove rather than the huge open medieval fireplace that belched smoke and soot over the food being prepared. Her mother had loved having fires in every room and the light the big rectangular windows provided.

At the bottom of the driveway, Lucy turned right and headed along the main thoroughfare to Kurland Village. The ground was wet and muddy, and she was glad she had worn her stout boots. There was no one else visible on the road, but that was to be expected in the middle of the day. Despite the sunshine, her breath condensed as she exhaled, and she could still feel the brush of winter's icy fingers against her cheeks.

She walked past the first of the thatched cottages that housed the laborers who worked the fields of the Kurland estate. A woman was hanging washing out to dry, and nodded at Lucy through a mouthful of pegs. Lucy smiled and nodded back, aware as the wind picked up and flattened the woman's gown to her belly that she was expecting another child. Mentally, Lucy added another set of birthing clothes to the list of garments she needed to knit or sew for upcoming happy events.

The cottages grew closer together until Lucy was in the village proper facing the green and the square of buildings huddled around it. The ice had finally thawed on the duck pond, and Lucy was pleased to see that several of the local birds had returned to claim their spots at the side of the weed-choked pond. Something large Lucy couldn't quite identify stuck out above the surface of the water like an awkward elbow. She should speak to Major Kurland about that. It was his responsibility to keep the pond from becoming stagnant and overgrown.

In truth, she had no inclination to speak to Major Kurland about anything that might raise his ire. Perhaps it would be better to take her concerns to his rather obnoxious land agent. At least he might listen to her, even if he chose not to do anything.

"Miss Harrington?"

Lucy turned from her contemplation of the duck pond to find Mrs. Weeks, the wife of the baker, waving at her from the door of her shop. The fragrant scent of baking bread laced with a hint of cinnamon sugar tantalized Lucy's nostrils. When she was a child, Lucy had often saved her pennies and sneaked down to the village just to buy an iced bun or an eccles cake from the bakery.

"Good morning, Mrs. Weeks." Lucy stepped into the baker's store and closed the door against the chill. "Is there something I can do for you?"

Mrs. Weeks folded her arms across her chest. "I was wondering if you wanted me to make the cake for the rector's birthday."

"I would love you to make it, Mrs. Weeks, but there is the little matter that Mrs. Fielding might take offense."

"She always takes offense, but there is no denying that her cakes aren't as light as mine."

Lucy had heard variations of this argument her entire life. The rivalry between the baker's shop and the rector's cook had started before Lucy was born, when her mother had inadvertently begun the tradition of having a special cake made as a surprise for her husband's birthday. She'd asked Mrs. Weeks to make it, and Mrs. Fielding had never forgiven her. The problem was that Mrs. Weeks did make a far superior cake, which Lucy's father much preferred.

"Please make the cake, Mrs. Weeks," Lucy said, cutting through the other woman's long discourse on what Mrs. Fielding had said to her, and what she had said back. "I'm sure it will be as delightful as always."

She'd placate Mrs. Fielding by keeping her busy cooking a sumptuous dinner of all the rector's favorite foods, and hope she wouldn't notice the addition of an extra cake. Of course, she'd notice it eventually, but by then it would be too late for her to do anything about it. The strategy had worked quite successfully in the past few years and Lucy was confident it would be successful again—as long as Mrs. Weeks didn't boast of her triumph too loudly after church on Sundays.

Lucy realized that Mrs. Weeks was still speaking and tried to pay attention.

"My Daisy, Miss Harrington."

"I'm sorry, what about your Daisy?"

"She'll be wanting a new job soon and I was wondering if you'd have anything up at the rectory for her. She's a sturdy, hardworking girl, and she knows her place."

Lucy tried to recall Daisy and remembered thick braids,

brown eyes, and a permanent scowl. "Does she not wish to work in the shop with you?"

"Not anymore, miss. She *says* she wants to go up to London and become a lady's maid."

"And you do not want her to do that?"

"She's my youngest, and I was hoping to keep her by me for a while. I don't think she is ready to move up to London yet. She disagrees with me, of course. In fact, she's still sulking in her bed upstairs after our latest argument."

"How old is she?"

"Eighteen, miss."

Lucy reviewed the current staff of the rectory. "If my brother goes up to Cambridge, and the twins leave for school in the autumn, I will probably have to reduce the staff rather than increase it. I'm sorry, Mrs. Weeks. But I will inquire among the neighboring houses as to whether anyone needs a new maid."

"Never mind, miss. It can't be helped." Mrs. Weeks wiped her hands on her apron. "I'm sure with God's help, she'll find something. Now is there anything I can get you while you're here?"

Lucy departed with half a dozen iced buns and went next door to the haberdasher's and general store to replenish the contents of her sewing box. She chatted with the proprietor and then spent another quarter of an hour talking to the butcher about the excellence of the Christmas goose and tactfully mentioning that they would not require any more mutton in the foreseeable future. She was aware that she was dawdling because she didn't want to retrace her steps to Kurland Manor but, eventually, even she ran out of things to say.

As a child, she'd loved visiting the manor house. The major's mother had been a charming, welcoming hostess who had encouraged the rector's children to treat her home as an extension of their own. Of course, Lucy's mother had gently suggested that this was because Mrs.

Kurland was not wellborn and rather too familiar, but Lucy hadn't cared about that. She'd enjoyed getting away from her mother and running after the two Kurland boys.

Even then, Robert Kurland had been rather aloof and above their childish games. As the oldest son and heir, he'd had none of his younger brother's carefree spirit and had stopped taking any notice of the crowd of village children who gathered to swim and play in the extensive grounds of Kurland Hall. And, after starting at Eton and his brother's death, he'd withdrawn from them completely.

She trudged up the long drive to the major's ancestral home with all the anticipation of a cavalry unit sent uphill to dislodge some enemy cannon. The military cant made her catch her breath and wish painfully for Tom, her other brother, the one who now lay in the family crypt by the church awaiting the resurrection.

She forced herself to think of more cheerful matters. She was secretly glad that Major Kurland hadn't followed her father's example and replaced the Elizabethan manor with a modern stucco box. The house was shaped like an *E,* with thick beams, narrow windows, and fantastically tall, lopsided Elizabethan chimneys in the grand manner of Hampton Court. Local legend said that many of the internal beams had been salvaged from the destruction of King Henry VIII's naval ships, which would explain both their thickness and their inconvenient curves.

Generations of Kurlands had added to the manor house, some more successfully than others. It now resembled something of a hodgepodge with stairs that led to nowhere, large windows where once had been arrow slits, and a beautiful park laid out by Capability Brown.

Lucy knocked on the old oak door and frowned fiercely at the worn Kurland family crest carved into the panel. She should have more sympathy with Major Kurland. He had survived Waterloo, even if her brother hadn't.

Foley, the butler, opened the door for her and smiled.

"Good afternoon, Miss Harrington. Have you come to visit the major? He's tucked up in bed again."

"Then I won't disturb him," Lucy said rapidly. "Perhaps you might like to give him these newspapers when he wakes up."

"Oh no, miss. He's awake and I'm certain he'll want to see you." He lowered his voice. "The doctor called, and the major's been grumpy as a bear and complaining about a lack of decent company all morning."

Lucy tried to hang back, but Foley somehow had a firm grip on her elbow and was maneuvering her up the stairs. For such a slight man, he was difficult to stop. She readjusted her basket and stripped off her gloves. It was an opportunity to show Christian charity, and she should embrace it.

Foley knocked on the major's bedroom door and opened it wide. "Miss Harrington to see you, sir. I'll bring up some tea."

Chapter 2

"Good morning, Major Kurland, and how are you feeling today?"

Lucy fixed on a bright smile and advanced into the major's large bedroom. The curtains were half-drawn against the weak sunlight, but she could see just well enough not to bump into any of the rather forbidding oak furniture. Major Kurland was sitting up in his four-poster bed against a mound of pillows. Even from the doorway, Lucy couldn't help but notice his pallor and the lines of pain bracketing his mouth.

"Well enough, Miss Harrington."

Lucy hesitated. "I can come back tomorrow, if it would be more convenient."

"I doubt anything is going to improve by tomorrow, so you might as well come in."

"But I don't wish to impose."

"Miss Harrington, if I didn't wish to see you, I would have ordered Foley to deny you admittance at the front door."

"You *wanted* to see me?"

"You are a voice of bright reason amongst all the doomsayers." His words held a hint of impatience she had come to recognize all too well.

"I am?"

"Indeed. Your optimistic view of life never fails to entertain me."

Lucy raised her chin. Perhaps it was time to assert herself with the acerbic major. "If you intend to make fun of me, sir, I'll leave you in peace." She waited, her hand clenched on her basket as he continued to look out of the window.

"I'm not making fun of you. I've had an appalling morning being pulled around by Dr. Baker, and I'm in the mood for a little distraction."

Beneath his polite tone she sensed something defeated. Did he truly need her company? An all-too-familiar sense of guilt stirred in her chest. Her father would expect her to give the poor man the benefit of the doubt and stay to comfort him.

She brought out the folded newspapers from her basket and came up alongside the bed. "Father thought you might enjoy having the London papers."

He finally turned to face her and flinched away from the papers she brandished at him as if he were a rabid dog about to attack. Heat blossomed in her cheeks, and she stuffed the papers back in the basket.

"What happened? Your face is bruised."

He made a dismissive gesture. "I fell."

Without thinking, Lucy put down her basket and perched on the side of his bed to examine him more closely. "What on earth were you doing?"

He scowled at her. "Nothing that might concern you, Miss Harrington. You are neither my nursemaid nor my mother."

"Thank goodness," Lucy said under her breath.

"I beg your pardon?"

Unfortunately, his hearing was sharper than she had anticipated. She met his dark blue gaze without flinching. "You are an exceedingly difficult patient, Major, and I am sincerely glad that I no longer have the care of you."

His eyebrows drew together. "And I suspect I owe you another apology." He cleared his throat. "I am a little belligerent this morning. I overreached myself last night. Dr. Baker says I have set my recovery back by several weeks."

The bleakness of his tone conveyed far more than Lucy guessed he intended to reveal and impulsively she patted his hand.

"Dr. Baker is rather a pessimist, Major. I'm sure you'll recover far more quickly than he predicts." He didn't answer her, his attention seemingly fixed on the sight of her ungloved hand on his. "In fact, I should probably leave you to read the papers, and come back when you are feeling more the thing."

"Don't go." To her consternation he wrapped his long fingers around her wrist. "Despite what you might think, I have come to appreciate your visits, Miss Harrington."

"Indeed?" Lucy didn't try to pull away. Even in his currently weakened state, she reckoned Major Kurland was far stronger than she was, and she had no intention of getting into an undignified wrangle with him. "I am only doing my Christian duty, sir."

"Your Christian duty," he repeated. "Where is your esteemed father today?"

"I am not quite sure." *Was it wrong to lie about the doings of a rector even if he was her father?* "I expect he is tending to his flock in some capacity."

"Strange, because my valet told me there is a horse auction in Saffron Walden today and that the rector was set on attending it."

Lucy looked prim. "It is not my place to question the actions of my father, sir. I am here because he asked me to visit you."

"And you are a dutiful daughter."

"Obviously."

"Or else you would not have come."

Silence stretched between them. Eventually, Lucy raised her eyes to meet his, a challenge in hers. "You said that you appreciate my calling on you. If that is truly the case, then I am glad to be of service."

His mouth quirked up at the corner, surprising her. "I think that is why I have come to enjoy your visits so much. Despite the meekness of your words, I suspect you would quite like to ring a peal over my head. You are the only person who doesn't treat me like an invalid who has lost his mind along with his ability to walk."

It seemed that whatever had happened the night before had made the major resolve to be frank with her. Lucy decided the least she could do was be truthful back. It was also something of a relief.

"I truly feel sorry for your injuries, sir, but I don't believe it gives you the right to behave like a sulky bear to those around you."

He released her hand and leaned back against the pillows, his cropped black hair stark against the white linen. "I feel as if a brigade of horses is trampling through my head, my leg is throbbing like the devil, and I ache all over from my fall. A fall that was my own stupid fault as I thought I knew better than my physician. I think I have a perfect right to be ungracious."

"With yourself, perhaps, but not with those who are trying to help you. That smacks of self-pity."

This was the most unorthodox conversation she had ever had in her life. Whatever had happened to Major Kurland on the previous night had obviously brought him to this point and surely she was honor bound to listen to him? She was sitting, unchaperoned, on a gentleman's bed while he unburdened himself of his feelings. Feelings she, as an unmarried woman, should not be party to, and that she had never guessed were concealed beneath the major's tough exterior. But he'd said he valued her presence—that she was the only person who didn't fuss around him.

His abrupt movement brought her back to her surroundings. "I am aware that I am not at my best, Miss Harrington, which is why I admit very few people into my presence." He shoved a hand through his hair. "But as we are acquaintances of long standing, I will endeavor to present at least a veneer of politeness, just for you."

Lucy smiled at him and slid off the bed to fetch a chair. "Then I will stay for a while. It is laundry day at the rectory. In truth I have no wish to get back there too soon."

"Thank you, Miss Harrington." He shifted on his pillows as if trying to find a position that didn't pain him. "Is your family well?"

"Yes, Major, very well. I am attempting to civilize the twins before they leave for school in the autumn."

"They are old enough to go to school?"

"Indeed." Lucy summoned a smile.

"I remember my mother writing to tell me about their birth, and your mother's death. That must have been a difficult time for your father."

"I believe it was."

"He was lucky that you were there to support him, and take over the household so competently."

"It was my duty, sir."

"Ah, that word again." His fingers gathered up the sheet into a crumpled ball. "We all have our duties, don't we?"

"I suppose we do." Lucy tried to think of something else to talk about. Sometimes her family's demands felt suffocating, but she didn't think Major Kurland would want to know about that. He'd answered the call of duty for his king and country and been wounded as a result. Her pathetic complaints about being the daughter who had to stay at home were nothing in comparison.

"And how is your cousin, Paul, sir?"

He raised his eyebrows. "I have no idea."

"He hasn't even written to inquire about your health?"

"The last time I saw Paul, Miss Harrington, he asked me for a substantial loan for a new business venture. I refused to give him a penny. He hasn't spoken to me since."

"Oh." From the forbidding set of the major's mouth, Lucy knew he would not speak of his wayward cousin again. "Would you like to read the paper, or shall we play chess?"

"I don't have the concentration to play chess, and I can't read without getting a headache. Mayhap you could read to me instead?"

Lucy reached down to take the newspapers out of her basket and was interrupted by a knock at the door and the appearance of Foley with a tea tray.

"Here you are, Miss Harrington."

"Thank you, Foley." Lucy smiled at the butler, who placed the tray on a small table at her elbow.

Foley withdrew and Lucy looked over at Major Kurland. "May I pour you some tea?"

"Is there coffee instead?"

Lucy inspected the silver tray and shook her head. "No, just the tea and some toasted muffins. Are you hungry?"

"No, thank you. I'll just have the tea."

Lucy could tell that he was just being polite, but at least he was trying. She poured him a cup of the fragrant brew and walked with it over to the bed.

"Do you need help sitting up?"

"No, I can manage."

He struggled to push himself more upright, and Lucy fought down an urge to help him. She had no desire to be shouted at. Men were so ridiculous about their pride sometimes. She blew on the tea and held out the cup and saucer.

"Should I . . ."

"*No.*"

He snatched it from her, and the china wobbled danger-ously, the teacup rattling like a frail barque on the ocean. Even as she reached for the cup, she knew it was too late as hot tea cascaded down over the major's hand and onto the bedclothes.

"Devil take it!"

She ignored his appalling language and attempted to re-trieve the cup and saucer and mop up the tea. He clutched his hand to his chest, the tea staining the whiteness of his nightshirt. Carefully, Lucy took his clenched fist, unfolded his fingers, and examined them.

"I don't think you're badly hurt. Let me get you a cloth to clean yourself."

She went to his nightstand where a jug of water and a bowl stood ready. She poured some cold water in the bowl and brought it back to the bed with a soft drying cloth. Major Kurland didn't speak as she reclaimed his hand and placed it in the bowl of water on top of the wet cloth. Bending over the bowl, she studied his fingers.

"Do they still hurt?"

"There is no need for you to fuss over me."

She drew his hand and the cloth out of the water, wrap-ping his now cold fingers in the wet cloth and gently squeezing.

He hissed a curse and startled her. She looked straight up into his blue eyes.

"Are you all right, Major?"

"What do you think? I can't even drink a cup of tea without help. What kind of a man have I become?"

"You are not well, sir. In a few weeks, you will be much stronger."

"It's been months, Miss Harrington, and I can still barely stand."

Lucy picked up the basin of water and returned it to its place. She poured another cup of tea and brought it over to the bed.

Major Kurland made a sign of distaste. "I don't want any more damned tea."

"Then I'll drink it."

Lucy sipped at the hot beverage and waited until Major Kurland sank back against his pillows, his scalded hand clasped to his chest. He closed his eyes and a shudder ran through him. Lucy suspected he was about to apologize to her again. It disturbed her to see her most difficult patient at his lowest ebb, and it made it hard not to feel sorry for him. But from what she knew of him, trying to sympathize about his current condition would only rouse his ire.

"You wished to see me this morning. Was there something in particular that you needed?" Lucy put her cup and saucer down on the tray.

He slowly raised his gaze to meet hers and exhaled.

"I was wondering if there was any disruption in the village last night."

"What kind of disruption?"

"Theft of any kind?"

Lucy frowned. "Not that I know of. I was in the village earlier, and no one mentioned anything to me. Why do you ask?"

He smoothed out the tea-stained bedsheets. "I didn't sleep very well. I thought I heard some kind of commotion." He glanced over at the bay windows. "My windows face toward the church and the village."

"Is that why you got out of bed?"

"What does that have to do with anything?" he demanded. "I merely asked if you were aware of any disturbance."

Despite being glad that he seemed to be his old irascible self, she couldn't help but bristle at his tone.

"And I said that I wasn't." She glared right back at him. "Do you wish me to inquire further?"

"I wish that I could get out of this damned bed and inquire myself, but that is impossible."

"I know that you are scarcely at your best, Major, but perhaps you might refrain from using such language in front of a lady. It is the fourth time you have cursed this morning."

He inclined his head a stiff inch. "Then I apologize. I didn't realize you were keeping score."

Goaded by the lack of true remorse in his clipped reply, Lucy carried on. "I know I'm the rector's daughter and you've known me for years, but I *am* still a lady."

His slight smile was unexpected and set her on guard. "I do tend to forget that, Miss Harrington. Not many young unmarried ladies of my acquaintance would be lounging on my bed in the middle of the day without instantly expecting a marriage proposal."

Lucy felt herself blushing as she removed herself and reclaimed her chair. "I am my father's spiritual representative in this matter, and thus above such material things." She helped herself to one of the buttered muffins and chewed thoroughly.

After a while she dared look up at him again. His eyes were closed, and he looked almost as pale as his pillows. "If you truly wish it, sir, I will inquire further into the matter and report back to you."

"That would be most kind of you, Miss Harrington."

She stood and gently laid the newspapers on the bed. "Good-bye, Major. I'll call again tomorrow."

He didn't respond and she realized he was falling asleep. She picked up her basket and tiptoed out into the hallway, almost colliding with Foley and the major's valet, Bookman, who were huddled in conversation just outside the door.

"Is the major all right, Miss Harrington?" Foley asked.

"He seemed rather tired. I left him with my father's newspapers to read later."

Bookman shook his head. "He's worn out, miss, that's for sure. The doctor was very concerned about him this morning, threatened to amputate his leg if he didn't follow instructions and stay off it."

Lucy brought her hand to her mouth. "Amputation? I didn't realize things had become that bad. Is there still an infection?"

"Not that we know of, miss, but with all those broken bones to mend, the major needs to take his time recovering, and he is not the most patient of men."

"So I should imagine. What exactly happened last night?"

Bookman shrugged. "It appears that the major attempted to get up and refill his water glass, without ringing for me. He fell and couldn't get back into bed. I found him on the floor this morning."

Lucy wondered why Major Kurland hadn't discussed his suspicions about a robbery in the village with his servants. Did he think they wouldn't believe him?

"Oh dear. He said that he has trouble sleeping. Is there nothing he can take to help with his slumbers?"

"He doesn't like taking laudanum, miss. He says it dulls his senses, and he was quite unlike himself when he was forced to take it regularly—hallucinations and nightmares, and the like." Bookman shook his head.

"I hate to take it myself. Is there a way to carry the major to sit in a chair by the window for part of the day? Does he have the strength to sit up? I suspect he would feel much better if he could at least see what was going on outside."

"That's a good idea, miss. I'll ask Dr. Baker what he thinks when he visits on the morrow." Bookman sighed. "I don't like to see the master like this, I really don't."

Lucy turned to walk down the shallow oak staircase and into the medieval hall complete with the suits of rusting armor that had enchanted her as a child. Foley went ahead of her and opened the front door wide, his lined face still worried.

"Thank you for visiting, Miss Harrington. Despite what he might say, the major does appreciate it."

Lucy smiled. "I'll return in a day or so, and hope that he is feeling more the thing." She hesitated on the bottom step, and Foley looked inquiringly at her. "Did you hear any disturbance from the village last night, Mr. Foley?"

"Last night, miss?" Foley frowned. "Not that I can recall. Has something happened?"

"I'm not sure." Lucy hurriedly turned away. She had no ability to conceal her feelings, especially when she tried to fib. "I thought my father mentioned something before he left this morning, but I might have been mistaken."

"Well, let me know if there is anything I can do, Miss Harrington. We all want this village to remain a safe place to raise our families."

Lucy headed back down the drive, her thoughts consumed with the notion that there had been something going on in the village that she didn't know about. In such a small place, most people knew each other's business far too intimately. Had someone been robbed, as the major seemed to think, or had he been dreaming? If he *was* taking laudanum at night, he might be suffering from night terrors and have imagined the whole thing. It was odd that Foley hadn't heard anything, and that the major had failed to confide in his staff about his suspicions.

Lucy changed direction and took the path that led directly from the house to the church. It was a shortcut that allowed the occupants of the manor to avoid the longer walk around to the bottom of their driveway and up again to the front of the church. As she walked, she glanced back at the manor house trying to pinpoint Major Kurland's diamond-paned bedroom windows, which formed the end part of one of the three wings.

In the shadow of the high church wall, the temperature dropped suddenly. The gate that led into the churchyard proper hung open, and the mud beneath the stile was churned up as though several feet had tramped through it. A hawthorn bush grew on the other side of the gate, its branches ragged as though someone had recently forced a way through it.

She studied the gate and stile. Had Anthony brought his three hound puppies through here on a walk early this morning and left the gate open? It would be just like him to forget anything but the well-being of his dogs. Or had someone with more devious motives used the path to avoid the village as the major suspected? Sidestepping the mud, Lucy passed the gate and made sure it was latched. She followed the line of the wall toward the graveyard and the side entrance to the church, her breath freezing in the cold.

Just ahead of her, on the opposite side of the main road, was the rectory, and a welcome hint of sunshine. The path proper ended at the side door into the church, but Lucy kept walking. She braced her gloved hand against the huge cornerstone for balance and squeezed through the narrow gap between the wall containing the graveyard and the church. The rector didn't approve of his children using the shortcut, but they all did it. It was much harder to get through the gap than when she was a child, but it did save her valuable time.

As she walked toward the house, she could already smell the dank scent of lye, wet washing, and steam, and she inwardly sighed. Forsaking the front entrance, she took herself around to the kitchens, and found Anna directing operations, her face flushed, her apron soaked with water.

"I'm so glad that you are back, Lucy. Mary still hasn't come down, and Betty and I have been working like fiends!"

"Where is she? Is she unwell?"

Anna wiped her hands on her apron and bustled toward Lucy. "I haven't had time to find out."

"I'll go up and see where she is. Did Betty not say any-thing?"

"They don't share a room. She said she didn't know."

Lucy stripped off her gloves, tossed them onto the table, and walked toward the door. "I'll just take off my coat and then I'll be back to help you."

But Anna wasn't looking at her. She was staring at Lucy's gloves. "Oh my goodness. Are you hurt, Lucy?"

"Whatever do you mean?"

Anna pointed at the dark red stains now covering the cook's pine table. "Your gloves are covered in blood. Ugh, can't you smell it?"

Chapter 3

Lucy pondered the blood on her gloves and ran up two flights of stairs to the attic room Mary inhabited under the eaves of the house. She must have brushed up against something at the butcher's shop in the village when she stopped to talk about the Christmas goose and the mutton. But why hadn't she or Foley noticed the blood when she'd taken off her gloves at Kurland Hall?

Breathing rather hard, Lucy paused to knock at the door to Mary's room and, getting no reply, knocked again. She cautiously turned the door handle and peered inside. To her surprise the room was full of light. The small square-paned window that looked out over the circular driveway was open, and the checked cotton curtain flapped in the brisk breeze. Lucy shut the window, ducking her head, as the plaster wall sloped up at a right angle to meet the ceiling in the center of the room. Mary's narrow bed was not occupied and was already made.

Lucy frowned as she surveyed the immaculate chamber. Last time she'd inspected the maid's quarters she'd had to ask Mary to clean her room because the girl was naturally untidy. Now, not a trace of Mary's personality or her cluttered possessions remained. Lucy knelt in front of the clothes chest and opened the lid. It was empty apart from some hand-stitched sachets of lavender and pennyroyal to ward against moths.

"Mary, wherever have you gone?" Lucy's words echoed around the small space. "And why didn't you tell anyone?"

She checked under the bed, but there was nothing there, except an earthenware chamber pot and a tangle of dust. It seemed that Mary had taken everything she owned, but why?

She made her way back down to the steamy kitchen and pulled Anna aside into the hallway.

"Mary isn't up there."

"What do you mean?" Anna's face flushed with indignation. "Did she go shopping with Mrs. Fielding? Why didn't anyone ask me if it was acceptable for her to leave? Just because I'm not as intimidating as you are, I still need to be consulted."

"It's not quite that simple. All her possessions have gone with her."

Anna brought her hand to her mouth. "You mean she has run off?"

"It certainly looks like it."

"But why? She seemed perfectly happy here, didn't she?"

"As far as I know, she was well settled and content." Lucy took off her bonnet. "Was she particular friends with any of the other maids?"

"I'm not sure. Perhaps Betty might know."

"Let's go and ask her." She turned back toward the kitchen, but Anna grabbed her arm.

"Don't ask her now, or the washing will never get done!"

Lucy paused. "That's true. I'll help you, and then we can question her afterward."

"I don't know where Mary went, miss." Betty looked earnestly at Lucy. "She's been behaving a bit strangely the last few weeks, a bit distracted like, as if her mind wasn't on her work."

"But you had no notion that she intended to leave us?"

"None at all, miss." Betty shook her head so definitely that her dark ringlets bobbed around her face. "But she wasn't one to share her secrets with me."

"Was she close to any of the other servants?"

Betty nibbled her lip. "I know she spent some of her time with one of the servants from the Hathaways' house up the road. But here, she was closest to Jane in the nursery. I think she wanted to work as a nurse one day."

"She never mentioned that to me. But I suppose she knew there would be no more babies in this family. Perhaps she simply found a new position."

"Without a reference?" Anna stripped off her apron. "What respectable family would take on a servant, especially as a nursemaid, without first writing to her former employers?"

Lucy caught Anna's eye and nodded at Betty. Sometimes her sister could be a little indiscreet in front of the servants. "Is there anything else you can think of that might help us, Betty?"

"Not right now, miss." Betty tugged at her wet, clinging skirts. "After doing all that washing, I'm too tired to think."

"Well, if you remember anything, please don't hesitate to come and tell me at once." Lucy rose and Betty nodded.

"Yes, miss."

"If Jane isn't busy, could you send her down?"

"Of course, miss. I'll go and find her before I change my dress."

"Thank you, Betty. I'm sorry the whole burden of the laundry fell upon you today. I promise I will make it up to you."

Betty bobbed a curtsy. "That's all right, miss. But I hope

we find out what happened to Mary. I'll have a few words to say to her myself when I see her next."

After Betty left, Anna glanced at Lucy. "I wonder what has happened? Had you even paid her quarterly wages?"

"No, I haven't. She didn't strike me as the kind of girl who would save her wages, either." Lucy frowned down at her cracked hands, which now smelled strongly of lye soap. "Do you think she might have broken into Father's strongbox and taken some money?"

"Oh my goodness. I don't know." Anna brought a hand to her cheek, her blue eyes wide. "Unless she had an accomplice—a man who wanted her to run away with him, or simply pretended that he did to get her to steal from us."

"You have the most vivid of imaginations. Perhaps you should stop reading those horrid gothic novels Mrs. Jenkins lends you."

"You read them, too, Lucy, and you were the one who mentioned Mary stealing from us first."

Lucy ignored that remark and continued to think out loud. "It is far more likely Mary found a new position and simply decided to leave us. I suspect we'll get a letter from her in the mail eventually asking for her back wages."

"Which you won't pay."

"Which Papa won't pay. He won't be happy about this at all. I cannot think of a way to conceal what has happened from him. He'll be sure to blame me in some fashion."

"It is hardly your fault if one of the maids decides to change employment, Lucy," Anna said robustly. "You'll just have to stand up for yourself."

Lucy bit back her hasty reply. It was easy for Anna to suggest she should be more forthright with their father when she was his favorite child, and not the oldest daughter of the house whose duty had been laid out for her from the cradle. Even now, when she knew her father's air of authority hid only his appalling selfishness, she still hadn't found a way to break free of his oft-expressed expectations. What had once been unquestioning obedience had slowly turned into a bitter and unexpressed resentment she had to conceal to avoid telling him her true feelings.

There was a knock on the door and Jane, the twins' nursemaid, appeared, her pleasant face flushed and her gaze wide with excitement.

"Is it true, Miss Harrington? Has Mary gone?"

"It certainly seems so." Lucy invited Jane to sit down. "Did she mention anything about leaving to you?"

"Well, she complained a few times about how hard she worked, but no more than anyone else, miss."

"But did she say anything more specific?" Lucy smiled sympathetically at Jane. "I hate to ask you to share her confidences, but I am very concerned as to her safety. Did she mention seeking a new position?"

"I did say I would help her if she wanted to become a nursemaid, but I don't think she'd applied for any positions. I told her she needed more experience, and that she should ask you if she could help out sometimes."

"That was excellent advice," Lucy agreed. "When did she decide she wanted to become a nursemaid?"

"Quite a while ago, miss." Jane smoothed her apron.

"Was Mary walking out with anyone in the village?" Anna leaned forward, ignoring Lucy's glare.

"I don't think so, Miss Anna. There was a man she was seeing for a while who was working on the new stables, but he's gone now." Jane hesitated. "She did get letters occasionally. She said they were from her childhood sweetheart."

"Her new admirer wasn't a local man, then?"

"I'm not sure, miss."

"Perhaps he came to find her and asked her to marry him." Anna clasped her hands together. "Wouldn't that be romantic?"

"I suppose it would be, miss." Jane paused. "But why didn't he come to the front door and ask permission to court her in a respectable manner like a gentleman and a Christian?"

"That's a very good point, Jane. Did Mary seem agitated or out of sorts recently?"

"She did seem a mite distracted, but I had no idea that she planned to take off." There was a loud crash from the upper floor and Jane stiffened. "I told those two heathens to sit still and wait for me to bring up their supper. They are probably fighting again. I've never known two lads who can't resist starting a boxing match with one another."

"You'd better go, Jane." Lucy rose, too. "Tell the boys to behave themselves, or else I won't come up and wish them good night."

"I will, miss, and if I think of anything else to help with Mary, I'll tell you right away."

Lucy pressed a hand to her aching forehead. "Thank you, Jane."

Anna closed the door behind the nurse. "I still think there is a man involved somewhere, don't you?"

"It certainly is possible."

"Perhaps Mary's suitor went to her parents first to ask permission to marry her and then came here?"

"I don't think she had parents. I believe Father recruited her from the foundling hospital and orphanage in Cambridge."

Anna continued to pace the carpet. "It certainly is a puzzle, isn't it?"

"Indeed." The clock struck five. "I need to check that Mrs. Fielding has returned from the village and started dinner." She opened the door and then paused. "Is Anthony back? I wonder if he caught any fish?"

Anna stamped her foot. "Lucy, why do you have to be so practical? What about Mary?"

"There is nothing we can do about Mary until Father returns." Lucy swallowed hard. "Let's hope Anthony was successful and that a good dinner will mellow Father's temper before I have to tell him the bad news and ask him to check we haven't been robbed."

Robert sat up in bed and waited while Foley carefully placed the tray containing his supper on his lap. It was Bookman's evening off, and Foley was deputizing for him. Because of their many years away from home together during the war, Robert sometimes forgot that, like him, Bookman still had family and friends in the surrounding area.

"Now be careful, sir. We don't want you covered in hot soup," Foley warned.

After his humiliating experiences with Miss Harrington earlier that day, it was a sentiment Robert heartily agreed with. He picked up his spoon and studied the clear broth. "This is scarcely soup, Foley. There's no meat in it."

"It's what Dr. Baker ordered Cook to make you, sir, so don't go scowling at me. A good broth will help you recover your appetite."

"My appetite is quite recovered." Robert put down his spoon. "Will you go and fetch me a nice plate of roast beef? I still have all my teeth. I'd like to use them while I can."

"Now, sir, don't you be ordering me about like that when you know I'll have Bookman and Cook raising hell with me for disobeying the doctor."

"Then I'll just have to starve to death." Robert took a tentative sip. The soup was watery and quite unappealing, but he had to eat something.

"There's a nice custard for pudding, sir."

"How lovely. I feel as if I am back in the nursery again being coaxed to eat by my nurse."

Foley handed him a napkin. "How about I get you a nice hunk of Cook's newly baked bread and a glass of port?"

Robert smiled for the first time since Miss Harrington

had visited him that morning. "You are indeed an angel, Foley."

"But you must finish your soup first."

He picked up the bowl and drank the contents down in one gulp.

"I've finished. Now fetch me that port."

"That is hardly the way a gentleman should comport himself at the table, sir."

Robert placed his spoon in his bowl and handed Foley the tray. "I'm not at the table and I scarcely feel like a gentleman. You, of all people, should know that society regards my lineage as very spotty indeed."

Foley stuck out his chin. "Don't be funning with me now, sir. Your mother was perfectly respectable. You are a gentleman born, and you know it."

Deciding that he had teased his old family retainer enough for one evening, Robert asked, "Did you sleep well last night, Foley?"

"I did, sir. After our supper, Bookman and I played a few hands of piquet and shared a jug of ale. Then I took myself up to bed early and slept like a baby."

Robert wondered just how much ale Foley and Bookman had shared to make them both sleep through the racket he'd made when he'd fallen, bringing the chair down with him.

"By the way, sir, Bookman felt terrible that you didn't think to ring for him to help you back to bed last night."

"And destroy his night's rest as well as my own?" Robert countered. In truth, he had eventually rung the bell in desperation, but no one had come. He wasn't going to mention it now and cause a fuss. "I was scarcely on the floor for more than a few minutes before he found me."

That wasn't true, either, but he didn't want his trusted servants to feel guilty about what had happened. They had already started treating him like a permanent invalid, and he didn't want to encourage them any further. Trotting out a strange story of having seen something mysterious moving through the grounds would hardly enhance his credibility or his claims to be on the mend. He'd more likely end up in Bedlam.

"I'll fetch the rest of your repast, sir." Foley bowed and left the room.

While he waited for Foley to return, Robert put on his spectacles and studied the newspapers Miss Harrington had brought him. While convalescing, he'd avoided reading about what was happening in London and the rest of the country. He'd felt quite detached from the social order, the riots, and the fear of revolution wafting seditiously across the English Channel from France. His focus had turned inward to his own pain and loss—to simply surviving. But as Foley had reminded him, he was a gentleman, and at some point he would have to take his place in society, even if only at a local level. His family had held the position of squire and local magistrate for hundreds of years. He wanted that to continue.

He'd barely skimmed the first article about the latest peace treaty before his headache returned. Casting the paper aside, he took off his new spectacles. When Miss Harrington next visited, he'd ask her to read to him. She'd probably enjoy being a ministering angel. He found himself smiling at that thought. Despite her meek appearance, she was no milk-and-water miss, and she certainly wouldn't allow him to order her around. It was quite refreshing.

"Here you are, sir. A nice glass of port." Foley was already speaking as he entered the room. "I also brought the post up for you."

"Thank you. Is there anything of interest?"

"A letter from your aunt Rose, one with no return address, which we had to pay for, and something official-looking from your regiment."

Robert studied the mail and then returned his attention to the excellence of the port. He wasn't in the mood to decipher the spiderlike scrawl of his aunt Rose, and the military could wait until he drew his last breath. The unpaid letter from an unknown correspondent was probably his cousin and heir presumptive, Paul, and he was in no mood to read that, either. He put the letters to one side.

"Miss Harrington said there was a disturbance in the village last night. Did you hear anything, sir?" Foley handed Robert a plate filled with bread and rich yellow butter.

Robert stiffened. "What kind of disturbance?"

"She wasn't sure, sir. She said her father mentioned something on his way out this morning." Foley refilled Robert's port glass.

For some reason, Robert was glad Miss Harrington hadn't said that he'd been the one inquiring about the incident. He didn't want to have to explain to Foley *quite* how far he'd ventured out of bed. Foley would tell Dr. Baker, who would probably double his dire prediction of how long it would take Robert to walk again.

"I assume you told her we'd keep an eye out for anything suspicious."

"I did, sir." Foley deftly stoppered the port and removed it from Robert's reach. "Let's hope the rector was mistaken, although I have heard rumors that there are gangs of discharged soldiers roaming the countryside stealing from decent folk."

"What else are they supposed to do when the government offers them no recompense for their service to their country?"

"Easy for you to say, sir, until you are murdered in your bed." Foley rearranged the items on the tray. "I'll tell the staff to make sure they lock their doors tonight."

"Trust me, Foley, a locked door won't stop a determined rabble from getting in."

"Then would you like me to bring you your pistols, sir? Bookman has kept them in perfect order."

He fixed Foley with his most intimidating stare. "I do not want my pistols, and I do not want you alarming the staff over a potential threat that might not even happen. Do you understand me?"

"Yes, sir, although . . ."

"Foley . . ." Robert held out his hand. "Give me the port and retire for the night. I won't need you again."

With a martyred air, Foley handed over the glass decanter and headed for the door.

"I'll tell Bookman to check on you later, sir."

"You don't have to do that, I'll—" Robert realized he was speaking to himself as his loyal henchman had deliberately walked out of earshot. He let out his breath. There was no point in becoming agitated. After last night's debacle, he suspected Bookman would be coming in to see him at whatever time of the night he returned, regardless of Robert's commands.

He settled back against his pillows and refilled his glass. Were Foley's remarks about marauding soldiers true or a fabrication? He didn't like to think of the men under his command begging for food or work. After helping defeat Napoleon, it didn't seem right. But what was a landowner to do? He couldn't feed them all, or he'd bankrupt his estate in a week.

He slowly sipped at his port. What if the man he thought he'd seen last night was one of those displaced soldiers intent on robbing the villagers? Should he in truth be encouraging Foley to set his staff and his neighbors on their guard? A headache pushed against his temples, and he pressed his fingers into the pain. Whatever happened, in his present condition, he could do nothing to save anyone—not even himself. He swallowed down that bitter reminder and contemplated finishing the decanter of port. Perhaps he should have told Foley to bring him his pistols. Not for his own defense, but to put an end to his miserable existence once and for all.

Chapter 4

"I'm not sure what else you want me to do about this matter, Lucy."

With the air of a martyred man, the rector put down his knife and fork. They were enjoying a light luncheon, and the sun was shining directly over the newly laid out garden. After her siblings dispersed to their various pursuits, Lucy had lingered at the table to consult with her father.

He continued, "Mary has obviously disappeared. Luckily for us, she didn't take the silver with her. Where she has gone, I have no notion."

"But you will ask around on your travels, won't you, Papa?" Lucy encouraged. "You *will* be visiting the smaller parishes this week as usual."

The rector glanced across at his curate, who paused with a piece of toast halfway to his mouth. He swallowed hastily and spoke through a mouthful of crumbs.

"Actually, Miss Harrington, I will be visiting Lower Kurland and Kurland St. Anne in the rector's stead while he concentrates on writing his sermon." His cheeks flushed an unbecoming shade of red. "I would be honored if you wish to accompany me."

Lucy flashed him a distracted smile. "That is very kind

of you, Edward. Please let me know when you intend to go. If I'm able to leave my duties here, I will definitely come with you."

She returned her attention to her father, who had picked up his paper again. "Do you not think we have a responsibility to discover what happened to poor Mary? She was a foundling. As far as we know, she has no other family to care about what has become of her."

"The Bible has much to say about ingratitude, Lucy, of nourishing a viper in one's bosom." He stood up and looked down his nose at her. "Perhaps you might reflect on *that* before you presume to lecture *me* about my Christian duty to one who has sinned by leaving a perfectly good home provided to her by a loving, spiritual family."

Lucy opened her mouth to refute his argument, and then closed it again. She would never convince him of anything when he was offended by her suggestion that he was being less than Christian.

The rector folded his paper and tucked it under his arm. "In truth, Daughter, perhaps you should examine your own conscience more thoroughly. Mary was under your domestic care, not mine. Perhaps if you had been a little more diligent in your duties, this unhappy occurrence would not have arisen."

An all-too-familiar anger coiled in Lucy's stomach, but before she could speak, her father left the room, his demeanor that of a man who had nothing on his conscience at all. She'd forgotten he hated to be put in the wrong, especially in front of his curate. As soon as he had ascertained that Mary hadn't stolen anything from the house and had left without her quarterly wages, he considered his part in the matter closed.

Lucy stirred her tea with such unnecessary vigor that half the liquid trickled down onto the tablecloth.

"Miss Harrington?"

She looked up to find Edward staring at her. "Yes?"

"I'm sure the rector is concerned about Mary. He just has a lot on his mind at the moment."

"I understand that—what with that new horse to be broken, and the hunting season approaching."

The moment she said the words out loud, Lucy regretted them. Being angry with her own father was not new, but sharing that resentment with his curate was reprehensible. She forced a smile.

"I'm sorry, Edward. I am worried about Mary, and my father is right. I do feel responsible for her sudden departure. I had no idea she was so unhappy here."

Edward poured himself another cup of tea and took the last four slices of toast. He was perpetually hungry, and could always be relied upon to finish even the most unappetizing meals that emerged from the rectory kitchen. Despite his prodigious appetite, he was as thin as a rail, his pale complexion mottled with pimples and his hair a dull mouse brown.

"She did seem rather disengaged from her duties recently—as if her mind were elsewhere. She left your brother Anthony's garments in my room on several occasions recently, and I had to ask her to remove them."

Lucy handed him the dish of plum preserves, and he spread them lavishly on his toast. "You are the second person who has told me that she was distracted. I must confess I barely noticed her at all. She always performed her duties perfectly when she was with me."

"Naturally, you are the mistress of the house." He crunched his way through another piece of toast, sending crumbs all over the tablecloth. He gulped down some tea. "She was in awe of you—as we all are."

"I'm only the temporary mistress. One day, I hope to be in charge of my own establishment." Lucy longed for that day, but still couldn't quite see how to accomplish it. It wasn't as if she went out in society much and could look for a husband. Sometimes she wondered if her indolent father expected her to dedicate her whole life to him. Sometimes she awoke in the night from a horrible dream of being suffocated and was quite certain of it.

Edward smiled at her, a splodge of purple jam dangling from his top lip. "You will make some man very happy one day." He swallowed hard. "Very happy indeed."

Lucy avoided his beseeching gaze and started to gather up the breakfast dishes. Thank goodness Anthony was not present to hear Edward's remarks. He would be winking at her, clutching his chest, and making lovesick eyes. It was common knowledge that the curate would like to make Lucy his wife, but that didn't mean she had to encourage it.

"Well, please let me know when you intend to visit the other parishes. I would like to make sure that everyone knows Mary has disappeared." She paused while stacking the plates. "Do you know if anyone was courting her?"

"I don't, Miss Harrington. She did have a habit of loitering around the new stable block while it was being built, so perhaps she had a young man who worked there."

"That's an excellent point, Edward. I can find out the names of the men who worked on the construction from my father's bills. I intend to go into the village and ask if anyone there has any notion of what might have become of her."

It also meant she could carry out Major Kurland's commission and find out if there had been any recent robberies or disturbances. She would call at the houses of the local gentry and see if they had taken on any new staff. Poaching another family's servants was generally frowned upon. But as her father often pointed out, some of the new families in the area had money, but not the necessary breeding, and might think nothing of offering a trained servant a higher wage to entice her away.

Lucy rang the bell for the breakfast room to be cleared, and Edward hurriedly finished his repast. He dabbed at his mouth with his napkin and stood up.

"I'll wish you good afternoon, Miss Harrington. I will let you know as soon as I plan to visit the smaller parishes."

"Thank you, Edward."

Lucy nodded and continued to stack the plates. She wasn't sure why she found his regard so objectionable. He would be the most obvious person for her to marry. Her father had even hinted at the suitability of such a match. Such a marriage would only enhance his comfort, and bind both her and Edward to the yoke of carrying out the duties of the parish for the rest of their lives.

Betty came into the parlor with an empty tray and started piling the crockery onto it. "Any news about Mary, Miss Harrington?"

"I'm afraid not, Betty." Lucy picked up a knife that had fallen to the floor. "I'm going into the village now. Mayhap I can discover more there."

She hurried to put on her bonnet and cloak before anyone else in the household needed to speak to her, and escaped into the fine spring sunshine. She'd wasted several minutes looking for her best gloves until she remembered their bloodied state and several more trying to relocate her old pair. Her first call would be on the Hathaway household, where her friend Sophia resided with her parents and two brothers. If Mary had been a friend of one of the maids, it was a good place to start. As she walked along the narrow lane, Lucy wondered if either of the Hathaway brothers would be at home. She always enjoyed conversing with Rupert Hathaway, the younger of the two. Since he'd started to practice law in London, he came home very irregularly. In truth, she'd always hoped he'd develop stronger feelings for her, but he had never broached the subject, and it was unbecoming for a lady to ask about such a delicate matter.

She sighed and kicked a dried-up cowpat from her path. If only she might be allowed to visit London and persuade one of her father's sisters or cousins to let her stay for the

Season. But every time she suggested it, he put her off, insisting he needed her at home. And he had needed her; there was no doubt about that. But with everything about to change at the rectory with the twins and Anthony's departure, surely she would have her chance to escape her domestic duties now?

The main gates to Hathaway House were closed, but Lucy knew the way through the smaller, less obvious pedestrian gate behind the lodge. To her delight, the bluebells in the ancient wood incorporated within the park were in bloom. She extended her walk to pass through the middle of them, inhaling the peppery scent and marveling at the waxen nature of the tiny bell-shaped petals. As children, they'd rolled down the hill through the bluebells until the nursemaids grew tired of trying to get the stains out of their clothing and complained to their parents.

Reluctant to disturb such perfection, and determined to bring her sketchbook on her next visit to capture the view, Lucy picked just one and tucked it in her buttonhole before heading for the kitchen door of the large stone-built house. The distracted cook and youngest scullery maid were busy at the range, their backs turned toward her. Lucy inhaled the smell of roasting beef and immediately felt hungry.

"Good afternoon, Mrs. Lucas, and how are you today?"

"Very well, Miss Harrington." The cook poked her young assistant with her spoon. "Curtsy to the lady and say good afternoon, Maggie."

Maggie's thin face flushed red, and she mumbled something inaudible before bobbing a curtsy.

Lucy smiled at them both. "Do you have a moment to speak with me, Mrs. Lucas?"

"Of course, miss." Mrs. Lucas pushed the scullery maid in the direction of the pans. "Keep an eye on these pots for a minute."

Lucy waited until the cook joined her by the table. "Mary Smith from my kitchen has gone missing. I wondered if you had heard anything about where she went, or why?"

Mrs. Lucas wiped her hands on her apron. "Gone, has she? Taken another job, or run off?"

"At this point, I don't know." Lucy studied the cook's kind face. "I didn't think she was unhappy with her lot, but obviously one could be wrong."

"From what I've heard, you treat your servants very fairly, miss. Your Mary was quite friendly with our junior parlor maid, Susan O'Brien. Would you like to speak to her?"

"If that would be possible, Mrs. Lucas. Obviously, I'll ask Mrs. Hathaway's permission when I go up to see her."

"And I'll check with Mr. Spencer, the butler. He might prefer to be present at any interview you hold with a member of staff."

"Naturally." Lucy nodded and turned toward the stairs that led up to the main floor of the house. "I'll go up and see Mrs. Hathaway immediately."

She ascended the uncarpeted stairs and pushed open the door that led through into the hallway of Hathaway House. It was strange how as a rector's daughter she had equal access to all classes of society. She was just as at home in a kitchen as she was in a drawing room. She supposed she should thank her father for that at least. The austerity of the servants' quarters gave way to a large airy hall with paneled walls, marble floors, and an elaborately plastered ceiling. The Hathaways considered themselves the second highest family in the village—after the Kurlands—and conducted themselves accordingly. They had always been very kind to Lucy, and she was a welcome and valued visitor.

Lucy found her way to the back of the house, where Mrs. Hathaway had a bright and sunny informal sitting room, and knocked on the door. After being told to enter, she went in and was rewarded by a smiling welcome from both the ladies present. She often wondered how it might have been if her own mother had lived and hoped they would've been as close as Sophia and her mother.

"Lucy!" Sophia leapt to her feet and ran to hug her friend. She was dressed simply in a soft green muslin dress with a single flounce, her blond hair braided around the crown of her head rather than curled. "How nice to see you. Mama and I were just speaking about Major Kurland. I'm quite certain you have all the latest gossip about him."

She kissed Sophia's cheek and sat beside her on the sofa. "Good day, Mrs. Hathaway. Are you feeling better?"

Sophia's mother smiled in reply. "I am, thank you. I suspect I was just tired from the journey back from London. A few days in my own home have restored my spirits and my health quite wonderfully."

"I'm glad to hear it." Lucy patted Sophia's Cavalier King Charles puppy on the head. "Did you find both your sons in good health?"

"Indeed, Perry is rattling around in a manner that makes my husband threaten to cut off his allowance, and Rupert is advancing steadily in his career."

"Neither of them made the journey back with you?"

"Unfortunately not, but I expect them both at Easter. You will all have to come to dinner and catch up on all the news from Town."

"That would be lovely."

Sophia elbowed her in the side. "Are you deliberately ignoring my question about the dashing major, or are you simply displaying your superior manners?"

"I have nothing of interest to tell you about Major Kurland. He is still bedridden and remarkably argumentative."

"In my experience, men never make good patients," Mrs. Hathaway said comfortably. "They either behave like children, or imagine they are the only mortal in the entire world to ever be so sick, or near death." She set a stitch in her embroidery. "Mind you, I'm not surprised Major Kurland is a difficult patient. After his distinguished career in the military, it must be hard for him to be idle."

Lucy didn't argue the point. The whole village seemed intent on hero-worshiping Major Kurland, and wouldn't hear a word against him. Only she, Foley, and Bookman seemed to know what it was really like to tend the oh-so-ungallant major.

"Has he made any progress at all?" Sophia fed her dog a crumb of cake.

"It is hard to tell. He certainly isn't walking by himself yet." After seeing the depths of the major's despair, she felt guilty even saying that. "But I'm sure he'll come about."

Sophia rang for some more tea, and Lucy guided the conversation back to more mundane matters such as the weather and the new piece of embroidery the very talented Mrs. Hathaway was working on for the church altar. She succeeded so well that when the butler appeared with the tea tray, and loudly cleared his throat, she almost jumped.

"I understand that Miss Harrington wishes to speak to a member of my staff, ma'am."

Mrs. Hathaway looked inquiringly at Lucy. "Do you?"

"Oh yes! I hadn't quite gotten around to mentioning it. One of our servants has gone missing. I understand that she was a friend of your parlor maid, Susan O'Brien. I was hoping to ask whether she had any news about Mary."

"How very strange," commented Mrs. Hathaway. "Did your servant not leave a message or a forwarding address?"

"No, she just disappeared, apparently without a word to anyone."

Mrs. Hathaway looked at her butler. "Then, of course Miss Harrington must speak to Susan. Make sure she is in the kitchen when my guest is ready to depart."

"As you wish, ma'am." The butler bowed and departed, leaving Sophia to pour the tea at her mother's direction.

Lucy accepted a cup and then looked up at Mrs. Hathaway. "Are you sure you don't mind me talking to Susan?"

"Of course not, my dear. I'm sure you are worried about what has happened to your Mary." Mrs. Hathaway sipped her tea. "Don't worry about Spencer. Sometimes I think he believes he is head of this family rather than Mr. Hathaway."

"He's never really liked me," Lucy replied. "I think he believes my whole family are too socially inferior to be invited here."

"Scarcely that," Sophia chimed in. "In fact, Spencer sometimes reminds me that your father is the son of an earl, and that your mother was related to a viscount. He believes I should strive to behave more like you."

"Me?" Lucy smothered a laugh by drinking her tea.

"You are very well behaved, Lucy, and a credit to your family," Mrs. Hathaway said. "I only wish your mother was here to see how well you have turned out. She would be so proud of how you have taken her place and brought up her children as if they were your own."

Lucy's smile died. "Sometimes I wish I didn't have to take her place, but I had no choice. I wish . . ." She stopped speaking and busied herself with choosing a slice of cake from the nearest tray.

Sophia squeezed her hand. "Mother and I think you are a saint to carry such a burden. Those twins would have sent most parents straight to a madhouse!"

"They are old enough to go away to school in the autumn, can you believe that?"

"That will leave you with more time on your hands to look about you and decide what you want to do next." Mrs. Hathaway hesitated. "Has your father made any suggestions as to your debut into society?"

"My debut?" Lucy put down her cup. "I think he believes I am far too old to hanker after such a thing."

Sophia and her mother exchanged a cryptic glance. "And if you weren't?"

"Weren't what?"

"Averse to a Season in London." Sophia studied her closely. "I have decided it is time for me to enter Society again. It is five years since Charlie's death at Badajoz. He always told me that if anything happened to him, I should marry again." She drew in a sharp breath. "You might think me callous, but I yearn for all those things Charlie's death has denied me—a husband, children, a home of my own. I'll never love anyone the way I loved him, but I hope I can find a man who will care and respect me for myself."

Lucy stared at Sophia, who steadfastly held her gaze. Her friend had married her dashing cavalryman when she was barely seventeen, but had never regretted it. His death during the siege of Badajoz had shaken her to the core. Lucy had wondered if Sophia would ever fully recover from it. It seemed that she had, although her prosaic approach to looking for a new husband sounded rather cold-blooded to Lucy. But who was she to criticize? In her more desperate moments, she had considered marrying anyone who offered for her, regardless of his age, social standing, or financial stability.

"If I do go to London, I'd like to take you with me as my companion. Your father can hardly object to that. We can look for a husband together." She leaned forward and took Lucy's hand. "What do you think?"

Lucy stared at Sophia as a thousand new possibilities flooded through her brain. "I would like it above all things."

Sophia sat back. "I'm so glad you said that. Mother will come and chaperone us, so it will all be perfectly respectable."

"I'll have to speak to my father about it. When do you plan to leave?"

Mrs. Hathaway laughed. "There is no need for haste.

We probably won't be ready to go until much later in the year, or even next spring. Sophia might even change her mind."

"I will not," her daughter interjected. "I wanted to ask you whether you would accompany me, so that you would have something to look forward to when the boys go away to school. I know that you will miss them dreadfully."

"I will miss the little scamps. But the prospect of a Season in London will certainly help reconcile me to their loss. Thank you so much for the invitation. I am quite undone."

Sophia grinned at her. "I would rather face the gorgons of London society with you by my side than with any other woman. I'm delighted you want to come with me."

The clock struck the half hour, and Lucy rose to her feet and hugged Sophia hard. "I hate to leave you, but I must speak to Susan, and then go to the village to see if anyone else has news about Mary."

She sped down the stairs, her heart lighter than she could ever have imagined. A Season in London! After the boys were safely ensconced at school, how could her father possibly deny her that? It took her all her efforts to control her exuberance and face the Hathaways' butler with a serene expression.

"Miss Harrington?" He opened the door into his sitting room and followed her inside. "This is Susan O'Brien."

A small redheaded girl with freckles bobbed Lucy an awkward curtsy.

Lucy took a seat and gestured for the girl to sit opposite her. After a wary glance at the butler, Susan sat down.

"Did you know that Mary Smith planned to leave my employment?"

"Mary said a lot of things. I didn't think she'd ever do any of them. She was a mite excitable, if you know what I mean."

"So she did mention she planned to leave?"

Susan glanced down at her folded hands. "She wanted to go to London, I know that for sure."

"And did she go?"

Susan steadfastly refused to look up. "I suppose she must have if she isn't here."

"But she didn't tell you her plans?"

"She's hardly been around the last few weeks." Susan sniffed. "Taken up with someone new, no doubt. She was like that, always chasing something she couldn't have."

"Would you describe her as restless, then?"

"I suppose so. She always wanted a better life, but who could blame her?"

"But how did she define a better life?" Lucy sat forward. "A better job, a man to marry her?"

Susan briefly looked up. Lucy plainly saw the resentment in her gaze, but whether it was for her question, or for the position Mary's disappearance had placed her in, Lucy couldn't tell.

"I'm not sure what you want me to say, Miss Harrington."

"Let me make myself plain. Do you think Mary might have left the village to secure another position, or to get married?"

"Knowing Mary, it could've been either of those things. She wasn't without ambition, or plenty of suitors, Miss Harrington, even if they weren't always hers to have."

Lucy studied the parlor maid for a long moment. "Did you have a falling-out? You almost sound glad that she has gone."

Susan's expression darkened. "I didn't do anything to her, miss. She's the one who liked to have everyone's attention on her, not me."

"Thank you, Susan."

Lucy glanced across at Spencer to indicate that she had no more questions for the girl, and he opened the door to usher Susan out.

"That will be all, Susan. If you think of anything that

might help, come and see me and I'll make sure the information gets back to Miss Harrington."

"Thank you, sir." Susan curtsied and made her way through the door, which Spencer closed behind him.

"I'm not quite sure what has got into the girl lately, Miss Harrington. She's been rather surly."

"Perhaps she and Mary quarreled over something, and now she feels badly about it."

Spencer sat down heavily in his chair. "That might be the way of it. Female servants are much harder to deal with than men. There is always something going on, be it about tall tales or talk of marriage."

"I know." Lucy joined in his sigh. "What I can't decide is whether Susan is annoyed because she doesn't know what Mary planned, or if she is lying for her. I got the distinct impression that the news of her friend's disappearance came as a shock."

"I'll keep an eye on her, Miss Harrington. She might be prepared to divulge more to me than to you."

Lucy rose and retied the ribbons on her bonnet. "Thank you, Spencer. I appreciate it. Now I must be off to the village. I have several commissions to fulfill there."

She walked slowly down the elm tree–lined drive, her thoughts full of the missing girl. If Mary had left to get married, why hadn't she simply informed Lucy of her decision, been paid her outstanding wages, and been sent on her way with a smile? It didn't make sense. The most obvious answer was that the girl had found a better position and not bothered to tell her former employer. But was it more complicated than that? If Mary had a new beau, had she wanted to leave the village with some funds behind her and been seen escaping by Major Kurland?

Lucy considered that as she approached the village high street. It seemed the most obvious answer to both the problems. In such a small village, it was unlikely that two such significant events would be unrelated. She suspected

Susan knew more than she'd said, but she could only hope the girl would confide in the butler. Had Mary stolen her young man? If Mary had such an accomplice, who was he, and wouldn't he also be missing? That might be worth inquiring about, too.

The door to the general store, which was housed in a low timber-framed building, was open, and Lucy decided to start there. Two spinster sisters ran the small shop, which provided basic necessities for the villagers, including foodstuffs, household goods, and linens.

Miss Amelia Potter nodded as Lucy entered the shop. She was a plump, elderly woman with soft, faded features and gray hair braided into a coronet on top of her head. She wore an old-fashioned gown of brown muslin covered with a large linen apron.

"Good afternoon, Miss Harrington. Back again so soon? What may I assist you with today?"

Lucy put her basket on the counter. "I need some black wool to darn the twins' stockings, and six more buttons for their shirts."

Miss Amelia tittered discreetly behind her lace-mittened hand. "Those boys of yours are such a trial with their clothing."

"Indeed, they are." Lucy waited while Miss Amelia found a skein of black wool. "Soon we will have to outfit them for school. I'm quite dreading that."

"I'm sure you are, Miss Harrington. I've heard it is quite a task for one child, let alone for two."

"My father says he will take them to his tailor in London for most of their garments, but that still leaves a lot for me to do."

"I'm sure it does, my dear." Miss Amelia carefully counted out six identical buttons from the jar and put them into a twist of paper along with the skein of black darning wool.

"And how fares your sister?" Lucy asked. "Is she still unable to sleep?"

"Alas, Mildred is still waking at the most ungodly of hours." Miss Amelia shook her head, making the cap atop her hair tremble. "And as she is afraid of the dark, she has a terrible tendency to wake me up and tell me what she thinks she has seen."

Miss Mildred sounded remarkably like Major Kurland, but Lucy didn't share that interesting thought. She stowed the buttons and wool in her basket and handed over a coin. "What sort of things disturb her?"

"Cats fighting, dark shapes flitting around the village, raised voices . . ." Miss Amelia deposited the coin in a drawer. "In truth, I know far more about what goes on in this village when Christian folks should be in their beds than I ever wished to."

"Was Miss Mildred awake the night before last?" Lucy put away her purse. "I only ask because I was up myself, and thought I heard a disturbance in the village."

"Mildred heard something, too. She said there were several people out and about who *should not have been there at all.*"

"Oh my. Did she say who she saw?"

Miss Amelia lowered her voice. "Some young girls who should know better, and several *men.*"

Lucy tried to look disapproving. "Together?"

"Mildred didn't say, and I don't like to encourage her. Sometimes she expects me to go out and reprimand the miscreants." Miss Amelia shivered delicately. "I cannot bring myself to do that. What would people think?" She picked up the jar of buttons and answered her own question. "I know what they'd think, that my sister and I were a pair of old gossips who had nothing better to do with our time than make up stories about our neighbors."

Lucy nodded sympathetically. "Can you not give your sister a sleeping draught?"

"They don't appear to work on her delicate constitution." Miss Amelia put the jar back on the shelf. "Dr. Baker says he has nothing else that she can try. I cannot afford to send her to London for treatment, the cost would be prohibitive." She looked around the small shop. "We make enough to be comfortable, but not for the extravagancies of life, and since I had to let young Joseph go . . ."

"Whatever happened?" Lucy, who had picked up her basket, put it down again. "I thought he was proving most satisfactory."

Another customer came into the shop, and Miss Amelia lowered her voice even more. "I thought so, too, but—certain things have gone missing from the store—small things, but they all add up. When I questioned Joseph, he grew very sullen with me, and insisted I was blaming him because of his family history. But he does come from a troubled background, Miss Harrington, we both know that, don't we?"

There was a hint of self-righteous censure in Miss Amelia's remark that made Lucy bite back a sharp reply. It was true that Joseph's family were well known in the village for their casual attitude to work and generally sly natures. But she'd thought better of Joseph, which was why she had prevailed upon Miss Amelia to take him on as an errand boy and general dogsbody.

"Has he returned home? I'll go and speak to him as soon as I am able." Lucy picked up her basket.

"I won't take him back, Miss Harrington."

Lucy did her best imitation of her father. "Surely everyone deserves a second chance?"

Miss Amelia's expression took on a stubborn turn. "Not in this shop."

"Then who will do your deliveries for you?"

"I'll do them myself until I can find someone satisfactory."

"Would you like me to help?"

"No, thank you, Miss Harrington. I think you've done enough."

Lucy forced a smile. "Then I'll be off. Thank you for your assistance, and my good wishes to your sister."

She shut the door with rather more force than necessary, aware that Miss Amelia's attitude toward the unfortunate Joseph was unlikely to change, and that she was probably correct that the boy had been stealing things. She doubted Major Kurland had any knowledge of young Joe, who had been born while he was away, but maybe he knew of his father, Ben? He was a large, powerfully built man who had been a boxer in his youth. If there had been any kind of disturbance in the village, it was highly likely that Ben Cobbins had been part of it.

Lucy continued along the street. Despite her disappointment about Joseph, she had found out some information about who had been out that night that might interest the major. There had definitely been some unusual activity. Perhaps Mary had been one of the girls out and about in the village.

A waft of cinnamon-flavored warm air flowed around her, and she found herself being waved down by an agitated-looking Mrs. Weeks from the open door of the bakery.

"Miss Harrington!"

"What is it, Mrs. Weeks?"

Mrs. Weeks clasped one large floury hand to her bosom. "It's my Daisy."

"Has she found a new situation?"

"No, Miss Harrington—she's up and run away to London!"

Chapter 5

Lucy thrust her cloak and gloves at Foley, picked up her skirts, and hurried up the shallow stairs toward Major Kurland's bedroom. She knocked on the door and barely waited for his peremptory command to enter. The major was sitting up in bed reading a newspaper, a pair of gold-rimmed spectacles perched on his aristocratic nose.

"Are those my spectacles?" Lucy asked, her attention momentarily diverted.

"I don't know, are they?" Major Kurland studied her over the top of the frames. "I found them by my bed the other morning, and assumed that Bookman or Foley had acquired them for me." He whipped them off his nose. "Do you want them back?"

"Not if they are helping you. I have another pair at home because I am constantly misplacing the dratted things."

"I don't wish to inconvenience you. I'll ask Bookman to arrange for a pair to be made for me."

Lucy walked over to the side of the bed and observed the major more carefully. He looked rested, the dark shadows under his eyes less visible. "Please keep them until your own pair is ready for you."

"Thank you, Miss Harrington. I will, although I still find reading a strain on my eyes."

"Would you like me to read to you, sir?" She drew up a chair and sat beside the bed. She indicated the pile of letters on the nightstand. "You appear to have some outstanding correspondence."

"I'm aware of that. I haven't even attempted to open most of it yet." He grimaced. "It's even harder to read handwriting than print."

"Don't you have a secretary to attend to such matters for you?"

"I've never needed one before."

"Perhaps you should advertise for one."

"Indeed." He stared down at her, one eyebrow raised until she felt herself blush.

"I apologize. My brother often describes me as a 'managing' female. Your lack of a secretary is obviously no concern of mine."

"Obviously." He put the newspaper down. "How are your brothers? I don't suppose either of them needs a job, do they?"

Lucy focused her gaze on the major's capable-looking hands. "Anthony is studying for Cambridge, and Tom . . ." She swallowed hard. "Tom died at Waterloo."

Silence greeted her stark words, and she looked up to see a stricken expression cross Major Kurland's face. His hand slowly clenched into a fist.

"Why didn't anyone tell me?"

"You were so ill when you returned that my father ordered us not to mention it."

"And now I have blundered and made you remember him."

She lifted her gaze to meet his. "I always remember him. I pray for his soul every day."

"I am sorry for your loss. Tom was my friend." He exhaled. "And from all accounts, he was an excellent officer."

"Thank you. My father was very cast down by Tom's death. Now all his hopes are focused on Anthony, who doesn't find such attention easy to deal with."

"I know the feeling, Miss Harrington."

"But you were always the oldest son and heir."

"But after Matthew's death, my parents only had me. I felt that responsibility quite heavily."

Lucy allowed the silence to fall between them again as they both considered their lost siblings. The major was the first to speak.

"Did you bring me news?"

Lucy was quite willing to be distracted. "According to Miss Amelia and her sister, there *have* been some nocturnal activities in the village."

"What exactly does that mean?"

"I'll have to speak directly to Miss Mildred to find out. Her sister was rather vague."

"Spinsters are the devil. What did she say?"

"That various young men and women, who *ought not to be out at all,* are running amok through the village streets."

"And what does that have to do with potential thievery?"

"According to Miss Mildred, there was just such a disturbance on the night you heard something, too. It does indicate that there is more going on in this place than I ever realized."

"What else?" the major demanded.

"Miss Amelia did say there had been some petty thefts from her store, but she is quite convinced her errand boy, Joseph Cobbins, is responsible for those."

"I know the Cobbins family. She's probably right."

Lucy raised her chin. "I'm not sure I agree. Joe is not like the rest of his family at all. In fact, I—"

The major cut across her again. "The person I saw was an adult, not a scrawny child like Joseph."

"You *saw* someone? Doing what?"

"Carrying some kind of load past the church."

"You didn't mention that before."

He rubbed a hand over his scalp where his black hair was just starting to curl again at the nape of his neck. "I didn't want to appear unhinged. Bookman and Foley are already worried about me. Insisting I saw strangers traipsing across my property in the dead of night would certainly not aid my claims to sanity and reason. They'd think I'd been at the laudanum again."

Remembering his staff's concerns on the previous day, Lucy privately agreed. "I wonder if you saw Joe's father, Ben?"

"It's possible. The Cobbins family has always been shiftless. It wouldn't surprise me if Ben was encouraging his son to steal from his employers."

"Poor Joe is no longer employed. I intend to speak to him as soon as I can."

He frowned. "Be careful. I don't want you tangling with Ben Cobbins."

"I don't think he'd hurt me."

"You have no idea what he might do if he felt you threatened his livelihood. Keep away from him."

"Now who is being managing? I am quite capable of looking after myself."

His skeptical expression signified his disbelief, but to her relief he didn't say anything more. "What else has happened in the village?"

"After I spoke to Miss Amelia, I was hailed by Mrs. Weeks from the bakery."

"And?"

"Her daughter, Daisy, has run off!"

"How old is she?"

"Eighteen, I believe."

"Let me guess, she's run off to London to seek her fortune on the stage. Is she pretty?"

"Not particularly. I gather her ambitions are more practical. She dreams of becoming a lady's maid."

He snorted. "She's more likely to end up on her back."

"It's highly likely, Major, but according to her mother, she is both a resourceful and a stubborn girl. I've no doubt she'll contrive to steer clear of the brothel keepers."

He stared at her for so long that she began to fidget. "What's wrong?"

"In some ways, you are quite remarkable, Miss Harrington."

"What do you mean?"

He gave her one of his rare smiles, and she was amazed at how it changed his face. "I should be apologizing for my crudeness."

"You only spoke the truth. Most girls who venture into the city do end up on their backs."

"But most young ladies of your standing do not know about it."

"You forget I'm the daughter of a clergyman. We see far more than most women of our class."

"So it seems."

"Is it possible you saw Daisy leaving the village? The quickest route from the village to the main road where the mail coaches run is past the church."

"No, it wasn't a girl."

Lucy sat back. "Could it possibly have been more than one person?"

"Why do you say that?"

"Because one of our maids has disappeared, as well." She quickly recounted the basic elements of Mary's disappearance. "I was wondering whether the two girls left together, or whether they were accompanied by at least one man."

"Why?"

"Because Susan O'Brien, who is a parlor maid for the

Hathaways, indicated that Mary had taken up with a new friend and neglected her. If Mary was planning to leave the village with Daisy Weeks, her head would've been full of those plans, and she would not have had time for her old friend."

"I suppose that is possible, although it didn't look like two girls."

"How can you be sure? It was dark and you were quite far away."

"The moon was very bright. That's why I got up in the first place, to close the damned curtains." He shifted against his pillows. "Why do you think there might have been a man involved?"

"Because Mary was interested in some man who helped build the new stable block for our house. Anna and I wondered if perhaps she had eloped with him."

"And taken Daisy along with her to play propriety? It seems unlikely."

Lucy sighed. "I know. I just can't work it out. If Mary decided to go to London with Daisy, why didn't she wait until quarter day to receive her wages, and hand in her notice? It makes more sense that she left with a man. Mayhap you only saw him because she was hiding under his cloak."

Major Kurland stared out of the window as if he was reconstructing the events in his head. "That might be it."

"Then what should we do?"

"There are several avenues to explore. Firstly, you need to talk to Miss Mildred Potter about exactly whom she saw 'cavorting' in the village the other night. Then you need to speak with Joseph. Or if you wish it, bring him here and we can question him together. He might respond better to me."

Lucy held up her hand. "Wait. If you are going to start issuing orders, I really need to write them down. Do you have ink and paper here?"

"In the desk."

She went over to the dainty escritoire that stood against the far wall and pulled out the chair. The major was looking more animated than she had ever seen him and, despite his peremptory tone, she was loath to interrupt his flow of enthusiasm. She opened the inkwell and dipped her pen in it.

"Speak to Miss Mildred. Bring Joseph here to question him about the thefts." She wrote these down and turned to him, pen poised above the paper. "Anything else?"

"Yes, check and see if anyone else in the village has lost any property."

"Why do I need to do that?"

"Because we need to ascertain the scope of the problem. Is there a gang stealing from the village, is it a single person such as Joe Cobbins or your maid, or a band of roaming ex-soldiers terrorizing my tenants?"

"That last one seems rather extreme."

"In these troubled times it could be any of those things. Foley was worried enough to mention our lack of security here at the manor to me last night."

"What does he expect you to do, take up the drawbridge and pour boiling oil over the walls?"

A flash of amusement lightened the major's drawn face. "I believe he'd like to do just that, but if he doesn't feel safe in a place where he has lived all his life, neither do I."

Lucy studied the list. "It might be simpler than you think. Over the last few months, Daisy and Mary could've stolen a few trinkets to finance their journey to London. The man you saw might have been hired to drive them to the city and was merely carrying their baggage to his cart."

The major just looked at her. "You are a strange combination of the practical and the romantic, Miss Harrington."

"I'm just considering all the scenarios, sir."

He tapped his finger against his chin. "I'll speak to

Foley about the servants here and whether we've suffered any thefts."

Lucy wrote everything down and then blew carefully on the ink to speed the drying process. "Do you want to see the list?"

"Yes, please." He held out his hand and she walked over to him.

She waited while he read, his brow furrowed. "That will do for now. Come and see me tomorrow and bring young Cobbins with you."

Lucy took back the sheet of paper and fought an inclination to salute. "I will if I have time, Major." She hoped her discouraging tone indicated that she wasn't one of his lower-ranked soldiers or his servant to be ordered around.

"Naturally, Miss Harrington. I wouldn't dream of inconveniencing you."

She put the note in her basket and made her escape, torn between her delight at seeing her patient so enlivened, and her annoyance with his high-handed manner. While he had nothing to do all day except lie around in bed and issue orders, *she* had a house to run. Unfortunately, she now had the task of returning home and negotiating with Mrs. Fielding about dinner, a daily task that continued to terrify her.

In the hallway she met Bookman carrying a pile of laundered nightshirts toward the major's room.

"Miss Harrington. How did you find the major today?"

"He seemed a little brighter."

Bookman smiled. "He slept better last night."

He was a good-looking man of about thirty with brown hair, hazel eyes, and a pleasant, respectful demeanor. He'd grown up on the Kurland estate, so Lucy knew him almost as well as Major Kurland. He'd gone away to war with the major as his batman and was now employed as his valet. Gossip said that it was Bookman who discovered the unconscious major on the battlefield of Waterloo, dragged him clear of his fallen horse, and saved his life.

"Did you have the opportunity to ask Dr. Baker about allowing the major to sit up in a chair by his window?"

"I haven't seen the good doctor yet today, but I will be sure to mention it to him." Bookman glanced at the bedroom door. "He needs something to keep his spirits up."

It was on the tip of Lucy's tongue to tell Bookman about her inquiries, but she managed to curb the impulse and nodded instead. If Major Kurland wished to discuss the matter with his valet, it was his business. She lived in fear of becoming known as a terrible spinsterish gossip.

"Thank you, Mr. Bookman. Let's hope Dr. Baker agrees with you."

Robert glanced up from his newspaper as Bookman came into the room with a pile of folded linen.

"Are you ready for your luncheon, Major?"

Robert took off his borrowed spectacles. "I believe I am."

"That's good to hear, sir." Bookman opened one of the drawers and deftly slid the shirts inside. "It sounds like Miss Harrington cheered you up."

"She is very kind to me."

"You probably don't remember much about when you were brought back here. After we discovered the nurse we'd hired to take care of you was guzzling gin, Miss Harrington stepped in and nursed you herself. And very capable she proved to be, too. In fact, you might say that between her, Dr. Baker, me, and Foley, you owe us your life."

"I am quite aware of that, Bookman." How could he explain to his longtime servant and companion that at his most wretched, he'd wanted to die and had bitterly resented their efforts to keep him alive? "Is Dr. Baker coming to see me today?"

"He'll be here around six o'clock."

He couldn't repress a shiver. Bookman walked over to the bed and fussed over straightening the covers. "Not to worry, Major. He just wants to see how you do."

Robert glared at his valet. "I'm scarcely *worried*. I'm not that much of a coward."

"I know that. I've seen you in battle many times, but there's no denying that doctor does like to maul you around." Bookman hesitated. "It's different here, isn't it? On a battlefield, you accept the horror of death and pain because it's all around you, and it's all you know. But in Kurland St. Mary? Pain and suffering seem somehow out of place."

"That's very profound, Bookman."

He gave an embarrassed laugh. "Just thinking aloud, sir. Pay no attention to me."

He turned toward the door, and Robert watched him carefully. Bookman and he had shared a lifetime of atrocities and probably the same nightmares. It was no wonder his valet found the contrast between tranquil, pastoral England and war-torn Europe as jarring as he did.

"If you have time to ponder such things you must be very bored indeed. Arranging my nightshirts is hardly a task for a man of your capabilities."

"I don't just do that, Major. I help old Foley manage the staff. He's getting on a bit, you know, and is quite forgetful."

"I appreciate your hard work and your loyalty, but I must ask you to reconsider my offer."

"Trying to get rid of me again, sir?" Bookman turned to study Robert. "I thought we'd been through this before. I'm staying right here."

"Thank you, Bookman."

"You're welcome, sir." His valet saluted and opened the door. "I'll get your rations now."

Robert eased back on his pillows and slowly let out his breath. He didn't deserve such loyalty. Bookman, at least, knew the worst of him, but the gently reared spinster daughter of the rector should have no ability to understand him or the brutal military life he'd led overseas. Robert frowned. She did understand him, and sometimes surprised him with her matter-of-fact common sense. He'd never thanked her for her care when he'd been delirious with fever and begging for someone to put an end to his agony. In some strange way he supposed he now shared a bond with her, too.

Pushing such unsettling thoughts to the back of his mind, Robert considered the information Miss Harrington had gathered for him in the village. He suspected she was far better at getting people to talk to her than he would ever be—even if the information were disgorged in a particularly fragmented and feminine way. In his role as local magistrate, Robert had the power to affect people's lives. Such a position also made his tenants and the villagers more afraid of him, and wary of giving offense.

He would have to rely on Miss Harrington's haphazard methods of detection and use his more ordered male mind to unravel the tangle of information and make sense of it. The thought of Ben Cobbins being involved in the matter made him uneasy. He didn't want Miss Harrington to approach such a rogue, especially in his own dwelling. He could only hope she would heed his advice and bring the boy, minus his father, to Kurland Hall on the morrow.

Bookman reappeared with a tray in his hands, and Robert inhaled the scent of baked ham and onions. For the first time in a long while, he was actually hungry. Bookman placed the tray across his knees and removed the cover with a flourish.

"While the cook's back was turned, I poured away the gruel, and got you what the servants were eating. It's not fancy, but I reckon it will put some flesh on your bones."

Robert picked up his knife. "Thank you."

"You're welcome, sir." Bookman bowed.

"Can you ask Foley to come and speak to me after I've eaten?"

"Yes, sir." He paused at the door. "Is there anything I

can help you with? As I said, I've been trying to take some of the burdens of managing this old place from the old duffer. He's neither as young nor as observant as he used to be."

"Foley does well enough." Robert looked up. "Do you have a sudden ambition to become my butler?"

Bookman's smile flashed out. "Maybe in about twenty years when Foley toddles off to his maker, I'll take you up on that."

"When Foley *retires,* consider the position yours." He pulled off a hunk of warm bread and dipped it in his gravy. "But send him up to me anyway."

When Foley came in, Robert found himself judging the familiar figure with fresh eyes. He guessed the butler, who had been hired by his mother, must be in his late fifties or early sixties. He was a thin man with wispy gray hair who looked as if he might blow away in a strong breeze. He often complained about the cold draughts that gusted through the old house, comparing it unfavorably with the modern stuccoed box the rector had built beside the church, which Robert privately thought was an eyesore.

"Thank you for coming to see me so promptly." Robert waved at the chair beside his bed. "Would you like to sit down?"

Foley raised his chin. "It wouldn't be fitting, sir."

"It's just you and me, Foley. No one need know."

"I'd prefer to stand."

"Have it your way," Robert said briskly. "I wanted to ask you about your concerns for the safety of this house."

"You told me I was overreacting, sir."

There was a hint of reproach in the butler's voice that made Robert want to squirm like a schoolboy. "I've been thinking about what you said. I wondered what prompted your fears."

"I told you, sir."

"About the gangs of soldiers on half-pay? Have you actually seen any evidence of such a gang around here?"

"Not exactly, sir."

"Then what else worries you?"

Foley looked down at his feet. "It's hard to say. I just have a sense that something isn't right. You'll think me a fanciful old fool who should be pensioned off."

"Not at all."

"I know Bookman thinks he could do my job, sir, but he doesn't understand the complexities of it at all."

"Foley." Robert waited until the butler looked up at him. "I have no intention of getting rid of you, or of promoting Bookman in your stead. I value you both too highly. However, if the position *is* getting too much for you, and you do wish to retire, that is a different matter."

"Whatever Bookman says, I don't wish that, sir. I'm quite capable of running this household."

"I'm sure you are." Robert paused. He hoped his butler and his valet weren't going to be at permanent odds with each other. "Then maybe you will have the goodness to tell me what worries you, fanciful or not."

"Just little things, sir. How to integrate your military staff into the existing household, deal with the estate business that you haven't been able to—"

"What problems have you encountered with my staff?"

Foley shifted his feet. "Nothing much, sir, just that when you were gone, we got into the habit of doing things a certain way, and now with you back, some things have had to change."

"Is Bookman the problem?"

"Oh no, sir! As I said, there's nothing in particular. It's just a sense of things having altered."

"Perhaps I should go away again and leave you in peace."

Foley fixed him with an intimidating stare. "You know

that's not what I meant, sir. You have a perfect right to reside in your ancestral home."

A slight suggestion of a headache made Robert lean back against his pillows and momentarily close his eyes.

"Are you all right, Major? Shall I fetch Bookman?"

"No, you can ask him to come to me when you leave. What else is concerning you?"

"What do you mean, sir?"

"Out with it, man. There is something you're not divulging to me."

Foley blinked. "I was going to tell you about this the other day, sir, but you told me to stop worrying about nothing."

Robert held on to his temper and his patience with something of an effort. "What?"

"Well, I hardly liked to bother you with it now, but we've lost a few trinkets here and there from some of the less frequently used rooms on the ground floor."

"What kind of trinkets?"

"Candlesticks, pieces of porcelain, a few books from the library."

Robert sat up. "We have a thief in our midst?"

"We thought it better not to worry you, sir. Petty theft is not unknown in such an environment as this. These old houses have far too many doors and windows to keep an eye on them all. Now that we are aware of the problem, we will apprehend the culprit fairly speedily."

"You know who it is?"

"Not exactly, Major, but—"

"When did this start happening?"

"I'm not sure, sir. I only became aware of it quite recently when one of the maids noticed footsteps in the dust leading out of one of the closed-up rooms on the west side of the house."

"My mother's old rooms?"

"Indeed, sir. When I ventured into the rooms in question, I noticed that several small pieces had either been re-arranged, or had disappeared."

"Then perhaps it is time we cleaned the whole dratted house and made an inventory of every item in each room."

"That is exactly what I was going to suggest to you—when you were ready to open up the house again to guests."

"I'm still not ready for guests, but do it anyway."

"As you wish, sir." Foley bowed. "I might need to engage some more servants to accomplish such a task."

"Then go ahead. We're financially sound at present." Foley moved toward the door. "And next time, don't treat me like an invalid. Tell me what is going on in my own damned house."

He bowed again. "Of course. I'll send Bookman to you." At the door he turned and looked over his shoulder. "I'm glad that you don't intend to replace me yet, Major."

Robert mock-frowned at him. "If I tried to replace you, my mother would come back and haunt me from beyond the grave. Now, go away, Foley and start mustering the new staff."

He sat back against his pillows and glanced over at the windows. It was already dark, and the black shape of the church tower threw an even gloomier shadow across the lawn and the front of his house. His thoughts circled endlessly like crows over a battlefield. What was going on in Kurland St. Mary? Were the thefts connected to the two girls attempting to finance their journey to London, as Miss Harrington suspected, or were there wider, more unscrupulous forces at work? Whatever it was, and despite his current infirmity, Robert was determined to get to the bottom of it.

He fought against an overpowering wave of fatigue. The thought of death wouldn't relinquish its hold on him, and for a moment, he allowed himself to consider the fate of the two girls. Was he just so used to the excesses of war that he immediately assumed the worst? Could the connection between the missing females and the petty thefts be a more dangerous one? Perhaps on their flight the girls had inadvertently interrupted a thief.

Somewhere in the house a door slammed. Like the battle-scarred veteran he was, Robert reached for his nonexistent sword. For the first time in his life, he felt more vulnerable in his own home than he had on any battlefield. Maybe he would order Bookman to bring his pistols up to his room after all.

Chapter 6

The next morning, Lucy approached the ramshackle cottage Joseph Cobbins called home with some trepidation. She'd had to hide in the copse at the end of the lane until she'd seen Ben Cobbins stride past, a poacher's bag on his back and a thick cudgel clasped in his meaty hand. Picking up her presence, his dogs fawned and jumped around him, barking and snapping at each other until he cuffed the nearest on the head and quieted them down. All she could hope was that he wouldn't decide to return home too quickly. His dogs were a nuisance in the village and their owner was even worse.

A thin wisp of smoke emerged from the lopsided chimney, encouraging Lucy to believe that someone was at home. The Cobbins house was on the end of a row of four stone and brick-built cottages and was in terrible repair. The thatch was sliding off the roof, and the front door was without a latch or a lick of paint on its scarred surface. Unlike most of its neighbors, the long front garden bore no evidence of neat rows of tilled earth or fruit trees awaiting the promise of spring. The grass was knee-high, and several objects Lucy failed to identify had been left to rust or mold in situ.

One couldn't entirely blame the Cobbins family for the state of the property. The cottage was owned by the Kurland estate and did not reflect well on Major Kurland's land agent's management at all. She'd heard complaints that the elderly agent, Mr. Scarsdale, was a penny-pinching Scot and couldn't help but agree. He seemed more inclined to spend his days in his own well-maintained cottage and his nights in the arms of the Widow Gavin at the Whistling Pig.

With that thought hastening her up the path, Lucy knocked on the thick oak door. There was no answer, but she could hear the wail of a baby and the roar of an enraged toddler. With a sigh, she took herself around the back of the house, picking her way through the debris and glad of her strong boots. The back door sagged ajar, and the top hinge appeared to be in the process of falling off.

She knocked again and then felt a tugging on her skirt. Looking down, she saw a young child, his face smeared with porridge, grinning up at her.

She smiled back. "Hello, is your brother Joseph at home?"

"Timmy! Come back 'ere, before I wallop you proper!"

Joe erupted from the house, making the disheveled child hide his face in Lucy's skirts and start to bawl. She carefully disengaged Timmy's sticky fingers from her dress and picked him up.

"It is all right, dear. Please don't cry. Good morning, Joseph, how are you?"

Joe's expression darkened. "What do you want?"

"That's hardly a civil way to greet someone. Is your mother at home?"

He shoved the door shut behind him. "She's sick."

"Well, it is good of you to take care of your siblings in this manner for her."

"Got no choice. Pa said I had to make myself useful, seeing as I had no job anymore."

His cheek was discolored and bore the marks of a fist.

Lucy tightened her hold on the squirming toddler and angled him more firmly on her hip. "I was sorry to hear about that, Joe."

"I didn't steal nothing." He met her gaze. "I liked working there with the old ladies. They didn't thump me."

"Would you like another job, then?"

He looked away, his lip stuck out rather pugnaciously. "Who would have me now? Everyone thinks I'm a thief like me dad."

"If you would care to present yourself at Kurland Manor this afternoon at three, Major Kurland wishes to ask you some questions."

"About what?"

She smiled encouragingly at him. "Maybe your future employment?" She hated to use subterfuge, but if her suspicions were correct, and Joe was innocent, she intended to ask Major Kurland to offer the lad a job on the estate that would keep him away from his father for good.

"I'll see."

"I hope your mother can spare you."

He shrugged. "She won't care either way as long as I'm not under her feet." He held out his arms. "Hand Timmy over. I have to get him dressed."

A warm feeling spread down Lucy's thigh, and she held Timmy at arm's length. A dark stain now ran down the length of her walking dress. Timmy grinned at her and so did Joe.

"Sorry, miss. He ran off before I put his breeches on."

"So I see."

Lucy relinquished her damp burden and patted the little boy on his no-doubt lice-ridden head. "I'll be at the manor later, too, Joe. I look forward to seeing you."

"All right then, miss." Joe nodded, grabbing his small brother by the collar as he made another run for it. "Come 'ere, you."

There was nothing left for Lucy to do but pick up her

wet skirts and retrace her steps through the garden. Despite her plans, she had no choice but to head home and change into something a little less malodorous.

"But what if I don't want to sit at the window and admire the view?" Robert demanded.

Foley and Bookman, for once united, exchanged a glance and then looked back at Robert.

"Doctor's orders, sir," Bookman said cheerfully. "If he wants you sitting up, that's what we need to do. We'll put a bell beside you so that if you need anything, you can ring it, and someone will come."

"How long do I have to sit in this damned chair?"

"Dr. Baker said to take it easy. An hour or so the first day, and then we're to see how it goes."

Robert eyed the new footman lurking behind Bookman, who was pretending not to listen to the conversation. Did he sound as petulant and invalidish as he feared?

"All right, then. I'll try it."

"That's the way, sir," Foley cried. "We'll have you up in a flash."

Bookman was consulting with the footman, and they both advanced on Robert.

"If you would let me assist you, sit up and swing your legs over the side of the bed. We'll make sure your feet are firmly on the floor."

Robert didn't tell Bookman that he'd already mastered this part, and meekly let his valet help him. He set his teeth as his bare feet touched the wooden floor and a jagged pain lanced up his left leg. Foley rushed to kneel in front of him.

"The major's slippers, Bookman!" Foley slid Robert's feet into his slippers and then gestured to the footman. "Fetch the major's banyan."

"His what, Mr. Foley?"

"His dressing gown. It's on the bed."

It took a few moments for Bookman to help Robert into

his loose-fitting robe, fasten the silk frogs, and settle it around his body. For a moment Robert considered how it might feel to be forced into one of the tight-fitting coats he had favored as a younger man. He doubted he could stand the effort required now.

"Would you like a sleeping cap, sir?" Foley asked.

"I thought the object of this exercise was to wake me up, not send me to sleep."

Foley's face fell and Robert regretted his acerbic comments. "If I feel cold, I'll make sure to ring the bell and summon help."

"Right then, sir." Bookman stood on his left. "Would you prefer us to carry you over to the chair, or shall we bring the chair to you?"

"Does it matter?"

"We'll carry you then, sir." He nodded at the footman. "All right, James. Let's lift the major on the count of three."

Robert fought an absurd desire to close his eyes as he was lifted carefully off the side of the bed and carried twenty or so feet to a chair facing the window. Foley hurried to place a footstool beneath his legs and Bookman rearranged the cushions.

"How's that, sir?"

Tentatively, Robert allowed himself to settle against the back of the substantial wing chair. He swallowed convulsively as black spots danced in front of his eyes and a wave of nausea coiled in his stomach. He inhaled through his nose, willing the sensations to pass, aware that his servants were all watching him.

"Perhaps a blanket to go over your legs, Major," Foley suggested and bustled off to procure one.

"Major?" Bookman asked quietly. "Would you like some brandy?"

Robert managed to nod, and a moment later, a glass was put in his hand. He held on to it with all his strength, noticing the way the crystal caught the sunlight and the amber jewel tones of the brandy sloshed around inside the glass. He concentrated on stopping his hand from shaking. As if at a distance, he heard Foley telling the footman he might leave and the sound of the door closing. He took another, deeper breath and the world settled back into place.

A tentative sip of brandy helped even more, so he took another.

"That's the way of it, sir," Bookman said, as Foley continued to fuss around, placing a bell at Robert's elbow, the latest London newspaper from the rectory, and his unread correspondence.

"Do you have the major's reading glasses, Bookman?"

"I do." Bookman handed them to Robert with a flourish. "Now, shall we leave him in peace for a while to enjoy the view?"

Before Robert could thank them, they both retreated, leaving him alone in his chair. He took a longer swig of brandy and contemplated the sight of his blanket-covered legs. The left one was already aching, but there was nothing new in that. It never stopped. Sometimes he wondered if it ever would. He was so used to the pain that it had become part of him, a new facet of his personality that turned him into a snarling, unreasonable monster.

A beam of weak sunlight fell on the woven pattern of his blanket and traveled upward toward Robert's lap. He placed his hand into the brightness and was shocked to see how thin and pale his fingers looked. He clenched his hand into a fist, marveling at his own weakness. Lying in bed for months was not conducive to a man's overall health in many ways.

He raised his gaze from the contemplation of his fist and studied the view outside. He'd lived at Kurland Hall all his life and inhabited this particular set of rooms since the death of his father, but how often had he really looked at his home? It had been so familiar, he'd hardly bothered.

After months of illness he was able to view the gardens with a fresh eye and appreciate them so much more.

To the right was the boundary hedge, beyond which was the bulk of Kurland Church with its Norman tower and nave. The church had been endowed by the Kurland family and was filled with the names of Robert's dead ancestors since the Crusades. At one point he and his brother, Matthew, had begged for permission to dig up the grave of Sir Roger De Kurland in the firm belief that the lost treasure of the Knights Templar was buried with him.

In front of him was a gentle grass slope that ran down toward what had originally been a moat and the fishponds for the medieval kitchens. The moat no longer surrounded the house, redeveloped by a later Kurland into a series of connected ornamental ponds that meandered through the formal gardens into a small lake with an island. The water wasn't particularly deep. Robert and the local children had spent many happy hours there learning to swim or handle a small rowing boat. To the left, a set of stone steps led down to a rose garden his mother had planted and a rather scrubby maze.

Robert narrowed his eyes and stared at the dark green ranks of hedges. He'd have to speak to the head gardener about either replanting the maze or taking it out. Damnation, he couldn't remember the name of the man. Foley would know. His hand hovered over the bell, and then he paused. Did he really want Foley coming back to see him so soon? In truth, he was enjoying the sensation of being alone and free of the smothering confines of his bed linen.

A male peacock strutted out from the maze and headed toward the slope of the lawn, his tail dragging behind him. Was it his mother who had introduced the dratted birds or his grandmother? Between his long absences fighting abroad and his recent illness, he'd lost touch with his heritage and his staff. Did he want to reach out and reclaim it, or was the effort required too great?

He gave in and rang the bell. The speed with which Foley reappeared made Robert think he'd been lingering outside the door the whole time.

"Yes, sir? Is your leg paining you, do you need your medicine, or should I send someone for Dr. Baker?"

Robert waited until Foley ran out of breath. "I'm fine, Foley. What I *would* like is my spyglass. Bookman will know where that is."

When Lucy entered Major Kurland's bedchamber, her gaze was drawn to the unoccupied bed and her hand went to her mouth.

Foley cleared his throat behind her, making her jump.

"As I was attempting to tell you before you decided to forge on ahead, Miss Harrington, Major Kurland is *sitting up* by the window." He mitigated the reproof of his words with a beaming smile and a wink.

"That's excellent news." Lucy walked over to the bay window, her basket on her arm. "Good afternoon, Major."

"Good afternoon, Miss Harrington."

She inspected him carefully, but although he looked pale, he seemed to be bearing up rather well. In place of his usual nightshirt, he was arrayed in a glorious green silk banyan with wide embroidered sleeves. He had his spectacles in his hand and a long metal tube in the other. For some reason he looked far more formidable sitting up.

"Oh, is that your spyglass? May I see?"

He handed it over without hesitation. "You need to close one eye to use it properly."

"I know that, Tom had one." Lucy brought the spyglass to her eye and rotated it around to the window. The maze swung suddenly into view and she gasped. "Oh my word, this is remarkable! Everything looks so close."

"I admit to having amused myself spying on the moles and the peacocks for the last half hour. It made the time pass rather quickly." He took the spyglass back. "Did you bring Joseph Cobbins with you?"

Lucy glanced at the clock on the mantelpiece. "I asked him to come here at three, which is in less than a quarter of an hour. I told him you wanted to question him. I also intimated you might have a job for him on the estate. I hope you don't mind, but it was the only way I could think of to ensure he turned up."

"The likelihood of my giving him a job, Miss Harrington, depends on the truthfulness of his answers."

"I understand that, but I do feel sorry for the boy. It was obvious his father had beaten him quite badly for losing his situation."

"Or for getting caught. The boy would probably prefer to stay home and terrorize the locals like his father rather than earn a proper wage."

"I don't think he would. Joe has always been different from the rest of his family, and no one would *want* to stay in that cottage." She shuddered. "It is in such a state of disrepair I wonder why it hasn't fallen down around their ears."

Major Kurland snapped the spyglass shut. "That's one of my cottages, isn't it?"

"I believe it is."

"Then why hasn't my agent either repaired it, or turned the family out? We have no obligation to house the family. Cobbins doesn't work for me."

"I believe Ben still considers himself on your payroll as one of your gamekeepers. I doubt Mr. Scarsdale wants to disagree with him."

"That's Scarsdale's job."

"I know, but—" Lucy hesitated, then plunged on. "He doesn't seem interested in carrying out any repairs to the property, or care to listen to any complaints from your tenants."

"And how would you know this?"

"Because everyone talks to me." She half-smiled. "I'm like Caesar's wife."

"I suppose you are." Major Kurland regarded her seriously. "I will speak to the man."

Lucy took the chair opposite. "That isn't for me to say, sir."

"Because you've meddled enough for one day?"

"Hardly 'meddled,' sir. I've just drawn your attention to a situation that is within your control to alleviate."

"If I choose to."

"Why would you not? This is your home, too. I doubt you wish to see it fall into ruin." With a sense of having pushed her companion as far as she could for one day, she contemplated the table beside the major's chair. "Would you like me to read the newspaper to you?"

"No, thank you. I believe I have been given quite enough to think about in my *own* small environment to be worrying about the state of the nation and abroad."

His tone was acerbic, but Lucy pretended not to notice. No man liked to be corrected, especially by a woman. It was better to make one's point, and leave the gentleman to make up his own mind where he could convince himself that it was all his own idea after all.

The major handed her a letter.

"Perhaps you might attempt to make head or tail of this correspondence from my aunt Rose. I must confess that I cannot read a word of it without bringing on a headache."

Lucy squinted at the crossed and then crossed again pages. She turned the page this way and that, but to no avail. "I *think* she is suggesting she might come and visit you, but I'm not quite sure when." She looked up. "The rest of it makes no sense to me at all, but seems to be about dates, and times, and what she intends to bring with her. Do you need laying hens?"

"That's all I made out of it, too." He took the letter back with a sigh.

"Do you want her to visit you?"

A smile flickered across his face. "If my aunt Rose decides to visit, nothing I say will change her mind."

"She is your mother's sister?"

"That's correct. She visited quite regularly when my mother was alive."

"I think I remember her. She was always very pleasant. Her company will do you good."

"I'm not so sure about that. I have no inclination to rejoin society at this time."

"She's your aunt. She scarcely counts as 'society.' "

"That's true, but she likes to amuse herself, so no doubt I'll be inundated with morning callers and invitations to all kinds of events."

"You don't have to receive anyone, or accept their invitations," Lucy reminded him.

"My aunt can receive her own guests, and I am hardly likely to be considered an asset at anyone's country ball." His smile was bitter. "Unless I employ two stout footmen to carry me from place to place in this chair."

"It's not beyond the realm of possibility, sir."

"I'd rather not bother." He took the letter back and handed her another one with an official-looking document with a red seal on it. "This one is from my regiment."

Lucy carefully broke the seal and spread out the single sheet of parchment.

"Thank goodness it is written in a far clearer hand. 'To Major Robert Kurland of the Prince of Wales's Own Royal Hussars. Your presence is requested at an evening reception to be held by our Right Royal Patron His Royal Highness, the Prince Regent, at Carlton House on the nineteenth of this month.' "

Lucy looked up. "Oh my, it is an invitation from *royalty*. How disappointing for you that you cannot attend."

"I'm not one of the prince's supporters. I probably wouldn't have gone even if I was able."

"Not *gone?*" Lucy stared at him. "To Carlton House?"

"I've been there before. It's always too crowded and too hot. The Prince Regent has an aversion to opening a window."

"But . . ." *How must it feel to be so blasé about things that she could only dream of doing?* "Isn't it an honor?"

"It sounds like an excuse for the prince to congratulate himself again on our success in battle."

"He is the patron of your regiment."

"But he's never fought with us."

"He's the heir to the throne. No one would want him to risk his life like that. Think of the succession!"

He grimaced. "The Prince Regent has several brothers, although I'll take your point that the thought of any of *them* on the throne is equally horrifying. My only hope is that King George recovers soon and takes up the reins of government before his son ruins us." He took the letter out of her unresisting fingers. "Perhaps you might be willing to assist me, and pen a short note back declining the invitation and explaining my present circumstances."

"Certainly, sir. Are you quite sure that you don't require a secretary?" Lucy stood up and gave him her best glare. "Shall I write the letter now, or would you prefer me to take it home?"

His smile was sweet enough to set her teeth on edge. "Whatever suits you best, Miss Harrington. I would hate to disrupt you with my petty errands."

A knock at the door made Lucy recollect her surroundings and place the letter in her basket. Foley entered the room with a sullen-looking Joseph Cobbins.

"Major Kurland, Miss Harrington. Apparently you are expecting this young person." He nudged Joseph in the ribs. "Keep your hands to yourself, Cobbins. I'll be checking your pockets myself before you leave."

If it was possible, Joe scowled even more. Lucy went across to meet him.

"Joseph, thank you for coming. Have you met Major Kurland before?"

She put a hand on Joe's shoulder and maneuvered him around the clutter of furniture until he faced the major's chair.

"Good afternoon, Joseph."

"What happened to you, then?" Joe stared at the seated figure.

Before Major Kurland could take offense, Lucy intervened. "Major Kurland was wounded at the battle of Waterloo."

Joe's eyes widened. "Cor, really? What regiment?"

"The Prince of Wales's Own Royal Hussars." This time the major answered before Lucy could speak.

"The tenth?"

"That's correct."

"Well, blimey. I didn't know that, sir. Me dad said all lords and ladies were lazy good-for-nothings who deserved to have their heads cut off like that lot in France."

"I'm a soldier, not an aristocrat. But your father does have a point."

"Well, I'm sure you wouldn't get beheaded, sir." Joe nodded. "Soldiers are great guns. Did you kill loads of Frenchies?"

Aware that the major's expression had tightened, Lucy smiled brightly at them both. "Joseph, I'm sure Major Kurland would prefer to talk about your recent contretemps with your employers than about his experiences during the war."

"Contre-what?" Joe scratched his head. "Do you mean that lying old biddy, Miss Amelia, who said I stole things from her store?"

"Why do you think Miss Amelia would call you a thief if she didn't think it was true?"

"I dunno, sir. Things have gone missing from the shop, there's no doubt about that. I was the one who first noticed! But she didn't give me any credit for that, did she?

Said I'd done it to distract her from my wickedness, or something." He sniffed and wiped his nose on the back of his sleeve. "The thing is, it could be anyone stealing stuff. Half the village is in there every day pawing over the goods."

"Is that true, Miss Harrington?"

"It is, Major. The Potters' store is always busy."

"Have you ever seen Mary Smith or Daisy Weeks in there, Joseph?"

"Yes, Major, they sometimes come in together giggling and carrying on and whispering like girls do."

"They were friends?"

"I suppose so." Joseph scratched his head again, inspected what he'd gathered on his finger, and crushed it. "But you know girls, they're always squabbling about something or other."

"Did either of them ever come into the store with a man?"

"What sort of man? Like their dad or something?"

"No, someone who wasn't familiar to you."

"I don't think so."

"Who else comes in the store?"

"Just about everyone, except you and the gentry from the big houses. They send their servants to do the work, and I deliver their orders right to the kitchen door." Gloom descended over his expression. "Well, I used to."

"Did your father encourage you to get a job?"

"That was all Miss Harrington's doing. My dad thought it was a fool's game, especially when I wouldn't bring home any leftovers or extras for him to sell on."

"He expected you to steal for him?"

"Yes, but it doesn't mean I did it." Joe raised his indignant gaze to the major's. "If I wanted to steal stuff, I didn't need to get a job. I could've just stayed with my dad and learned from the best."

"Then why did you take the position?"

Lucy was impressed by the calmness of the major's tone

until it occurred to her that he was probably used to dealing with young men and boys from his days in the military. She suspected that beneath his rather harsh exterior, he was a good judge of character.

Joe's skin flushed. "It's like this, sir. I wanted to help out my mum, and save a bit for myself so that I could run away and join the army. My dad never gives me a penny when I work for him."

Lucy met the major's gaze over Joe's head, and he nodded at her ever so slightly.

"How old are you?"

"Thirteen, sir."

"A little young to join up."

"I'm fourteen in a few months."

Robert sat back and studied the boy, who drew himself up to his full height. "I have a proposition for you, Joseph."

"What's that mean?"

"A proposal. If you accept a job in my stables and keep your nose clean for a year, I will use my influence to have you accepted into a good regiment, and will outfit you at my expense."

Joe's mouth fell open. "Why would you do that?"

"Because I am willing to give you a chance to prove yourself. Everyone deserves a chance, and I suspect the military will be the making of you." He pointed at the boy. "But understand this. If you steal as much as a head of corn from one of my horses' nosebags, you'll be turned off without a character, and I will wash my hands of you."

"What about my mum? Who's going to keep an eye or her and all the little ones?"

"Like all my staff, you will receive time off, and are welcome to spend it with your mother and siblings. I do not, however, expect to see your father visiting you at work or anywhere on my grounds. I will make that clear to him myself."

Joe studied Robert's face. "I don't want to see him, sir. I swear it, but I have to make sure that my mum is all right."

"That sentiment does you proud, Joseph. Between my efforts, and those of Miss Harrington, I think we can ensure that your mother is provided for. If you wish, I can even ensure that a proportion of your wages is paid directly to her. Do you accept my offer?" He held out his hand.

"Yes, sir. I do, sir. Thank you, sir." Joe grabbed Robert's hand and shook it vigorously. "When can I start?"

"If you will ring the bell, I'll speak to Foley right now. You can wait downstairs until he's made the necessary arrangements."

Foley came in and Robert nodded at Joe.

"Please take young Joseph down to the kitchens and make sure he is given something to eat. When he's settled, come back to me and bring Sutton with you."

"Sutton from the stables, sir?"

"Yes, Foley."

"Why do you want to see *him,* Major? He'll bring all that muck in with him."

"Are you trying to tell me who should be allowed in my own house?"

Foley dropped his gaze. "Of course not, sir. I'll find him right now."

Robert waited until the door closed behind his butler and Joe before he allowed himself to relax.

"That's the trouble with old family retainers, isn't it? They become rather proprietorial," Miss Harrington commented. "But that stare you gave him was positively glacial. I'm sure he won't forget himself in front of visitors again."

Robert turned to face Miss Harrington, who had remained seated opposite him. She'd taken off her bonnet to reveal her neatly braided mousey hair and clear complexion. Her dress appeared to be the same muddy brown as her eyes. Accustomed as he'd become to the dashing beauties of Europe and the ladies of the London *Ton,* she reminded him of a dusty sparrow.

"Since I came back from the continent, Foley and Bookman have been treating me like a child."

"I'm not surprised. There is something about being confined to bed that brings out the worst instincts in everyone. The person in the bed reverts to being an infant, and the provider becomes their mother. Sometimes one wishes to be comforted and cosseted, but not forever."

"Are you suggesting I *enjoyed* such treatment, Miss Harrington?"

"Not at all, Major. You were hardly a compliant patient. Your desire to be up and about was patently evident from the start."

"I *hated* being in bed."

"As a man of action, one would assume that would be the case." She smiled. "Do you wish to discuss Joe Cobbins, or are you too tired?"

"He wasn't much help about the thefts, was he?" Robert rubbed his jaw. "Almost the entire village visits that dratted place."

"But he did confirm that Mary and Daisy were friends and that they came into the shop together, but not with an unknown man. He also managed to convince you he hadn't stolen anything. If he isn't the thief, we need to consider who is."

"Foley said we have had some small thefts here, too."

"Here at the manor?" Miss Harrington shook her head. "Then we should definitely be looking beyond the village shop."

"As I suspected, Miss Harrington. I fear we are dealing with a more organized gang of criminals."

She raised her chin an obstinate inch. "I still think the two girls stole things to finance their trip."

"Well, we shall see what happens in the village now that the girls have fled to London. If the thefts stop, your theory will likely be proved correct, but if they do not, we will be searching for a more locally based band."

She smiled at him. "You were very kind to the boy. Thank you."

He waved away her gratitude. "He needs a new start in life, and the quicker we get him away from his disreputable parent, the better. Will you help Mrs. Cobbins? I apologize for enlisting your aid without consulting with you."

"Of course, I will. Will you be able to send someone to assess the state of the cottage and whether it is fit for her to live in?"

"That bad, is it?" Robert stared at her.

"Yes." Her brown eyes were unflinching,

"I will ask Foley to send for Mr. Scarsdale immediately."

Miss Harrington picked up her basket and reclaimed her bonnet and gloves. "You're looking a little tired, Major. I'm sure that can wait until tomorrow. Do you intend to keep Joe here, or should I stay and walk him home?"

"He'll probably need to go home to break the news to his mother, but I'll send Bookman with him. You need not trouble yourself."

She tied the ribbons of her plain bonnet under her chin. "I must confess to being a little concerned about what Ben Cobbins will do when he finds out his son has escaped him again."

"Leave him to me, Miss Harrington. I'll make sure he understands his position."

Her doubtful gaze drifted over his useless body and he stiffened. "I might not be able to beat the man in a fair fight, but I'm still the local magistrate. There are other ways to ensure obedience than brute force, Miss Harrington."

"I don't doubt that, sir. Power and privilege are often abused in such a fashion." She nodded and headed for the door. "Good afternoon."

She shut the door behind her with a definite snap that did nothing to aid Robert's budding headache. He realized he was clenching his jaw and gripping the armrest of his chair with all his strength.

"Meddling woman!"

While Robert waited for Foley to reappear, he focused on the view again. Miss Harrington had some nerve. Not only had she dared to suggest that he had *enjoyed* being stuck in bed, but then had gone on to imply that he was some kind of aristocratic bully. She had no idea how much he longed to take on Ben Cobbins in a bare-knuckle fight, to mark the man's face as he had dared to mark his own child's. . . .

And as for him wanting to languish in bed and be treated like an infant. He stared hard at the scurrying white clouds. Had she guessed that some deep cowardly part of him had dreamed of that—of staying in bed forever, of relinquishing control over his pain, his status in life, his military career? Being forced to sit up and literally take notice of his surroundings had made him reconnect with his world. He wasn't sure if he was ready for that at all.

A knock on the door distracted him from his thoughts. He waited until Foley and the head of his stable yard, Jack Sutton, who had also been to war with him, entered the room and then set out his plans for Joe Cobbins's future.

Chapter 7

Lucy sat at her father's desk and ran her finger down the neat column of figures in his accounts book. She oversaw most of the household finances, and could easily decipher the cryptic scrawls he made in the margins regarding each entry. Thankfully, the amounts spent on building the new house and grounds had tailed off in the last year, and their debts were minimal. He tried to live within his means, but his passion for horseflesh sometimes overcame his good sense, and left Lucy scrabbling to make up his excesses with household economies of her own.

She turned back a few pages and rested her finger under an entry for a payment for the interior and exterior woodwork of the new stable block. The recipient of the payment was a carpenter called Isaiah Bridges who resided in Lower Kurland. Had the man Mary been interested in worked for the Bridges family? When she accompanied Edward to the outlying parishes, she would make sure to stop at their residence and ask after him.

"Lucy?"

She heard Anthony shouting her name and shut the accounts book.

"I'm in the study."

He came through the door, buttoning his waistcoat. "Have you seen my blue coat?"

"When did you last wear it?"

"A week or so ago. There was a button loose. You said you'd fix it for me."

Lucy rose to her feet. "I was so busy I asked one of the servants to do it." She saw Betty passing through the hall. "Do you know what happened to Master Anthony's blue coat?"

"The one with the big shiny buttons?"

"Yes, that one. Have you seen it?"

"I remember Mary sitting with it on her lap sewing on a button a few days ago, but what happened to it after that, I have no notion."

Lucy had already started up the stairs. "Edward said that Mary accidentally put several of your garments in his room. I'll go and see if that included your coat."

She continued up the second flight of stairs and headed along the narrow hallway toward Edward's door. She assumed he had already left the house for the church, but she knocked anyway. To her surprise, the door was flung open and Edward appeared. When he saw her, his expression took on a hunted quality. He stepped outside and shut the door behind him.

"Miss Harrington."

"Good morning, Edward. Are you all right?"

"I woke up rather late." He made as if to duck past her. "If you will excuse me, I'm rather behind in my tasks."

"Before you dash off, could you look in your cupboard and see if Anthony's best blue coat is there?"

"Anthony's coat?" He looked at her blankly. "Of course! Let me just check for you."

He disappeared inside the room, shutting the door firmly in Lucy's face. Within moments, he was back, the coat draped over his arm.

"Is this the one? I'm surprised I didn't notice it before. It is rather too showy for my tastes and my profession."

"It is rather too showy for a clergyman's son, as well, but Anthony was determined to have it." She laid the coat over her arm. "Thank you, Edward. Anthony will be very relieved."

She took it down to the hallway and found her brother restlessly pacing while he waited for her.

"Well done, sis! Where on earth did you find it?"

"In Edward's closet. Mary was obviously quite distracted before she left us."

"Thank you." He examined the coat. "You don't think old Edward took it deliberately and has been prancing around in it, playing the dandy?"

"I doubt it." Lucy fought a smile. "It is hardly his style."

Anthony's grin faded. "Dammit, Mary sewed the button on in the wrong place and with white thread." He held it out to Lucy. "Lord! I can't wear it like that."

Lucy inspected the badly managed repair. "No, you cannot. Leave it with me and I'll make it right."

"But I want to wear it now."

Lucy raised her eyebrows. "Your best coat? Whatever for? Aren't you supposed to be meeting with your tutor this morning?"

Anthony mumbled something and looked away.

"You *are* seeing Mr. Galton, aren't you?"

"Can't a fellow have a day off occasionally?" Anthony demanded. "Even our Creator rested on the Sabbath."

"It isn't Sunday, brother mine, and you scarcely work for your daily bread."

Color gathered on Anthony's cheeks. "And you aren't my mother, so what does it have to do with you?"

Lucy refused to look away. "I care about your welfare. If Father finds out you are neglecting your studies, you will have to answer to him."

"And what will he do? Nothing! All he cares about are his damn horses."

"That's not true." Lucy went forward and touched Anthony's arm. "What's really the matter?"

He shrugged off her hand. "I'll be back in time to see Mr. Galton, so you don't need to go telling tales."

"That's not fair. I have always been your staunchest supporter."

"I'm going to get something else to wear." He turned away and headed up the stairs, leaving Lucy standing at the bottom still clutching his now abandoned coat. For a moment, she considered going after him, but what could she say? If he didn't wish to confide in her, she could hardly force him to do so.

With a small sigh, she went to the parlor at the back of the house where the light was brightest in the morning. Her sewing basket sat beside her chair and already contained several of the twins' shirts, a few socks to darn, and a half-finished knitted silk reticule. Despite her concerns about her brother's prevarications, she would sew on his button and leave the coat in his room. She selected a skein of brown silk and carefully snipped the white threads off the hastily sewed-on crooked pewter button. Why Anthony needed his best coat on a weekday morning was a mystery she was less close to unraveling. Was he going off to meet someone? And if so, why was it a secret?

As she sewed, she mentally reviewed the neighborhood and considered if anyone new had engaged Anthony's interest. She paused, her needle poised above the coat. Was he hanging around with some of the wilder younger sons of the gentry who came to hunt, or was it more to do with a young lady? He *had* wanted to wear his best coat. . . .

The thump of boots on the stairs and the crash of the front door slamming heralded Anthony's tumultuous exit. Lucy finished attaching the button, secured the thread, and cut off the excess. She smoothed the coat over her knees, checking the other buttons were still secure, and straightened out the pocket flaps. There was a bump in one of the pockets and Lucy dipped her hand inside the silk lining. She brought out a small box, which on closer inspection appeared to be made of porcelain, and was painted with an intricate pastoral scene on the hinged lid. She carefully examined the box, but there were no inscriptions on it apart from the usual maker's marks on the bottom.

Where had Anthony acquired such a thing? It certainly didn't belong at the rectory, and to her knowledge, he hadn't taken up the habit of inhaling snuff. Had he won it at cards, or had someone given it to him as a keepsake?

Ashamed of her thoughts, Lucy put the box back into the pocket. She wasn't his mother, and even though she cared for him greatly, she didn't have the right to pry into his private life. If he told her what was wrong, she would, of course, help him, but his earlier criticism of her becoming her father's watchdog stung. He was an adult, and she had no right to interfere in his life. She stood up, put the coat over her arm, and decided to return it to his room, intact.

The sounds of an altercation woke Robert from an uneasy nap. For a moment, he couldn't recall where he was. With an oath he threw off the blanket someone had carefully covered him with, and strained to turn his head toward his bedroom door, from behind which came the thump of feet and more than one angry voice.

The door was flung open so hard that it crashed into the wall and made everything in the room shake. Robert had no problem identifying his unexpected visitor. Ben Cobbins was a fearsome sight, the sort of man who enjoyed hurting those who were weaker than him and always had.

"Where's my boy?" Cobbins demanded, striding across to tower over Robert.

Robert stared up at him. "Mr. Cobbins."

"I said, where's my boy? What did you and that inter-fering bitch from the rectory do to him?"

Foley rushed to Cobbins's side. "You just leave the major alone, Ben Cobbins. He's not well, and he doesn't need to be disturbed by the likes of you!"

Robert waved Foley to one side and concentrated his at-tention on Cobbins. "If you are referring to your son Joseph, he has accepted an offer of employment in my sta-bles and has started work there today. As he went home last night to gather his belongings, and tell his mother where he would be staying, I find it difficult to believe you were unaware of the circumstances of his departure."

"You have no right to take my son from me." Ben was breathing heavily, his face mottled purple, his eyes nar-rowed like a bull about to charge.

"I hardly 'took him,' Mr. Cobbins. I merely offered him a job, an offer that he accepted. I fail to see why you are so enraged."

"His wages should come to me, not his mother."

"His wages are his own," Robert said gently. "If he chooses to share them with his mother, that is his business. Not mine."

He was aware that both Bookman and James, the foot-man, were now coming through the door, and he was con-scious of a cowardly sense of relief. Cobbins's enraged gaze swept the assembled company. His hands clenched into fists.

"I want to see the little bugger."

"He's working at the moment. I'm sure he'll be happy to see you when he comes home on his day off on Sunday. Perhaps you might meet him at church. I encourage all my employees to attend the morning service."

"Not bloody likely."

"I don't understand your anger, Mr. Cobbins. Most fathers would be pleased to see their sons working for a living."

"Not for the gentry."

"Is that so? But aren't you in my employ, as well? If that offends you, I'm sure we can stop any wages you receive immediately."

Cobbins spat onto the wooden floor. "Damn you, Major Kurland. I do a good job for you. Ask Mr. Scarsdale if I don't."

"I believe your business with me is done, Mr. Cobbins. Will you leave quietly, or do you require assistance?"

Bookman stepped forward, one of Robert's dueling pistols cocked and ready to fire.

Cobbins's gaze swept over Robert. "It's lucky you're already a useless cripple, Major Kurland, or I'd be telling you to watch out that one dark night you don't slip and get your pretty face beaten in."

"Thank you for the warning, Mr. Cobbins. When I'm on my feet again, we'll have to put your theory to the test, won't we?"

Foley stepped in front of Robert. "Go home, Ben, and leave the major in peace."

Cobbins threw one last threatening look over his shoulder, and then left, accompanied by Bookman and James.

Robert stared down at his useless legs and struggled to contain the wave of frustrated anger that shook through him. The contempt in Ben Cobbins's face had reminded Robert all too forcefully of his pitiful state. If Cobbins hadn't been in the mood to capitulate, he could've picked Robert up and snapped his neck with the ease of killing a chicken. And Robert wouldn't have been able to stop him.

"Are you all right, sir?" Foley asked, bending down to stare into Robert's face. "You look a bit shaken."

"Get me a brandy."

For once, Foley didn't argue, and poured Robert a hefty measure. "Here you are, sir. Well, I never. The gall of that man forcing his way in here as if he owned the place!"

He took another gulp of brandy, and it coursed down his throat like fire. "I can't say I'm surprised. He's always been an unpleasant individual, and losing control of young Joe's income must have galled him."

Foley refilled his glass. "He pushed past me in the hall. I had to chase him up the stairs. Luckily, Bookman saw him, too, and fetched James before any harm was done."

"Make sure Sutton knows what happened, and tell him to keep Joe close by."

"I'll go and tell him right now, sir." Foley hesitated. "Unless you want me to sit with you for a moment?"

"I'm perfectly fine, Foley."

"Thank God for that, Major. I couldn't have borne it if that ruffian had set back your recovery."

"Go and speak to Sutton, and ask Bookman to come and see me after he's escorted our uninvited guest off my land."

Foley disappeared, and Robert let out his breath. Having lived quietly at home for several months, he'd forgotten how the outside world must view his current state. He was now a man who couldn't mount his own horse or find the strength to hold his sword.

A weak man.

The sort of individual his younger self would have pitied and secretly despised. He finished the brandy and glanced around for the decanter, but Foley had placed it on the side table where he couldn't reach it. He couldn't afford to get drunk at this time of day anyway. What would his servants think of him, then?

"I've got rid of him, sir." Bookman came in and closed the door behind him. "He's an ugly customer, isn't he? I wouldn't be surprised if he wasn't behind the spate of thefts in this house."

"Foley told you about that?"

"He did, Major. I agreed to help him assess the defenses of the house and decide how we are going to stop any more light-fingered ladies or gents from helping themselves to your possessions again." Bookman held up the brandy decanter, but Robert shook his head. "I told Cobbins that if I saw him anywhere near the house or the stables, I'd shoot him on sight and be damned to the consequences."

There was a hard note to Bookman's voice that Robert couldn't fail to miss. His valet had been a ruthless soldier, quicker to kill than his superior, and completely cold-blooded about their survival, a quality that had saved Robert's life on more than one occasion.

"Thank you."

Bookman's grim expression disappeared. "You don't need to thank me, sir. You would've done the same if our positions were reversed."

Robert doubted that. He'd always been a little too lenient for Bookman's tastes. "I hope Ben Cobbins stays away from Joe."

"He's a coward and a bully, sir. Now he's been warned off, he'll keep away, at least for a while."

"And his poor wife will have to bear the brunt of his anger. I'd like to terminate his so-called employment with me, but then his family would be thrown out of their cottage." Robert shook his head. "By the way, someone should go down to the rectory and tell Miss Harrington not to approach the Cobbins family until things settle down. I don't want her walking into that cottage while Ben is still on the rampage."

"Speaking of cottages, Major, Mr. Scarsdale just arrived in the hall. He says you wished to speak to him. Shall I put him off for another day?"

"No, send him up. I need to see him." He waited as Bookman picked up the discarded blanket and draped it over his useless legs again. "I'd like you to stay in the room while I conduct the interview."

"If that's what you wish, of course, I will." He hesitated. "Although I don't think you'll have much trouble with Mr. Scarsdale. He ain't exactly in his prime."

He took something out of his coat pocket and laid it on Robert's lap. "Does that make you feel better, Major?"

Robert examined the familiar weight of his pistol and curved his fingers around the handle. "Yes, it does."

"I'd hide it under your blanket, though, sir. We don't want Mr. Scarsdale pissing himself in fear now, do we? He looked worried enough as it is."

Robert fought a smile as he concealed the pistol under his blanket and waited while Bookman went to retrieve his land agent.

"Mr. Scarsdale, sir."

Bookman bowed and then went to stand against the wall, the picture of an unobtrusive servant. Mr. Scarsdale came around to face Robert and inclined his head an obsequious inch. He wore the clothes of a simple country gentleman, but they were of the finest quality. His gray hair was cut short at the sides and combed forward over his bald patch rather like Napoleon. He carried an indefinable air of his own consequence.

"Major, it's good to see you up and about again."

"Hardly up." Robert gestured at his covered legs. "But I'm determined to get back into managing my lands again."

An expression of discomfort flitted across Mr. Scarsdale's austere face. "There's no need to rush yourself, me lad. I have it all well in hand."

"I beg to differ, and I'm hardly a lad anymore." Robert turned to Bookman. "Will you fetch the accounts books from beside my bed? I spent a very interesting evening reading through them."

"You didn't need to do that, sir."

Robert fixed his agent with his most withering stare. "I believe I did, Mr. Scarsdale. There's no point in prevaricating. Why haven't you been maintaining my estate properly?"

"Well, as to that, sir, I've—"

"I'm not a fool, Mr. Scarsdale, and as you pointed out,

I'm no longer languishing in bed. There are large sums of money missing from the accounts, money that should have been spent on improving my properties and land. Nothing has been done to maintain the cottages or improve the home farm since I left!"

"You don't understand, sir. Everything costs more. It's the war you see. It's—"

Robert held up his hand. "This estate has more than enough money to survive the exigencies of a wartime economy. You, Mr. Scarsdale, have either exercised very poor judgment, or used the money for purposes of your own." He paused to stare at his now perspiring land agent. "If you cannot account for the missing money before the end of the week, I will expect your resignation."

"Are you suggesting I have *misled* you, Major Kurland?"

"I'm not suggesting it, I'm damn well saying it to your face! If you don't want to be hauled before the local magistrate, which happens to be me, and face charges of theft and dishonesty, I suggest you cut your losses and leave forthwith."

"But—Major Kurland, you've been ill, your mind is obviously confused and under a great deal of stress, you can't possibly mean I'm dismissed!"

"Mr. Scarsdale, I am perfectly in my right mind, and I can't make myself any clearer. Either return the money by the end of the week, or resign your position and leave the area." He waited for a moment to see if his agent would start arguing again. "If you stay here, I *will* press charges against you."

"But after all I've done for you! Keeping the estate running when you were away, never knowing if you would return—"

"Feathering your own nest."

Mr. Scarsdale glared at Robert and pointed his whip at him. "You'll live to regret this, sir. You'll never find a man who'll be as honest as I was when his master was too feeble-witted to keep an eye on things himself."

Bookman took a step forward. "I think it's time for you to leave, Mr. Scarsdale. I'll show you out. I'm sure you have a lot of packing to do."

"Thank you, Bookman." Robert nodded a curt dismissal to his land agent, who was visibly trembling with rage. "Good day, Mr. Scarsdale."

Mr. Scarsdale glared at him. "I'll see myself out, sir, and be damned to the lot of you!"

Bookman held the door open, and Mr. Scarsdale swept out, Bookman in his wake. Robert waited until he returned.

"He's gone, sir."

"And good riddance." Robert stared out of the window. "Does everyone around here see me as a permanent invalid?"

"You have been sick for quite a while now, sir, and folks will always gossip." Bookman replaced the brandy decanter on the sideboard and picked up Robert's empty glass.

"Which explains why Scarsdale didn't stop stealing from me even after I returned from the continent. The man thinks I am feeble-witted as well as bedridden!" Robert turned quickly enough to see Bookman's guilty expression. "Dammit, they all do, don't they?"

"You were remarkably direct with him, sir. I don't think he'll make the mistake of underestimating you again."

"He won't get the opportunity," Robert snapped. "I doubt I'll see him returning all the money he's stolen from me by Friday." He carefully eased the pressure on his aching left leg. "After dealing so badly with Cobbins, perhaps I felt the need to exercise my rank of 'power and privilege,' as Miss Harrington so adroitly put it, on Mr. Scarsdale."

"Nothing wrong with that, sir. The man deserved everything he got. Both of them do."

"No doubt he'll be telling everyone in the village that I've finally gone insane," Robert muttered. "Devil take it, sometimes I feel as if I have!"

Bookman drew the curtains. "I'll ring for James and we'll put you back to bed, sir. I think you've had enough excitement for one day."

Bookman's refusal to be drawn on the subject of his employer's sanity didn't mollify Robert in the slightest. He knew Foley and his valet had worried over him for months. But he was quite sane now. In truth, he didn't like being forced back into the world, but he had a duty to his tenants and his family to perform his responsibilities. Miss Harrington had reminded him of that. He found himself wanting to smile. If he were very lucky, she'd probably furnish him with the name of a new land agent, as well.

"And what's wrong with a good rabbit stew, Miss Harrington?"

Lucy made herself look into Mrs. Fielding's narrowed eyes. "There's nothing *wrong* with it. It's just that we had the same thing two days ago, and the rector will not be pleased if he is expected to eat it twice in one week."

"I don't hear him complaining." Mrs. Fielding folded her arms under her ample bosom in the manner of a woman who was not going to change her mind.

Lucy tried again. "Do you have anything else?"

"Do you expect me to go hurrying out to the village at this time of the day, miss, when I'm supposed to be cooking dinner?"

Behind Lucy, Anna cleared her throat. "I'll go to the village if you like, Lucy."

"There's no need for that, Anna." Lucy raised her chin. "I'm tired of fighting with you every day, Mrs. Fielding. If working at the rectory is no longer to your taste, perhaps you might consider finding employment elsewhere?" She nodded a dismissal. "Please make sure that rabbit is not the only main course on the table tonight, or I will be taking my concerns to my father. Good afternoon, Mrs. Fielding!"

Before the cook could retaliate, Lucy turned on her heel, took Anna by the elbow, and marched them both out of the kitchen and into the back parlor. She shut the door and swung around to her sister.

"Oh, that woman is *infuriating!*"

Anna clasped her hands together. "You were magnificent."

"I thought about how Major Kurland would deal with such habitual insolence and pretended I was him." Lucy smiled. "It was quite exhilarating."

"Do you think it will help?" Anna sat down and stared hopefully at Lucy. "Father always criticizes her cooking, but he seems curiously reluctant to terminate her employment. Do you think it is because Mrs. Fielding came with Mama?"

"No, I think it's because she provides him with more than just—" Lucy stopped speaking. "Well, never mind that. Let's just say that he is very fond of her."

Anna nodded. "Because of Mama."

"It's certainly not because of her cooking." Lucy paced the small room. "It isn't fair, Anna. I have all the responsibilities of the lady of the house, and none of the power. Mrs. Fielding knows I can't get rid of her unless Papa is agreeable. She treats me with no respect at all."

"I know," Anna agreed. "She is positively *uncivil* to you."

"I will have to speak to him." Lucy stopped walking. "He won't like it, but I refuse to be treated like this."

Anna rose from her seat and came across to kiss Lucy's cheek. "Wait until after he's eaten, won't you? After all that mutton last week, seeing the rabbit stew on the table again might tip the balance in your favor."

Lucy smiled and hugged her sister. "Let's hope so. Would you mind going up and reading to the twins for a while? I promised to do so, but I'm too agitated. I think I'll walk into the village and see if I can talk to Miss Mildred."

"And find something better for us to have for dinner?"

"If I encounter anything edible, I'll definitely consider it. Has Anthony come in yet?"

"Yes, he was in the stables earlier talking to Harris about his horse's shoe being loose. Why, did you want him to accompany you?"

"No, I just wanted to make certain he was home."

Anna paused at the door. "Why? What has he done?"

"Nothing in particular." Lucy didn't want Anna carrying tales to her brother. Despite their argumentative natures, they were very close. "I just wanted to make sure everyone would be here for dinner."

"Mr. Nicholas Jenkins was here earlier." Anna looked demure. "He *said* he had a message from his grandmother for you, but he quite forgot to give it to me. I think he was hoping that if he lingered in the parlor long enough, we might invite him to stay for dinner."

"You shouldn't tease him, Anna. The poor man is quite besotted with you."

"I know, but I am never cruel to him, you must know that." Anna clasped her hands to her bosom. "I *couldn't* be cruel to him. He *is* rather sweet."

"I wonder what his grandmother wants? She'd probably like us to visit her this week. Will you accompany me?"

"Of course I will." Anna held open the door. "Now you should be on your way, or we'll have nothing edible on our dinner table at all. In truth, Mr. Jenkins should be pleased he *wasn't* invited."

Lucy found her cloak and put on her bonnet. It was late afternoon, and although the clouds were gathering, it wasn't yet dark. As she walked down the driveway, she pulled on her second-best pair of gloves and attempted to gain control of her temper. It was ridiculous to get annoyed with Mrs. Fielding, but she hated the thinly veiled contempt in the woman's gaze, and her unmistakable conviction that the rector would never let her go. It made all Lucy's dealings with her feel tainted and had done so for years.

She took a deep breath of the rapidly chilling air and strode resolutely onward toward the village. The sound of a barking dog made her look up, but she couldn't tell from which direction the yelping was coming. She swung around with a gasp as a large body crashed through the undergrowth of the trees to her right. Within moments, she was surrounded by a pack of slavering dogs snapping at her heels and jumping up at her.

"Well, damn if it isn't Miss Bloody, Interfering Harrington."

She forced herself to look away from the dogs and saw Ben Cobbins stepping through the gap the dogs had made in the brushwood. He wore no hat, and his long overcoat hung open to display his stained leather waistcoat and grimy neckcloth. An ancient pistol was tucked into the waistband of his breeches.

"Call your dogs off, Mr. Cobbins."

He strolled closer, smacking the end of his billy club into his open palm. Lucy found she couldn't look away.

"Call them off? Now why would I do that? They know their own."

"I'm not a rabbit or a fox to be hunted down, Mr. Cobbins."

His lips drew back in a travesty of a smile. "What are you going to do about it, Miss Harrington? Scream for help?" He looked up and down the deserted road. "I don't see no one about to hear you."

"What do you want?"

"I know it was you that set the major to giving my boy a job."

"I would've thought you'd be pleased Joe was working again."

"Then you'd be wrong." He came closer until she could smell the rancid tang of his unwashed skin and the beer hops on his breath. His gaze wandered over her with insulting interest.

She flinched when he put his fingers under her chin and made her look up at him. "Don't interfere with what's mine, Miss Harrington, unless you want to suffer the consequences."

She forced herself to look calmly into his bloodshot eyes. "If you lay a finger on me, sir, my family will never let you live."

"On the contrary, if they thought I'd ruined you, they'd cast you out without a second thought." He gaze slid down over her. "Luckily for you, scrawny, flat-chested virgins don't hold much appeal for a man of my appetites. Just keep away from me and mine, or I might have to overcome my disgust and teach you a lesson anyway."

He chucked her under the chin and then stepped away, whistling to his dogs. Lucy remained frozen until he disappeared back into the forest. When she tried to move, her limbs trembled so violently she almost fell. She rubbed her gloved fingers across her mouth where Ben Cobbins had flicked her lip and fought the desire to vomit. She would not turn and run back home. She would not let him frighten her. Forcing herself to take a deep breath, she continued on her way to the village, determined that regardless of her own personal safety, Ben Cobbins would never get near his son again.

Chapter 8

"Ah, Miss Harrington, and how are you this fine day?"

"Good morning, Major Kurland."

Robert waited until his visitor put down her basket and took off her bonnet before looking at her more closely. Due to the constant rain, tendrils of her brown hair had escaped her tight braids and curled around her face, softening her uncompromising features. For some reason, she looked rather tense and her normally calm smile was absent. She took a seat opposite him and he put down his newspaper.

"Do you have any news for me?"

She fussed over the contents of her basket and then straightened again, a handkerchief clutched in her hand, to loudly blow her nose. Robert's fingertips started to drum on the arm of his chair and she looked up at him.

"I beg your pardon, sir?"

"I asked if you had anything of import to share with me."

"Oh yes, I spoke to Miss Mildred yesterday about who she had seen out and about in the village on the night you were awakened."

"And what did she tell you?"

"She definitely saw Daisy Weeks."

Robert sat back. "Which doesn't help us at all."

"I haven't finished yet." She shot him a reproving glance, which reminded him forcibly of his mother. "Miss Mildred also said she saw several of *your* servants, Major, and some unknown men who were heading from the Whistling Pig to a cockfight in Lower Kurland. Apparently, according to her, *all* the men were behaving foolishly due to the effects of too much alcohol."

"Ah, I wondered why it was so quiet here at the manor," Robert mused. "Everyone was probably off at the cockfight." It certainly explained where Bookman had gone after his dinner with Foley. His valet had an eye for the birds.

"Did she see your servant girl?"

"She doesn't remember doing so, but I suppose even if the girls left together, Daisy would've collected Mary on the way to the main road rather than expecting her to come back into the village."

"Are you beginning to doubt your own conclusions, Miss Harrington?"

"What do you mean?"

"Do you no longer believe the girls left together?"

"If they didn't, what has become of Mary? I can only pray that if she didn't leave with Daisy, she ran away with the man she was interested in." She hesitated. "But what if that isn't true, either? Wherever can she be?"

Robert studied her closely. Should he acquaint Miss Harrington with his theories as to what else might have happened to the unfortunate girls, or leave her in blissful ignorance? He had no basis for his suspicions apart from his knowledge of all manners of hell on earth. But had his battle experiences distorted his perception or enhanced it? As Bookman had mentioned, the idea of violent death in the tranquil village of Kurland St. Mary seemed ridiculous, but a girl was missing. Two of them, in fact.

"What is it?" He looked up to find her staring at him just as closely as he had studied her. "What do you fear?"

"Maybe neither of the girls managed to escape to London. If there is a thief in our midst, perhaps they interrupted him, and he decided to dispose of them."

She shook her head as if trying to push back his words. "That's ridiculous. Why would anyone want to hurt Mary or Daisy?"

"He wouldn't *want* to hurt them. He might have felt he had no choice."

She looked away. "I devoutly hope you are wrong, Major."

"So do I." He felt like a callow youth who had inadvertently trampled all over a delicate bed of spring flowers. "I hardly wish them dead."

She shivered. "If most of the men were out of the village at a cockfight, it would've been a good opportunity for both the girls to escape and for our thief, or thieves, to take advantage of the empty homes."

"Indeed."

"We must find out if anyone else has suffered any losses of this nature." Miss Harrington nodded. "I'll ask the Hathaways and the Jenkinses tomorrow."

"An excellent idea." Robert gestured at the bell. "Would you like to ring for some tea?"

"I can't stay for very long, Major. I have to speak to my father about replacing our cook."

"Mrs. Fielding?"

"Yes, do you know her?"

Robert only knew that local gossip insisted Mrs. Fielding was the rector's longtime bed partner, and he wasn't going to discuss that with Miss Harrington.

"Only that she's been at the rectory for as long as I can remember. What has she done to earn your displeasure?"

"Her cooking is appalling and she treats me like a child."

"You are much younger than her, and she is a very experienced cook."

"In her case, experience is not an advantage. My father complains about the food he's forced to eat on a daily basis, but he expects me to deal with Mrs. Fielding's unpleasantness. And I know why he avoids terminating her employment, he—" She stopped with a gasp and put her hand to her mouth.

"Ah, so gossip doesn't lie," Robert murmured.

"I beg your pardon?" Miss Harrington's cheeks reddened even more.

"Nothing, Miss Harrington. I was just thinking of all the reasons why the rector might not choose to terminate his cook's employment. I'm quite certain he doesn't want to deal with the hiring of a new one."

"I would be in charge of that, sir, and I'm quite happy to do it." Miss Harrington rifled through the contents of her basket. "Sometimes I feel as if I have all the responsibility of the lady of the house and none of the power."

"Surely the best thing to do in that instance would be to set up an establishment on your own?"

She stared at him. "It's not quite that simple for a woman, Major."

"It is if you get married."

"And how would I have managed that in the last seven years while I've been caring for my siblings?"

"A determined man would've taken you away, anyway."

"I'm not the sort of woman to inspire such devotion." Her smile was tight. "Nor would I have allowed myself to leave. How is Joseph doing at the stables?"

Acutely aware that he had veered into unacceptably personal territory, Robert accepted her change of subject.

"He is doing very well. That brings to mind something else I wanted to say to you. Stay away from the Cobbins place for a while. Ben is extremely angry about being deprived of his son."

She shuddered. "I know. I had the misfortune to cross paths with him on my way to speak to Miss Mildred yesterday."

"He dared to accost you?" Robert demanded.

"He told me in no uncertain terms to keep away from his family." Miss Harrington rang the bell and gathered her possessions. "When I returned home, I was told you had sent a messenger down to warn me not to go to his cottage."

"Did I?" Robert frowned. "I believe I mentioned it to Bookman. I'm glad he followed my orders, even if it came too late for you to avoid Cobbins entirely."

"I'll keep away from the cottage, Major, I swear." Miss Harrington put her bonnet on again. "The curate is going to visit the other two parishes later this week. I shall accompany him."

"And what do you hope to achieve there?"

She tied the damp ribbons in a no-nonsense bow directly under her chin. "The man whom Mary was interested in works for a carpenter from Lower Kurland. I thought I might check and see if he is still employed there."

"An excellent idea. And you will speak to the Hathaways and Jenkinses discreetly about any thefts?"

"Yes, Major." She glanced over at the window. "And how are you enjoying sitting up?"

He considered her. "Was that your idea? I thought it was a bit revolutionary for our dear Dr. Baker. I am enjoying it more than I thought, although it also reminds me of all the things I am not yet able to accomplish."

"You can write a list, so that when you are able to march around the estate issuing orders to your heart's content, you will know exactly what needs to be done." She paused. "Oh, I almost forgot! I found the very thing for you yesterday when I was perusing a copy of *Ackermann's Repository*."

He waited as she dug into her basket and drew out a

slim volume. "There is an article and a diagram about a contraption called Merlin's Mechanical Chair."

"And what exactly does that have to do with me?"

She came back and placed the book on his knees, opening it at a marked page. "The writer says: 'This curious machine of which a correct perspective view is given in the annexed engraving. It is expressly catalogued for the accommodation of invalids who from age or infirmity are unable to walk about—' "

Robert picked up the book and studied the engraving of the blue chair, which was furnished with a selection of wheels, cogs, and rods to rival any clock or newfangled steam-driven power loom.

"This is ridiculous."

Miss Harrington leaned over him, and he smelled lavender and a hint of rain that made him ache to be outside. She pointed at the wheels. "It looks fairly ingenious to me."

"Are you suggesting that I would attempt to sit in such a thing and be wheeled around like an infant?"

"I don't see why not, Major. It would mean you could go outside and take the air. Wouldn't you like that?"

"It would only work if you stayed on the path," Robert objected. "It hardly looks substantial enough to last for more than a few minutes outside."

"But think of the possibilities, sir." She jabbed at the text. "The author even suggests that with some accommodations, small cannon could be strapped to the chair and it could be used in military situations."

"Poppycock!" Robert shut the book. "I appreciate the thought, Miss Harrington, but I scarcely think this is feasible."

She moved away from him. "Perhaps you should read the whole article before you make your mind up, sir. I'll leave it with you."

Robert resisted the urge to throw the book at her head. Despite her calm exterior, she was far too used to getting her own way. He couldn't ever imagine himself agreeing to be walked around the grounds in a glorified baby carriage. But he had to admit that Miss Harrington was trying to help him in her own unique way.

He found himself smiling at her. "I dismissed Mr. Scarsdale yesterday."

"You did?" She clasped her hands to her bosom, and he congratulated himself on his successful attempt to distract her from her latest cause. "What did he do?"

"Apart from treating me like a complete fool? He underestimated me, Miss Harrington. I reclaimed and read through the accounting books and found he has been fleecing me for years."

"That doesn't surprise me at all. When I questioned him once about the state of repairs to one of the cottages, he was very unpleasant and recommended I mind my own business. I tried not to deal with him too closely after that, although it was hard not to speak out sometimes."

"Perhaps you might do me yet another favor, Miss Harrington, and ask my tenants to come up to the manor and report any issues they've had with Mr. Scarsdale over the last few years."

She paused at the door. "You'll be inundated, Major. You might be better off waiting until you hire a new agent who can deal with the problems himself."

"But will he?" Robert smoothed the cover of the book. "I want to hear from my tenants directly, so that I can see how matters stand before someone new takes over. We can start with a clean slate, so to speak."

Miss Harrington smiled at him.

"What is it?"

"It's nice to see you taking an interest in your land again."

He raised an eyebrow. "Isn't that what you hoped to accomplish with all your badgering?"

She lifted her chin. "A lady never badgers, sir, she merely 'requests.' "

He inclined his head. "Good afternoon, Miss Harrington."

She curtsied. "Good afternoon, Major Kurland."

After she'd gone, Robert turned his attention back to the article she'd foisted on him about the magical mechanical chair and read it through. Trust Miss Harrington to find something so infinitely fantastical and expect him to embrace it as wholeheartedly as she had. He contemplated the chair by the desk. The idea did have possibilities, though. . . .

"Major Kurland!"

A hasty knock on the door and the appearance of Foley, his mouth agape, made Robert snap to attention.

"What is it, man?"

Before Foley could answer, he was pushed to one side and an all-too-familiar female bore down on Robert, arms spread wide.

"My favorite nephew. How good it is to see you!"

"Aunt Rose." Robert submitted to his aunt's perfumed embrace with as much grace as he could muster. "Whatever are you doing here?"

She planted a kiss on his cheek and beamed at him. "I told you I was coming to stay in my letter, love! Didn't you read it?" She straightened and turned toward the door.

"And look, my dearest boy, I've brought you something even more precious to cheer you up!"

With a premonition of dread, Robert turned to the beautiful but unsmiling figure framed in the doorway.

"Miss Chingford."

"Major Kurland." She curtsied, but didn't approach him—as though he carried the plague rather than was recovering from his wounds.

Aunt Rose smiled brightly. "Isn't this wonderful, Robert?

Dearest Penelope was so anxious about you that she begged to accompany me. How could I deny her?"

Robert kept smiling as his heart plummeted to his boots. He wished to God his aunt had denied Miss Chingford access to him. He hadn't wanted her to see him like this. With an inward sigh he held out his hand.

"I cannot rise to greet you properly, Miss Chingford, but may I at least shake your hand?"

She took a step back. "In your bedchamber, sir? I hardly think that would be prudent." She turned to Foley, who was standing beside her. "Perhaps you would have the goodness to instruct your butler to take me to my room. I am rather fatigued from the journey."

Robert caught his butler's attention. "May I suggest you escort the ladies downstairs until you have prepared the bedchambers for them? And may I also suggest you make this a priority?"

"Naturally, sir." Foley bowed. "If you would like to accompany me down to the small parlor, Miss Chingford, Mrs. Armitage? I'll send for some tea, and have those rooms ready for you as quickly as possible."

Miss Chingford retreated immediately, but his aunt stayed to smooth his hair from his brow and kiss him again. "Don't you worry, love. We'll have you all right and tight soon enough."

The familiar burr of her northern accent reminded him of his mother and made him want to press his face to her bosom and howl like a child. He managed to keep his smile firmly in place until his aunt went out, and then he covered his face in his hands and groaned. When he opened his eyes, Bookman was studying him quizzically.

"Is everything all right, sir? Foley said we have guests."

"We do."

"That's nice, sir. You could do with a bit of company."

"Not this company."

Bookman paused as he replenished the glass of water by Robert's bed. "I thought I saw Mrs. Armitage."

"You did. It's not her I'm worried about."

"Who else did she bring? Not your cousin, Paul?"

"Oh no, far worse than that." Bookman looked politely puzzled, and Robert continued. "She brought Miss Chingford with her."

"Miss Chingford?"

"The woman I foolishly asked to marry me."

Chapter 9

"May I assist you, Miss Harrington?"

Lucy gathered the skirts of her serviceable riding habit in one hand and turned toward Edward.

"That would be very kind of you." She placed her foot in the stirrup as he boosted her upward, and grabbed for the pommel, arranging her skirts decorously around her. "Thank you." She gathered the reins in her gloved hand and stuck one of the pins more firmly into her hat.

Despite her father's love of horses, the mounts he provided for his curate and his eldest daughter could hardly be described as dashing. To be fair, Bluebell was old, placid, and never likely to cause Lucy a moment's anxiety. Unfortunately, the curate's mount was a young horse the rector wanted exercised and seemed far too skittish for Edward to handle.

He mounted only after a groom stood at the horse's head to hold his tempestuous steed still.

"Shall we be off, Miss Harrington?" He glanced up at the cloudy sky. "Let's hope the weather holds."

It wasn't that far to Lower Kurland and Kurland St. Anne, which nestled together at the far end of the valley against a series of gentle hills. Lucy enjoyed the opportu-

nity to get out of the house. As a child, she and her brothers had often ridden out to the other villages, but she
rarely got the opportunity now.

She glanced sideways as Edward came into view and
then had to skitter away like a crab as he tried to control
his horse. She fought a smile. If he had intended to converse with her on the journey, she reckoned he was destined to be disappointed. After following the road for
about ten minutes, they cut across a field of winter cab-
bage to approach Lower Kurland from the rear.

Out here amongst the barren fields there were very few
signs of the approach of spring. Like a miser spending a
coin, winter seemed reluctant to release its icy grip. Lucy
inhaled the hint of frost in the air and slowly breathed
out. If she went to London with Sophia and found a husband, she might never come back here at this time of year
again. . . .

"Miss Harrington?"

She looked across at Edward and wondered how long it
had taken him to get her attention. "What is it?"

"Do you wish to accompany me on my visits, or do you
have other business to conduct in the village?"

"I'll come with you, but perhaps as we go around you
can help me find Isaiah Bridges. Do you know him?"

"Bridges? I don't think he is part of our flock. I believe
he might be a Methodist."

"One of those fire-breathing, Bible-thumping heretics
my father speaks about so disparagingly?"

"It isn't a cause for levity, Miss Harrington. These men
are *subversives* who deny authority."

Lucy stared straight ahead so that he wouldn't see her
smile. "Then I'll be very careful how I approach Mr.
Bridges. God forbid he try to convert me."

Edward dismounted to open the gate that led back onto
the road, and Lucy guided her horse through the gap. As

she passed, he caught hold of her horse's bridle in a tenacious grip.

"Miss Harrington, sometimes your tendency to make light of everything, to *mock* that which is sacred to my profession, is a character flaw I cannot admire. I try to persuade myself that it is just your sense of fun, but perhaps you might aspire to behave in a more Christian manner?"

Lucy lowered her gaze to meet his. "If I ever put you in a position to *give* me advice, Mr. Calthrope, I would gladly listen to your concerns." She waited until he took his hand away from her horse's bridle. "But as that is *extremely* unlikely, I don't believe you have the right to either correct or chastise me. Your horse is about to bolt. Shall we move on?"

Edward flushed an unbecoming shade of red and hurried back to catch his horse, who insisted on dancing away every time he tried to mount. Lucy made no offer to help him and simply set off again down the trail, her teeth clenched together as she rode. His anger surprised and unsettled her. But she wasn't in the mood to be cowed by another man. Whether it was the effect of associating with Major Kurland, or that several people had tried her patience recently, Lucy was more willing than usual to express her own opinions.

In front of her was a short run of parallel thatched cottages that made up the bulk of Lower Kurland's high street. She didn't recall there being a carpenter's shop in the rows of dwellings and businesses, but she might have missed it. The first substantial building was the Cock Inn, and Lucy turned her horse's head in that direction. Lower Kurland was so small that she could usually walk up and down the high street and conduct all her business in less than an hour.

"Morning, Miss Harrington! Leaving the old nag here for a while?"

She smiled down at the ostler who emerged from the stable yard of the Cock and ambled toward her.

"If that is all right, Bob. I won't be long."

"I'll keep an eye on her for you, miss, don't you worry." Bob led the horse to a mounting block and helped Lucy dismount. "Is Mr. Calthrope stopping here, too? I see him just coming over the hill."

"I assume so." Lucy untied her basket from the back of the saddle. "Do you know where Mr. Isaiah Bridges resides?"

"You going to try your hand at converting him, miss?" He winked at her. "I wouldn't bother. He's with his lord, and he's very happy about that."

"I just wondered where he lives. I have a bill to settle with him for his carpentry services."

Bob shaded his eyes and pointed up the street. "You won't find him in the village proper, like. His family owns Beech Cottage. It's just past the common to the left of the duck pond."

"Thank you." Edward rode up, his face red and perspiring as he wrestled with the recalcitrant horse. "Will you inform Mr. Calthrope that I will meet him after I've conducted my business with Mr. Bridges?"

"Yes, miss."

Lucy set off down the high street, ignoring Edward's attempts to call out to her. How dare he presume to tell her how to behave? She was no more answerable to him for her conduct than she was to Major Kurland! Indignation made her walk faster and she was soon breathing rather deeply. The heavy wool of her riding skirts weighed far more than her usual light muslins. She passed the duck pond, which still bore patches of ice on the surface, and studied the cottages ahead of her.

It was relatively easy to decide which one belonged to the Bridges family, both because of the barn adjacent to the property and the large wooden cross that graced the front garden. Hearing the sound of activity, Lucy walked around the side of the cottage toward the barn, where the pleasing smell of freshly cut wood permeated the air. When she saw the man splitting wood with his ax, she immediately remembered him being at the rectory overseeing the building of the new stable yard.

"Mr. Bridges?"

"Aye?" He looked up and stepped away from the stack of wood, wiping his brow on his shirtsleeve. "It's Miss Harrington, isn't it?"

"Yes." She curtsied to him. "I wonder if you might help me with a particular matter?"

"Is it about the work I did on the house?" He put the ax down and came toward her. He was tall and broad and much younger than she had anticipated. "If it's money you're after, you'll have to talk to my father. He still does the books."

"This is a more personal matter, Mr. Bridges. It concerns one of your workmen."

His smile disappeared. "Which one?"

"I'm not quite sure. One of my kitchen maids has gone missing."

"And you think this man of mine has something to do with it?"

"From what I've been told, Mr. Bridges, Mary Smith was quite close to one of your workers."

"Aye. I remember Mary. She was a pleasant girl and very willing to bring a man a cold drink on a hot day. Mind you, if she was sweet on one of my men, that might explain her willingness." Isaiah Bridges rubbed the back of his neck, ruffling his dark red hair. "I employ several men, but not many of them are young. Can you be more specific?"

"According to my other maid, this particular man was fair-haired and very tall."

"It sounds like young William Bowden. He's the only fair one I can think of. Do you think they've run off together? I haven't heard any gossip. I suppose he might have taken her back to his family at the farm and not mentioned it to anyone. I haven't heard of no bans being read in the church for them, either." He cleared his throat. "Not that I hold with such heathen practices, seeing as I've been personally saved by the Lord and do His holy work in chapel."

He eyed her speculatively, and Lucy prayed he wouldn't feel moved to try to save her. "Do you think I might speak to him?"

"Will doesn't live in the village, Miss Harrington. He lives out on one of the farms in the valley with his parents. He comes and works for me when the fields lie fallow or before harvest."

"Do you have his direction?"

He glanced up at the sky, which was clouding over in an ominous fashion. "It's quite out of the way, Miss Harrington. I wouldn't risk it today in this weather. You'd probably do better to write to him. He can read well enough. If he comes into the village, I'll tell him you've been looking for him. Come into the house, and I'll write down the address and some directions for you if you choose to go after him."

"Thank you, Mr. Bridges. That is very kind of you."

He smiled down at her and she noticed he had a dimple in each cheek. "It's the least I can do. As I said, Mary was a nice little thing. I wouldn't want any harm to come to her."

"Neither would I. I must confess I'm very worried about her." Lucy waited until he opened the back door and stepped past him into the kitchen of Beech Cottage. A woman with faded auburn hair was busy making pie at the kitchen table.

"Ma, I brought Miss Harrington to see you. Make her welcome while I fetch her Will's address."

Mrs. Bridges brushed her hands off on her apron. "Oh, Miss Harrington! How good to see you!" She glared at her son's departing back. "I do apologize, miss, he should've taken you into the best parlor."

"I'd much prefer to be here. Kitchens are always the warmest and best places in the house, aren't they?" She dislodged a patchwork cat from one of the chairs and reestablished him on her lap as she sat down. "What kind of pie are you making?"

"Ham and leek, miss."

Lucy inhaled. "They smell delicious. I don't suppose you'd like a job at the rectory, would you?"

Mrs. Bridges laughed. "If I didn't have to feed my own family, I'd be delighted to oblige you, miss. Imagine getting paid just to cook the dinner!" She went back to rolling out her pastry, and Lucy sat and watched as she petted the purring cat.

All too soon, Isaiah returned with a folded piece of paper. "Here you are, Miss Harrington. My father wishes to send his regards and apologizes for not coming to greet you properly, seeing as he's laid up in bed with the gout. He wanted me to ask you if the rector was happy with the work we did on the stables."

Lucy stood up and the cat jumped from her lap. "The carpentry was excellent. My father is recommending your services to all his acquaintances."

"I'll tell him. He'll be pleased as punch to hear that."

Mrs. Bridges held out one of the pies that had been cooling on the table. "Take this with you, Miss Harrington. It's still a bit hot, but it will make a lovely dinner for you tonight. I'll wrap it up for you."

"Thank you, Mrs. Bridges, that would be delightful."

Lucy carried her prize back toward the village and spied Edward leaving one of the thatched cottages. He stopped to wait for her.

She held up the pie. "Look what Mrs. Bridges gave me."

He hastened to her side. "Let me take that for you, Miss Harrington."

She relinquished the pie, which was remarkably heavy. "Where are you headed next?"

"Mrs. Ward, two doors along, has been sick for quite a while. I promised to visit her."

"Then I'll come with you." He stood back to let her precede him. It seemed he had taken her rebuke to heart, and she certainly didn't want to argue with him anymore. He had little *but* his faith in his life to defend, so she shouldn't mock that. "When we've finished these visits, I must venture into the village shop and ask about Mary."

"As you wish, Miss Harrington."

His manner was again that of the obsequious curate and she was profoundly grateful. She hadn't even realized he had a temper until he'd caught hold of her bridle like that. It reminded her that everyone had an unpleasant side, even Edward. Sometimes it was just more obvious, as with Ben Cobbins and, to a lesser extent, Major Kurland. But in some ways that was easier to deal with.

She knocked on the door of Mrs. Ward's cottage and waited to be admitted. If Mrs. Fielding did decide to retire in a huff after Lucy spoke to her, then the pie would make an excellent dinner.

Several hours later, Lucy had changed out of her riding habit and sat in the back parlor darning one of her stockings. No one in Kurland St. Mary or Lower Kurland had seen Mary, but they had all promised to keep a lookout for her. The general opinion was that young girls were flighty and far too eager to forget their responsibilities and disobey their elders. But at least she now had the address of the young man who might know more than anyone else about Mary's present whereabouts.

She put the darned stocking back in her basket and went to the small writing desk near the window. She opened the lid and discovered the letter from Major Kurland's regiment sitting on the blotter. After she wrote to William Bowden, she'd craft a reply to the prince's invitation in far more suitable language than she imagined the major would use. She strongly suspected he would simply scrawl the word "no" on the reverse of the invitation and send it back like that. Her father always said that a prudent man never burned all his boats. She didn't intend to let Major Kurland offend his royal patron, either.

Her letter to William Bowden was short, and asked him to contact her as soon as possible either in person or by letter. She didn't mention Mary, thinking that such a declaration of intent might make him suspicious or cause him problems at home. Of course, if he saw Isaiah Bridges before he received her letter, he'd know she was looking for Mary anyway. She sanded the letter and sealed it with wax before writing William's name and direction on it.

She found another sheet of foolscap and dipped her pen in the inkwell. Whom exactly should she address the letter to—the Prince Regent, or Major Kurland's commanding officer? Lucy considered the matter and then decided to address her reply to them both. She gracefully declined the invitation, adding that Major Kurland was still laid up in bed with injuries from his heroic conduct at Waterloo. With a private smile, she signed herself *L Harrington,* secretary to Major Robert Kurland.

Just as she finished addressing the second letter, the door opened and Anna appeared.

"Oh Lucy, there you are. I've been looking for you. Michael stabbed Luke through the ear with a penknife, and there was blood everywhere! Jane was in complete hysterics."

"Is Luke all right?"

Anna slumped into the nearest chair. "Of course he is. He thought it was highly amusing. Apparently, he and Michael saw a picture of some of the savages from America and decided they wanted to pierce their ears and put big hoops through them."

Lucy started to get up. "Where are they?"

"It's all right. They've been sent to bed without any supper, and Jane is guarding the door. There's nothing for you to do."

Lucy subsided onto her seat. "Those boys will be the death of me. The moment my back is turned, they are up to something."

"Just remember that in six months' time they will be somebody else's responsibility. I shudder to think of the poor teachers at their school." Anna leaned against the cushions and tucked her feet underneath her.

"Where did the twins get the knife?"

"Oh, it was Anthony's. He's not very pleased with them for taking it from his room, either. He shouted at them that they had no right to invade his privacy."

"As if he wasn't just as bad at taking Tom's things when he was a boy."

"He misses Tom."

"We all do."

"But it's different for Anthony, isn't it? He worshiped him. I fear he's been rather adrift since Tom died."

Lucy closed the desk and turned to Anna. "Have you noticed Anthony's been behaving oddly, too?"

"Yes. I asked him what was wrong, but he said I would never understand."

"I asked him, and he accused me of snooping for Papa. I was hoping he'd confided in you."

"Unfortunately not, and before you ask, he hasn't borrowed money from me again, either."

"After he promised not to? I should hope not." Lucy shut the inkwell. She was reluctant to share her suspicions with Anna, but she had no choice. "If he hasn't borrowed money from either of us, I'm worried he's gotten himself into debt again, and is too scared to tell Papa."

"Lord, I hope not!" Anna clutched her hands together at her bosom. "Papa was furious with him for weeks!"

"Which means he's unlikely to confide in us if he's in the same position again. I don't want to compromise your relationship with Anthony, Anna, but if you can get him to talk to you about any of this, please do."

"I will." Anna nodded. "And if he does confide in me, I promise to tell you what's going on if I feel it is necessary."

"That's very good of you." Lucy rose to her feet and smoothed down her skirts.

"By the way, Lucy, Mrs. Fielding was looking for you. Someone left a heavenly smelling pie in the kitchen, and after I mistakenly complimented her on it, she demanded to know where it came from."

Lucy groaned. "I should have eaten it all myself, but I foolishly wanted you all to share in my good fortune."

"That was very noble of you, but now Mrs. Fielding is extremely cross and threatening not to cook anything at all."

"Really?"

Anna sat up. "Yes. Why are you smiling?"

"Because if she doesn't cook *anything,* Papa is sure to notice and call her to account for it, especially if it means the reoccurrence of the rabbit stew."

The sisters smiled at each other in perfect accord.

"You can't stay in your bedroom forever, Robert."

"I am aware of that." Robert turned to look at his aunt Rose, who had taken a seat by his bed with a determined air. It was late in the evening, the curtains were drawn, and a small fire blazed in the hearth. "Are your rooms satisfactory?"

"No, they are not. I don't know what your staff have been doing while you've been bedridden, but they haven't been airing out the beds and the draperies. I had to go into Miss Chingford's room and clean out at least a dozen spider's webs!"

"I wondered what all that shrieking was about." Robert took his aunt's hand. "My staff hasn't been neglecting their duties. I haven't had any guests to entertain. There was no point in keeping the upstairs rooms in order because they weren't being used."

Aunt Rose squeezed his fingers. "You can't let this turn you into a recluse."

He'd forgotten how blunt his northern relatives were compared to southerners. They certainly didn't mince their words. "I'm not. It just seemed like a false economy to waste my staff on cleaning rooms that were never occupied. I'm sure the downstairs is perfectly fine apart from the west wing."

"While I'm here, I'll set everything to rights for you. Perhaps Miss Chingford can help me." Rose chuckled. "I don't think she's been very impressed so far with her future home."

"As to that—"

"By the way, she made it very clear that she won't come and see you while you're in your nightclothes and in your bedchamber."

"Why ever not?"

"Because she doesn't consider it seemly."

"Even if I'm sitting up by the window in my banyan?"

"She's a lady, Robert, and according to her, you're still in a state of undress. Her reputation means everything to her, and I did promise her parents I'd keep her safe. They were fairly reluctant to leave her in my care, seeing as I'm so vulgar, but money won out in the end. It usually does."

"How did you meet Miss Chingford? Forgive me, Aunt, but you hardly move in the same social circles."

"Nor would I wish to. I only visit London to see Henrietta and my grandchildren. I know I'm not welcome at their grand home, either, despite the fact that Hen's dowry paid for it all."

Robert allowed himself to be diverted. "I have no idea why she chose to marry Northam, a duller, more pompous individual I've never met."

"She married him because he's a baron, and she gets to

call herself Lady Henrietta. He married her because his finances were all to pieces and he needed the capital."

"A match made in heaven, then."

She swatted him with her lace handkerchief. "Don't be so dismissive. Men have always married for money and women for position. No one considered it odd when your father married my sister."

Robert found himself smiling. "By all accounts, it was a love match."

"They were lucky and they left you in excellent financial shape."

"I know. I thank God for it every day." He brought his aunt's hand to his lips and kissed it. "If Miss Chingford won't come to my room, how am I supposed to speak to her? Why make the effort to visit me and then not take advantage of it?"

"I don't think she realized how badly injured you were, Robert. Did you not inform her?"

"I believe my commanding officer wrote to tell her I'd been wounded, and I dictated a note to Foley once I regained consciousness here."

"That's all?" Aunt Rose shook her head. "No wonder the poor girl felt obliged to come and see for herself."

He was aware of a strong sensation of guilt. "Well, I can hardly ignore her now."

In truth, he wished he could, but he was a gentleman, and he'd made a commitment to Miss Chingford that he'd tried to ignore. He hadn't seen her for so long that he'd almost forgotten how beautiful she was. Had she really decided she'd waited long enough for him to crawl out of his shell? He smoothed a hand over his covered legs. He hadn't wanted her to see him like this. He'd been vain enough to dream of returning to London in perfect health to claim her again.

"Did she say exactly why she wanted to come with you?" Robert asked.

"Not directly. I met her at Henrietta's, and once she knew I was related to you and was fixed on visiting, she insisted on coming with me. She certainly didn't confide in me on the journey here. In fact, when she forgot her society manners, she treated me more like a poor governess than a potential relative."

"Her father is a viscount. Her lineage is impeccable."

"So she told me—as if I should be kneeling at her feet thanking her for deigning to share my carriage and join our worthless family." Aunt Rose gave an unladylike snort. "She might be mighty high in the instep, but she's still after your money."

"I'm certain of it. I know only too well that the Kurland estate is in this robust condition because of the wealth my mother brought into it."

"Don't you ever forget it, nephew, even though there are many of your class who will try to make you feel inferior because of it. Now, what is this that Bookman tells me about you having nightmares and using opiates to sleep?"

Robert blinked at the sudden change of subject. "What?"

"There's no need to sound so alarmed. Both Bookman and Foley are loyal to you. They only told me because I nagged them to death."

"I . . . did take laudanum for a while to dull the pain. But I didn't like the effect it had on me. I felt quite unlike myself."

"Indeed. Bookman suggested they feared for your sanity at some points."

"He never said that to me."

"You probably would have dismissed him for being insolent. It's much easier for him to confide his worries in me."

"But I've practically stopped taking the damned stuff!"

"There, there, don't get agitated, my love." Aunt Rose felt his forehead as though he were six again. Robert felt as frustrated as his childhood self. Did no one truly believe he was capable anymore?

"Tomorrow morning I will get up, get properly dressed, and have my chair taken down to the best parlor so that I may converse like a gentleman with you and Miss Chingford. Will that convince you that I'm not some raving lunatic huddled in his bed?"

Aunt Rose kissed his brow. "Of course, my dear. I look forward to it." She stood up with the happy air of a woman who had achieved her purpose and headed for the door. "Sleep well, nephew."

Robert glared at the closed door for a good few minutes. In her own way, she was just as manipulative as Miss Harrington. God save him from interfering females who thought they knew what was best for him. He drank the barley water she had placed by his bed and wished he had some brandy to put in it. Did Bookman really think he was still addicted to laudanum? He hadn't said anything about it, but he and Foley had been rather overattentive the past few weeks. He'd sometimes wondered if Bookman and Foley had been secretly adding laudanum to his food to make him sleep.

He studied the black glass bottle beside his bed and licked his lips, tasting the sickly opiate. Was it possible that what he'd *thought* he'd seen at the church was a figment of his drugged imagination? If he was addicted to the stuff, surely his most trusted employees should share some of the blame?

Robert settled back against his pillows. Thank God he hadn't mentioned what he'd seen outright to his servants. Even if he had "imagined" the man at the church, someone was stealing things in Kurland and something had happened to the two girls. These were problems that still needed solving, and if he refused to take any laudanum from now on, he was quite capable of solving them—wasn't he?

* * *

"I don't take kindly to food appearing in my kitchen that I haven't cooked!"

Mrs. Fielding glowered at Lucy and then returned her gaze to the rector, who sat behind his desk, hands folded on his blotter, his expression beleaguered.

"The pie was a gift from a parishioner. I could scarcely refuse it." Lucy didn't even bother to look at Mrs. Fielding. "And you have to admit that it tasted very good. You remarked on it particularly, Father."

"It shouldn't have been put out on my table!"

"I put it out, Mrs. Fielding, because I knew that the rector would not be satisfied with a dinner comprised of leftover rabbit stew and boiled mutton." Lucy noticed her father's shudder and pressed her point home. "The pie was excellent."

"It's not your business, Miss Harrington, to be telling me what to cook, or what not to cook. It's the rector that pays my wages."

"I manage the house and the staff for my father. I have done so for the last seven years. I'm sure he doesn't wish to be bothered by domestic issues when his mind should be on higher, more spiritual matters." Lucy stared hard at her father. "Do you *want* me to hand over the management of the house to you? Do you want to deal with Mrs. Fielding yourself, because I am more than willing to relinquish my responsibilities, if it suits you."

"I want harmony in my own house, Lucy, which you are not providing," the rector snapped. "And I do not want reheated rabbit stew and tough mutton!"

Lucy turned to Mrs. Fielding, who was breathing rather heavily. "Did you hear what the rector said?"

"He said nothing about you being in charge of me."

"Father—"

The rector stood up so suddenly that Lucy jumped. "Mrs. Fielding, you will take your orders from my daughter. Lucy, you will respect Mrs. Fielding's opinion on culinary matters where she has more experience than you have. Now both of you go away, and leave me in peace!"

"Well." Mrs. Fielding straightened her cap. "If I'm supposed to take orders from Miss Harrington, I will have to think seriously about my position here, Rector. Very seriously, indeed."

She swept out of the study and shut the door with a definite bang behind her. Lucy let out her breath.

"I hope she leaves. She has no intention of doing anything I say."

He groaned. "I don't understand why you bring me your troubles like this, Lucy. Why can't women get along with each other?"

"That is hardly fair. Mrs. Fielding is rude to me on a daily basis. I am tired of it."

He lined up his pens on his desk. "She has a right to her opinion in her own kitchen."

"So you are happy with the meals she produces? Papa, you are the one who complains the most about her food!"

"And it is your job to tell her that! Not to come running to me like a child every time you feel slighted."

Lucy curled her hands into fists. "This is unfair. I am your daughter, not your wife."

"But no longer a child."

"I feel like a child when you treat me like one, and refuse to back my authority."

"Don't be silly. Didn't I just tell Mrs. Fielding to obey your orders?"

"With the proviso that I have to listen to her about what she cooks, which defeats the whole purpose of this conversation!"

The rector sat down again and looked at her over the top of his spectacles. "I do not appreciate your tone or your anger, neither of which are appropriate for a gently born female."

"And I do not appreciate being put in an impossible position." Lucy took a deep breath and slowly let it out. "I manage your house and children, and yet I am not your wife and I do not have the authority of a wife."

"As my eldest daughter, it is your duty to do so."

"But what about *my* life, Papa? When do I get a chance to have a family of my own?"

"Your selfishness appalls me. Do you think I complained when God took my wife from me? I took up my burden and kept on despite everything."

"And I helped you willingly, but things are changing now. Anthony will be off to Cambridge in the autumn and the twins will go to school. You will no longer need me quite so much."

"What are you suggesting?"

"I think it is time for me to find my own husband and home." Silence fell and he simply stared at her. "Don't I deserve that?"

"I've never stopped a man from courting you, Lucy. No one has asked for your hand."

She bit her lip. "Are you suggesting I'm not good enough?"

"Of course not, my dear. But unlike your sister, you certainly aren't that young anymore."

"You assume Anna will marry and I won't?"

He avoided her gaze. "She is the acknowledged beauty of the family."

"And I don't begrudge her that in the slightest, but I have other abilities a man might find attractive. I'm an excellent housekeeper and already know how to bring up a child."

"Daughter, you misunderstand me. There are probably many men, older men who have been widowed as I was, who would welcome a woman with your qualities into their home." He hesitated. "But I always assumed you would stay here and look after me."

Lucy's heart jolted in her chest. "You would deny me the opportunity to even seek a husband?"

"I'm sorry, my dear, but it is hardly my fault that you have scarcely stirred much notice in our local community. Both of the Hathaway boys have expressed an interest in Anna, as has Nicholas Jenkins. I believe even Major Kurland views her favorably." Her father brightened. "Now there's an idea. Why don't you take her with you next time you visit the manor house?"

"You've always told me that beauty is in the eye of the beholder, and that such physical attributes are ephemeral and not to be trusted."

"In a spiritual sense, that is true, but beauty is much prized in the marriage market. It is the way of the world, my dear."

"But what if I was offered the opportunity to go to London and seek a husband there?"

He sat back. "I'm not willing to go to the expense of sending you to London for a Season." His voice gentled. "It would be cruel to raise such hopes only to have them dashed. You don't need to go to London to find a husband. If you are set on it, I'm sure young Edward would be honored to marry you."

"Your curate?" Lucy shuddered. "I would not marry Edward if he was the last man on earth."

"There's no need to be so dramatic. If you seriously wish to marry, he would make the perfect candidate. You could continue to live here, and life could go on the same as always."

Didn't he know that was what she feared the most? At her continuing silence, he carried on.

"In fact, as I've already arranged for Anna to go up to London next year, I will need you here more than ever."

Lucy's fingernails dug into her palms. "Anna is going to London?"

"I haven't mentioned it to her yet, but I've been corre-

sponding with my eldest brother's wife, the present count-
ess, and she is willing to bring Anna out with her youngest
daughter."

"But what about me? I—"

"Enough, Lucy!" He slammed his hand down on his
desk. "I can only deplore your appalling self-interest and
advise you to read your Bible very carefully tonight to remind yourself of your familial obligations."

"But—"

"Enough." He stood up. "Your ingratitude hurts me
deeply, child. Now go to your room."

She stared at him, her throat hurting with unshed tears.
She curtsied and left, closing the door quietly behind her.

"Miss Harrington?"

Briefly, Lucy closed her eyes. "What is it, Betty?"

"The twins have been asking for you."

"Thank you."

She picked up her skirts and started up the stairs.

"Miss Harrington?" Betty followed and held something
out to her. "What with all the excitement over Mary, I forgot to tell you that Mrs. Fielding found your gloves in the
kitchen the other day. She threatened to throw them on the
rubbish heap, so I cleaned them up as best as I could. I
wasn't sure if you wanted them or not."

Lucy held out her hand. "Thank you, Betty. I'd forgotten all about my gloves. I'll take a good look in the morning and decide what to do with them. Good night."

"Night, miss." Betty nodded and went back down the
stairs.

Lucy carried on upward and paused at the second staircase that led up to the nursery. At this moment, she didn't
want to see the twins. They would sense she was upset, and
she didn't want to cry in front of them for something that
wasn't their fault. Her father's comments about her ingratitude and lack of filial responsibility revolved through her
thoughts like a whirlpool. Hadn't she done enough for

him? Would he ever consider that she had? Why hadn't she flat-out told him about her invitation from the Hathaways?

She went into her bedchamber, appreciating the warmth of the small fire, lit a candle, and sat beside the hearth, her feet tucked under her. Despite the heat, she was shivering. How could he have spoken to her like that? His remarks were a mixture of pitying condescension and selfishness that had made her yearn to scream at him. She'd always done her duty. It was hardly surprising that none of the local men had ever considered her as a potential wife. She already appeared to be one!

She found herself smiling. How ironic that Mrs. Fielding provided her father with the one thing she couldn't. In truth, as far as he was concerned, between the two of them, he had the perfect substitute wife. Why would he want to change anything? And to suggest that she marry Edward was adding insult to injury. She would rather die.

A strange smell wafted up from her lap and she realized she still held her gloves clenched tightly in her hand. There were bloodstains on the right glove that even Betty's scrubbing had failed to remove. Where had it come from? She forced her mind not to dwell on the crushing of her hopes, and instead reconstructed her journey on the day of Mary's disappearance.

She remembered putting on her gloves after leaving Kurland Hall. As neither she nor Foley had noticed blood on them at that point, she had to assume she'd touched something on the way back to the rectory. But what? She pictured the trampled pathway and the open gate. She didn't recall any blood on the wooden posts but had wondered if there had been a disturbance there. Had she rested her hand anywhere else?

Tomorrow, when she returned from her visit to Major Kurland, she would take the shortcut past the church and retrace her steps. If there was any blood to be found, she was sure to discover it.

Chapter 10

"Father asked me to accompany you on your visit to Kurland Hall this morning. Do you need me to carry something?"

Lucy shut the drawer containing the twins' socks and turned to Anna. Her youngest siblings were in the village having a supervised walk with Jane, and for once, all was quiet in the rectory.

"You are welcome to come with me if you wish, but I don't have any special commissions for you."

"I wonder why he was so insistent, then?" Anna followed Lucy down the stairs into the hallway. "He must know Major Kurland isn't receiving visitors."

"You are hardly a visitor. Isn't it obvious? Papa thinks the sight of your beautiful face would do the major good."

Anna's smile dimmed. "There's no need to be sharp, Lucy. I swear I didn't ask if I could come with you."

"I know you didn't. It's just that . . ." Lucy paused. "Papa would be delighted if you managed to ensnare the major."

"Don't be silly. I have no intention of even *trying* to engage the major's attention. He is far too old and obstinate for me to manage." Anna bowed with an elaborate flourish. "I leave the way clear for you."

"I doubt he's about to propose to me. He thinks I'm an interfering busybody."

Anna mock-sighed. "Oh well, perhaps neither of us will be lady of the manor." She picked up a letter that lay on the hall table. "Did you see this? It's addressed to you. Another secret admirer?"

Lucy glanced down at the letter, but there was no return address written on the outside, only her name in a script she didn't recognize. Was it possible that William Bowden had replied to her so quickly? She went through to the back parlor and used her paper knife to split the wax seal.

"It's from Susan O'Brien."

"The maid who was a friend of Mary's?" Anna followed her in.

"Yes. She says she has something to tell me, and would I please visit at my earliest convenience." Lucy reread the note and then placed it on her desk. "I wonder what she wants."

"And why she couldn't simply write it down, and save you a journey," Anna remarked.

"She didn't write this herself. I doubt she can. Mr. Spencer, the butler, wrote it for her. She probably didn't want him to know her secrets." Lucy put away the paper knife. "I intended to visit the Hathaways today on another matter. I'll make sure to speak to Susan while I'm there."

Anna turned back to the door and groaned. "And I promised Jane I'd help sort out the twins' linen closet this morning. I suppose I'd better make a start while it's quiet. Give my regards to the Hathaways and to Major Kurland."

"Anna, I don't mind if you want to visit Major Kurland in my stead," Lucy said. "My usefulness to him is at an end. He no longer needs a nurse, and he would probably prefer a charming companion like you to keep his spirits up."

Anna looked back over her shoulder. "I don't want him, Lucy. Even if he begged me to be his bride, I'd still say no.

I want to go to London. I want to have choices, and marrying the first eligible man I ever met is not in my future." She pressed her hand to her heart. "I know it, here."

Lucy let her go without saying anything further. Anna had no idea that she was likely to get her wish and have the opportunity to meet as many eligible men as she wanted. Lucy didn't begrudge her the opportunity. She just wished she could persuade her father that she deserved the same chance. On that lowering thought, Lucy went upstairs to put on her bonnet and cloak.

"I didn't know you were engaged to be married, Major."

Robert angled his head so that Bookman could shave his jaw more cleanly. "I think you were wounded at the time and missed all the fun."

"When I had that nasty bullet wound in my thigh that wouldn't heal? That would be the year before last."

"That's right. I came to London to celebrate my cousin Henrietta's marriage to that bore, Northam. I met Miss Chingford then."

"You didn't mention it."

"To be honest, I almost forgot about it when we returned to France. It seemed somehow . . . unreal."

"Hmmph." Bookman expertly wiped the blade. "I don't recall her writing to you."

"I told her not to. I wasn't convinced I was going to survive."

"Sounds rather odd to me, sir."

"Just because you got letters from your sweetheart doesn't mean that everyone was so lucky. How is she, by the way? Ouch." Robert winced as the knife grazed his skin.

"Sorry, sir. You've talked at just the wrong moment." Bookman dabbed at the blood. "Keep still for a moment while I finish your throat."

Robert held his tongue until Bookman placed a warm towel under his chin and applied a piece of sticking plaster to the stinging wound. "There you are, sir."

"I'm not sure if my aunt told you, but I plan to go downstairs and hold court in the front parlor. Can you and James get me down there in my chair?"

"Yes, sir."

"It is necessary because Miss Chingford refuses to come into my bedchamber and speak to me."

"So Mrs. Armitage said." Bookman picked up the bowl of soapy water and threw it out the window. "Is Miss Chingford from a good family, sir?"

"Naturally."

"I thought as much. I heard her tell your aunt that the house was much smaller than she had imagined and that it needed a lot of improvements."

"Did she." Robert wiped shaving soap from his chin. "Do I detect a lack of enthusiasm for my potential bride?"

"It's not my place to say anything, sir."

"You'll just hint at your disapproval instead, then." Robert threw the towel on the floor. "In truth, Bookman, I don't know what I was thinking when I proposed to the woman. I'm not even sure that I did. I danced with her, took her out in my curricle, and visited her at home. Suddenly everyone assumed we were a couple and, even worse, she seemed to think so, too."

"I thought you were adept at avoiding such matrimonial lures."

"So did I." Robert grimaced. "And as a gentleman, I cannot withdraw from the agreement."

"Why not?" Bookman retrieved the towel, his expression uncompromising. "Why is it right for a woman to let a man down, and not the other way around?"

"Perhaps that's why she wanted to see me—to break it off."

"I don't know about that, sir. The way she's walking

around the house telling everyone how she's going to improve it, and get rid of all of your servants in favor of new
staff, I think she's planning on staying."

"Then I'd better make it clear to her that none of my
staff are going anywhere."

"Trust me, they'll be leaving if she marries you."

"Thank you for that vote of confidence, Bookman."

"You're welcome, sir. Now, let's get you dressed. Do
you want to wear your uniform?"

"Good God, no." Robert shuddered. "That's what got
me into this situation in the first place. Women love a scar-
let coat. I'll wear my usual breeches, a shirt, and a cravat,
and cover it all up with my banyan. I'm not struggling into
one of my coats, even for Miss Chingford."

"As you wish, sir."

As Bookman helped him into his clothes, Robert
checked the time. Would Miss Harrington visit him today?
He still wasn't sure if he should call her off. There was still
the matter of the thieving and the disappearance of the two
girls to be discussed. But how could he do that in the presence of his aunt and Miss Chingford? He picked up the
copy of *Ackermann's Repository* that Miss Harrington had
left with him.

"Bookman, what do you make of this contraption? Do
you think the estate carpenter is capable of making me a
wheeled chair of some sort?"

"I didn't broach the matter of my accompanying you
completely, but my father led me to understand that he intends to send Anna to London next year to stay with my
uncle and aunt." Lucy tried to force a smile. "If that is his
intention, I can hardly leave home, as well."

"Why not?" Sophia sat down next to Lucy on the couch
with a thump. "That's not fair. You are the oldest."

"I know." Lucy contemplated the Turkish rug. "But—"

"But nothing, Lucy. If Mama and I are willing to take

you, and it will hardly cost him a penny, there is nothing more to be said. How can he deny you such an opportunity?"

"He said that if I went, I would only be disappointed because no one would want to marry me."

"What a horrible thing to say." Sophia squeezed her hand hard. "You might not be as beautiful as Anna, but you have other attributes that any man of intelligence would be sure to recognize."

Lucy looked up into Sophia's indignant face. "Thank you. I must confess I was feeling rather sorry for myself."

Sophia embraced her. "Try not to fall into a fit of the dismals quite yet. Mayhap my mother and I can put our heads together and find a way to circumvent your father. He cannot keep you all to himself, and you are *definitely* not marrying the curate."

Lucy kissed her on the cheek. "I have to go. Give your family my love."

"I will, and I'll ask my mother if we've had anything stolen recently."

"I visited the Jenkins house before yours, and Lady Foster said she would look into the matter, as well."

"Was Nicholas there?"

"No, only his grandmother. He probably saw Anna hadn't accompanied me and ran away."

Sophia laughed. "You underestimate yourself."

"On the contrary, I know my own worth. Nicholas Jenkins is smitten with my sister, who, of course, has no intention of returning his regard even though his grandfather is a viscount." She sighed. "It must be pleasant to be beautiful and aspire to marry a duke."

Sophia hugged her. "You are so funny, Lucy."

"Thank you." She blew her friend a last kiss and headed down the stairs to the kitchen, where she hoped to find Susan. Luckily for her, the maid was sitting at the big table having a cup of tea.

"Good morning, Susan." Lucy nodded at the girl and then turned to the cook. "May I speak to Susan for a moment?"

"If you are quick. She has the beds to finish yet."

Susan left her seat and followed Lucy out into the deserted corridor that led toward the back door.

"What exactly did you want to tell me, Susan?"

Her companion stared down at the black-and-white-tiled floor. "It was about Mary, miss."

"What about her?"

"She wasn't a good friend to me!" Susan burst out. "She stole my man."

"Indeed. Which man would that be?"

"My William."

"William Bowden?"

"Yes. He came to work at your rectory after he'd been here, and she stole him from me!"

"Do you think that's where she's gone? To William?"

"Probably, miss. She would love to hold that over me for the rest of my life."

Susan's voice rang with resentment and echoed around the narrow space. "And she had plenty of beaux to choose from. She didn't need to steal mine."

"I'm sorry, Susan." Lucy touched the girl's rigid shoulder. "I'll try to find out what happened between William and Mary. If she *has* gone to live with him, I'll be relieved to hear that she is safe, but sad that she took something precious from you."

Susan stepped away. "Don't you worry about me, miss. If he was so easily led astray by that worthless piece of skirt, then he wasn't worth having in the first place, was he?"

"An admirable sentiment, Susan. I'm sure you'll find someone much better. I'll be on my way. I'll let you know what happens."

"Thank you, Miss Harrington. I just thought you

should know that Mary wasn't quite as sweet as everyone seems to think."

"And I'm glad you told me." As Susan turned back to the kitchen, Lucy remembered something. "I meant to ask, have there been any unexplained small thefts in the house?"

"What, you mean like money?"

"I'm not sure."

Susan paused. "Well, there have been a lot of little things going missing recently, like Mrs. Hathaway's embroidery scissors and her silver thimble. Mr. Spencer thinks someone has light fingers, but Cook and I think it's the fairies. Why do you ask?" Susan's expression lightened. "Do you think Mary was *stealing* things?"

"Not necessarily. Major Kurland up at the manor mentioned they'd had some petty thefts, and I was wondering about the other big houses." Lucy hitched her basket higher up her arm. "Thank you for talking to me, Susan, I appreciate it."

"You're welcome, miss." Susan bobbed a curtsy and headed back to the kitchen, leaving Lucy to walk out into the sunshine.

Should she wait for William Bowden to contact her, or borrow the gig and drive out to the address Isaiah Bridges had provided her with? It was tempting to confront William in case he decided to ignore her, or worse still run away. If Mary wanted to marry William, a man known at the rectory as a respectable individual, why hadn't she simply asked for permission? No one would have prevented the match. In fact, they would have welcomed it for her.

Lucy let herself through the gate and out onto the main thoroughfare. Had Mary kept it a secret because she feared Susan's reaction? It was highly likely. Lucy reckoned Susan would make a formidable enemy. A wood pigeon flew close by her bonnet, wings fluttering, and Lucy ducked. Ever since her unpleasant encounter with Ben Cobbins, she'd felt vulnerable walking by herself and she hated that. She averted her face against the bite of the chill wind, and trudged onward, avoiding the turn to the village and heading straight for Kurland Hall.

As she approached the old manor house, she turned to the side and followed the path up to the back door. The hem of her petticoats and her boots were covered in mud. Foley would never forgive her if she walked clods of earth all over the major's newly polished wooden floors. She used the boot scraper, wiped her feet vigorously on the mat, and entered the kitchen, which seemed to have acquired several new servants. She paused by the door to review the unusual swirl of activity. Foley came toward her, his expression flustered.

"Miss Harrington. Did you come to see the major? He's in the front parlor. I was just about to take up his tea."

Lucy took off her bonnet. "He's come downstairs? That's excellent news. If you don't mind, Foley, I'll go up to him."

"Yes, miss, but—"

Lucy was already moving toward the stone passageway that connected the medieval kitchen to the slightly more modern part of the house, which Major Kurland's grandfather had renovated in the Jacobean style. As she walked, she rubbed her hands together for warmth and contemplated a cup of hot tea. She wasn't sure if the major would be pleased to hear of her progress with the matter of Mary's disappearance, or disappointed that there was a reasonable solution. After all, Mary was hardly his concern. Like most men, he seemed inclined to enjoy the vicarious thrills of violence and murder and would prefer there to have been foul play. He'd probably be far more interested in her news of the thefts in the Hathaway household.

"Good morning, Major Kurland. I'm so pleased to hear

that you have managed to come downstairs. I—" She stopped talking as she took in the other people clustered around the fireplace. "Oh, I do apologize. I didn't realize you had visitors."

Major Kurland waved her closer. "There's no need to apologize, Miss Harrington. You are most welcome. May I present you to my aunt Rose, that is, Mrs. Armitage, and her companion, Miss Chingford?"

His aunt came forward to take Lucy's hand. "I remember you, my dear. You live at the rectory, don't you?"

"That's correct, ma'am." Lucy shook Mrs. Armitage's hand. She was quite short and pleasantly plump. Her hair was the same black as her nephew's and her eyes just as blue. Her accent was from the industrial north and not fashionable at all, but decidedly warm and welcoming. "I keep house for my father and siblings."

"Oh, aye, that's right. My sister wrote and told me about what happened to your poor mother. Do you miss her very much?"

"Every day." Lucy managed a smile, and Mrs. Armitage patted her hand.

"You poor love." She turned to the woman who sat ramrod-straight in the chair opposite the major's. "May I make you known to Miss Chingford? She kept me company on my journey here from London."

Lucy curtsied and received a glacial nod in return. Miss Chingford might have accompanied Mrs. Armitage on her journey, but she was no paid companion. Her clothes were of the latest fashion ripped straight from the pages of *La Belle Assemble,* and created from the finest, most delicate of fabrics. She was also blond and quite beautiful in a cold way that made her seem somewhat less than approachable.

Foley appeared with the tea tray, and Lucy took the seat next to Miss Chingford that Mrs. Armitage had vacated.

"When did you arrive, Miss Chingford?"

"Yesterday evening."

"How long did the journey take from London?"

"Far too long."

Lucy tried again. "I ask, because I am hoping to go up to London myself next year. Is it as wonderful as everyone says?"

"You've never been to London?" Miss Chingford swiveled to look at Lucy more closely. "I suppose there is no point if you are already beyond marriageable age." She smoothed her silk skirts. "I must confess to feeling a little long in the tooth myself these days and I've just turned twenty."

"Then you are of an age with my sister, Anna. I believe my father means to bring her to Town next year to make her come-out."

"At twenty?" Miss Chingford tittered. "She will be quite ancient."

"But she is very beautiful. I'm sure she'll enjoy the experience." Lucy looked up at Foley, who hovered at her elbow with the tea tray. "Will you join me in a cup of tea, Miss Chingford?"

"Thank you. At least the tea will warm me up. The chimneys in this place smoke abominably, and it is always cold."

"That is one of the disadvantages of any ancient building, I suppose. My father completely rebuilt the rectory a few years ago, and it is far more suited to our needs, but sadly lacking in character." Lucy noticed that Major Kurland was staring at her intently. Did he expect her to abandon Miss Chingford and rush over to talk to him? She resolutely turned her shoulder on him and concentrated on the discontented face of the beauty sitting beside her.

"This is not how I pictured Kurland Hall at all," Miss Chingford said. "I expected something far larger."

"I seem to recall that there are sixteen bedrooms and three wings. That scarcely seems small to me."

"But you've never been anywhere, have you?" Miss Chingford sipped at her tea and then put down the cup with a shudder. "I've been to far nicer country houses than Kurland Hall."

It was on the tip of Lucy's tongue to ask why Miss Chingford had bothered to come to this one if all she intended to do was complain about it, but she continued to smile. Years of training as a rector's daughter had inured her to the vagaries of humankind, and given her the skills of a foreign diplomat. "How long do you intend to stay?"

"Until Mrs. Armitage wishes to leave, I suppose." Miss Chingford sighed. "There are many decisions to be made as to the future, and as it is, I have no idea when Major Kurland will be well enough to participate in them." She regarded the major. "He doesn't even look like the same man out of uniform."

"You met him before his accident, then?"

"Yes. I'm a friend of Lady Henrietta Northam, Mrs. Armitage's daughter. She introduced us at her wedding almost three years ago."

"When you were first out?"

"Yes." Miss Chingford continued to stare at Major Kurland as he talked to his aunt. "He looks so much older now, and much less dashing and heroic."

"He's been very badly injured. In time, he will return to full health."

"I suppose so." Miss Chingford bit down on her lip, her doubtful gaze on his covered legs.

Lucy felt an unexpected flare of anger on the major's behalf. "Major Kurland is exceptionally brave. Not many men survive after being left for dead on a battlefield. Did you know he was mentioned in dispatches for his exemplary conduct at Waterloo?"

"Miss Harrington?" The major's peremptory tone echoed across the parlor.

She raised her chin, the light of battle in her brown eyes. "What is it, Major?"

"May I have a moment of your time?"

"Of course, sir." She nodded at Miss Chingford. "It was a pleasure to meet you. If you are staying for a while, I will bring my sister Anna to make your acquaintance."

Her companion didn't reply. Lucy was left with the distinct feeling that Miss Chingford was decidedly lukewarm about the prospect of meeting anyone else from the Harrington family. She walked across to Major Kurland and took the seat next to him while Mrs. Armitage engaged Miss Chingford in conversation. He wore his green silk banyan over a white shirt and brown breeches that had been split up one side to accommodate the splint on his left leg.

"Good morning, sir. It seems that your aunt's arrival date was even more precipitous than we imagined from her letter."

"I think it is more to the point that it took me a long while to read it, and most of it was indecipherable." Major Kurland put down his cup. "Have you seen any more of Ben Cobbins?"

"No, I haven't, thank goodness. Why do you ask?"

"Because you looked a little down in the mouth when you came in. That is not like you."

Lucy glanced quickly up at the major, met his unexpectedly concerned gaze, and looked away. "It's nothing in particular, sir, and nothing to do with the Cobbins family. I do have other news for you, though."

He shifted in his seat. "I've been meaning to say something to you about that. I regret involving you in this matter, Miss Harrington. I'm wondering whether I saw anything after all. Perhaps I was dreaming." He ran a hand through his short black hair. "But I was so certain. . . ."

"That's an interesting notion, sir, but whether or not you saw a man doesn't change the fact that two girls have gone missing from our village, and there has been a succession of petty thefts."

"A succession?"

"The Hathaways have experienced some losses, as well. I went there this morning to speak to Susan O'Brien about Mary. I also took the opportunity to ask her if there had been any thefts in the household."

"What did she have to tell you about Mary?"

Lucy raised her eyebrows. "I thought you just said you'd given up on that, sir."

"There's no need to be so cutting. I'm willing to be convinced otherwise. What did she say?"

Lucy fought down the urge to debate the inconsistency of the male mind. "That Mary, despite having more than one man buzzing around her, stole Susan's beau, William Bowden. If that is the case, it might explain why Mary left her employment so quietly. She probably feared Susan's wrath and had been avoiding her."

"William Bowden is the carpenter who worked on your stables?"

"That's correct, although he is actually a farmer who lives with his family a few miles out of Lower Kurland. I've written to him for information. If Mary is with him, I'm sure I'll find out."

"Well, that is progress of some sort at least." He picked up his cup and finished his tea in one gulp. "Now if only we could find out who is thieving."

"We still need to establish if anything else has gone missing since Mary and Daisy left."

"Agreed. I told Foley to start on an inventory of the west wing where the thefts here occurred so that we would know if anything else is stolen."

"That was an excellent thought." Lucy smiled her approval. "Whoever it is must have entry into all levels of society. I can't imagine Ben Cobbins being allowed into the Hathaways' sitting room to steal a thimble. I haven't noticed any losses from the rectory, but I will check with my father."

"I wonder why nothing has been taken from the rectory?"

"Probably because we have nothing worth stealing." Lucy pushed her worries for Anthony to the back of her mind. *What thief would foul his own nest?* "Although I suppose the twins might have decided to fulfill everyone's dire predictions by starting their disreputable careers early."

"I can just see those two daredevils running amok in the village, can't you?"

Lucy noticed Miss Chingford was glaring at her and hastily suppressed a smile. "Perhaps I should check their secret hiding places when I get home." Lucy rose. "I should be on my way. It was such a pleasure to see your aunt again." She didn't mention Miss Chingford. Her hope that the major might elaborate on his guest's reasons for visiting was dashed when he merely nodded.

"Miss Harrington is leaving, Aunt Rose."

Mrs. Armitage came over to Lucy and took her hand. "It was so nice to see you again, my dear. Please remember me to your father."

"I will, ma'am." Lucy curtsied and walked with Mrs. Armitage out into the hall. "I am so glad to see the major on the mend. Your arrival here can only hasten his continued improvement."

"I understand from Foley that you had a lot to do with his recovery, Miss Harrington. I thank you for that." Mrs. Armitage hesitated. "Robert is not the easiest of men at the best of times. I doubt he made a very pleasant invalid."

"He was in a great deal of pain, ma'am."

Mrs. Armitage squeezed her arm. "And you are a saint. You must be a great asset to your father." She paused and looked up at Lucy. "Do you think Robert will regain the use of his legs?"

"I hope so, ma'am, although I doubt he will recover all his abilities."

"I thought as much, but as long as he can walk and ride a horse, he will be able to take his place in society. I believe that is important to him."

"I'm sure he'll be able to do that, although I suspect his leg will cause him discomfort for the rest of his life."

Mrs. Armitage shook her head. "Thank you for setting my mind to rest. Miss Chingford is rather worried that Robert will remain an invalid."

Lucy paused at the door that led to the kitchen. "With all due respect, ma'am. What does the major's recovery have to do with Miss Chingford?"

"Why, didn't he tell you, my dear?" Mrs. Armitage smiled. "How typical. Miss Chingford is his intended wife."

Robert eyed Miss Chingford as she continued to sip her tea. Aunt Rose had accompanied Miss Harrington out of the parlor. He imagined they were now having an animated discussion about his character, and his progress, or lack of it, as his aunt was determined to help him get better. It was a good opportunity for him to talk to the woman who had agreed to marry him.

"Miss Chingford, could you possibly pour me another cup of tea?" He held up his empty cup and tried to look helpless.

"Of course, Major." She took the cup, filled it to the brim, and then set it down beside him. "Can you reach it from there?"

"Yes, thank you." He patted the seat next to him. "Would you sit by me? It is difficult to converse with someone who is halfway across the room without shouting."

"If you wish." She sat down and contemplated her folded hands in her lap.

"It was kind of you to accompany my aunt here." She didn't answer or look at him. "Miss Chingford?"

"Why are you and Miss Harrington on such familiar terms?"

"I beg your pardon?"

She finally raised her head. "I know that she is quite old, and obviously destined to be a spinster, but her manner toward you was *quite* proprietary."

"Miss Harrington is the eldest daughter of our rector. She helped care for me when I was gravely ill. I owe her an enormous debt."

"She *nursed* you? Surely that is an occupation only suited to the lower classes?"

"She had little choice in the matter as the nurse we originally hired was a drunkard. If it hadn't been for her and Bookman, I probably would have died. Your dislike is unwarranted and unfair."

"I didn't say I *disliked* her. She is obviously a country bumpkin quite beneath my notice. Did you see her muddied petticoats and outmoded gown? Imagine, she confessed she has never even been to London!"

"Perhaps one shouldn't judge on appearances." Robert concentrated on keeping his tone even. "She is far better connected than I am. Her uncle is an earl, and her deceased mother was the cousin of a viscount. Her family is well respected in this county and in Town. Perhaps you might care to reconsider your opinion."

Miss Chingford's lip trembled. "You are unkind, sir."

"I am merely pointing out that—"

She rose to her feet and paced in front of the fireplace, her yellow silk skirts rustling as she walked. "I should not even be speaking to you without your aunt's presence."

"I thought you considered us engaged? Aren't we allowed a little more latitude?" He glanced down at his legs. "With my current lack of mobility, I'm hardly likely to ravish you."

She gasped and backed away from him. "You are obviously unwell and not aware of the scandalous nature of your remarks."

Robert set his teeth. "In truth, I'm trying extremely hard to be polite." The door opened and his aunt came in. "Ah, there you are, Aunt Rose. Perhaps you can convince Miss Chingford that I have no designs on her virtue at this precise moment."

With a gasp, Miss Chingford turned and ran out of the room. Robert made no attempt to call her back.

"What on earth did you say to the poor girl to make her flee?"

"She insulted Miss Harrington. I corrected her false impression, and she took offense at my tone."

Aunt Rose sat next to him. "Robert, you must control your temper. It isn't fair to lash out at an innocent like Miss Chingford."

"Some innocent. She'd already decided Miss Harrington was beneath her, and wondered out loud why I would converse with such an unworthy person."

"Perhaps she was jealous?"

"Jealous of Miss Harrington? Ha! That's the most amusing thing I've heard in a long time. A glance in her mirror should reassure Miss Chingford that she is far superior in looks."

"You did speak to Miss Harrington for rather a long time."

Robert found himself glaring at his favorite aunt. "Mayhap because unlike Miss Chingford, she *wanted* to speak to me. Every time I try and engage my so-called betrothed in a conversation, she cuts me off or avoids answering me. I'm not even sure if she still wants to marry me or not."

"I'm not sure, either." Aunt Rose frowned. "Yet she was determined to come and see you."

"And perhaps finds me no longer to her liking." Robert swallowed hard. "She can hardly bear to look at me."

"She's young. Seeing you like this has been something of a shock. I'm sure she'll come to terms with it soon enough."

"I'll give her a few more days, but then I will have to speak plainly to her. We need to settle this one way or the other."

"I agree." Aunt Rose smiled at him. "Miss Harrington is very charming, isn't she?"

"Charming? In the manner of my favorite drill sergeant, yes, I suppose she is. She's certainly tougher than she looks. There were times when I was delirious with pain that I clung to the sound of her nagging like a raft in a stormy sea." He laughed at his aunt's raised eyebrows. "Hardly the most flattering of descriptions, but Miss Harrington is as formidable as you are, Aunt, and that's a compliment."

"Then let's hope she won't rake you down for failing to mention that you were engaged to Miss Chingford." Aunt Rose smiled sweetly. "She certainly looked rather taken aback when I told her."

Robert stifled a curse.

Chapter 11

Major Kurland was betrothed to that supercilious, condescending *nonentity?* Lucy stomped down the driveway of Kurland Hall at a speed that was most unladylike and possibly injurious to her health. It would have been nice if either of the happy couple had mentioned their engaged state to her. They hardly seemed to smell of April and May. She slowed to a more decorous pace and approached the shortcut to the church. Why did the major want to marry a woman like that? Was her father right that in the end, all men preferred superficial beauty to inner worth? If that were the case, the major would be far better off with Anna, who had both.

Just as Lucy glanced back at the gracious Elizabethan manor, the sun broke through the clouds and lit up the hundreds of diamond-paned windows. The house glittered like a faceted crystal glass reflecting back its secrets. If Miss Chingford had her way, Major Kurland would soon be busy rebuilding his house into a palatial mansion to satisfy his bride's delusions of grandeur.

"Three wings are not enough." Lucy mimicked Miss Chingford's high petulant tone as she approached the boundary wall of the property. "I'd be happy to have just one!"

The sunlight faded abruptly, shut out by the bulk of the Norman bell tower. Lucy buttoned her pelisse against the chill rising from the ancient stones. On her left was the stile and gate across a path that eventually came out on the main road. She stopped to examine the wooden posts and step, but there was no sign of any blood. The ground was still churned up, and the bushes that crowded against the posts needed cutting back. Hadn't the gate next to it been open when she'd passed by on the day of Mary's disappearance? A flash of something pink flapping in the breeze caught her attention. Entangled on one of the prickly hawthorn bushes was a piece of pink ribbon such as a woman might wear in her hair, or use to decorate a bonnet.

Lucy carefully untangled the ribbon and studied it. The frayed end was darker and the last inch was rusted with brown specks. She brought it up to her face and cautiously sniffed, catching the coppery tang of blood. With a shudder, she folded the ribbon and placed it in her handkerchief. The ribbon might have caught on the hawthorn bush or been left there by the wind. Had either of the missing girls liked pink? She couldn't recall.

She walked past the stile and continued along the path bounded by the church on one side and the flint wall of the graveyard on the other. As a child she'd asked her father why the church sat so much lower than the surrounding graveyard—had it sunk? He'd told her that, on the contrary, the church remained the same, but that over the centuries, all the burials had raised the level of the land around it. She'd thanked him for the information and had nightmares for weeks afterward.

Somewhat ahead of her, framed by the dark and narrow shortcut, was part of the honey-covered stone of the rectory. A flash of color made her pause as Ben Cobbins strode past, his coattails flapping, followed by only one of his dogs. Even though she knew he would be unlikely to see her, she pressed against the wall of the church and held her breath. After counting to fifty, she moved away from the wall and walked forward until she was at the cornerstone of the church. She now had a far better view of the street and the rectory and was grateful that Ben Cobbins appeared to have disappeared. The sound of raised voices from the graveyard made her stiffen. Had Ben gone in there, and for what purpose? She didn't have the nerve to go after him.

She turned sideways to squeeze through the gap between the cornerstone and the leaning wall of the graveyard. When had she last done this? She remembered the day of Mary's disappearance and looked up at the stone where her gloved hand rested. Was the surface darker there? She took out her handkerchief and scrubbed it against the stone before heading as fast as she could for the rectory.

When she reached the sanctuary of the kitchen door, she paused to look back at the church. Who would want to meet Ben Cobbins in the graveyard, and what had all the shouting been about?

"Are you all right, miss?"

Lucy jumped and swung around to find that Betty had opened the back door and was staring at her.

"I'm fine, Betty. I was just contemplating the state of the weather."

Betty peered up at the leaden sky. "Looks like it might rain, miss. You don't want to be going out in that unless you have to."

"Indeed, I think I'll come in and finish making those shirts for the twins."

She looked back over her shoulder again and saw Anthony and Edward approaching. Had they been in the church together? From the discontented expression on Anthony's face, she deemed it likely. If she asked him, he'd probably accuse her of spying on him and she didn't want that. As she walked into the kitchen, she glanced down at her handkerchief and saw the brownish stains from where she'd wiped it on the wall. Now she knew where she'd picked up the blood on her other pair of gloves. The question was, what did it mean?

The only person she could discuss her findings with was Major Kurland. She felt rather disinclined to walk back up the drive and speak to him at this particular moment. He'd probably be too busy attending to his guests to wish to consult with her anyway. She'd have to think this through by herself.

Lucy paused in the hallway. What if she wrote Major Kurland a note and had it delivered to him by hand in the morning? She wouldn't have to actually *see* him, and he wouldn't be able to stop her going ahead with her investigations until it was too late. Surely that was the best answer to her deliberations?

Anthony and Edward came in behind her, and although both of them bade her a civil good evening, neither of them seemed inclined to linger. For once she was happy to ignore their incivility and get on with devising a plan to discover exactly what Ben Cobbins was up to in the graveyard, and whether the trail of blood continued beyond the wall of the church.

The sun had disappeared behind a towering bank of clouds, so Lucy lit a candle and placed it on her desk while she wrote a short note to the major about her plans for the morning. Fragrant smells emanated from the kitchen where an offended Mrs. Fielding was intent on proving her culinary superiority to both Lucy and the rector. Lucy's stomach rumbled. She had no doubt that Major Kurland would be furious with her, but there was little she could do about that. He couldn't undertake the task and she could.

Rather than distracting Betty from laying the table for dinner, Lucy walked the note out to the stables herself and asked one of the stable hands to deliver it for her early the next morning. She didn't want to give Major Kurland the chance to stop her. The dinner bell rang as she returned to the main house, and she went to wash her hands and tidy her dress. Overhead in the nursery, she could hear the twins loudly protesting having to wash any part of themselves before eating and Jane's equally loud replies.

Lucy climbed the stairs, the scrap of ribbon carefully concealed in her bloody handkerchief. She'd have to wait until the morning when the light was better to carry out her plan, but at least she had an idea where to start. She paused on the landing and looked across at the church. What if Major Kurland was right after all and something far worse than petty theft had occurred in their picturesque, quiet little village?

"Are you all right, sis? You look as if you've seen a ghost."

Anthony walked toward her; his earlier glum expression had lifted. She noticed he was wearing his best blue coat.

"Are you going out after dinner?" Lucy didn't move out of his way.

"Yes, what of it?" His smile faded. "Do I need to ask permission?"

"Of course you don't. I—"

"You have to stop treating me like a child, Lucy. I'm almost nineteen. I'm a man."

"I do understand that, it's just—"

"You don't understand! This house feels like a prison these days, what with you, and Father, and that damned tutor all spying on me."

"I certainly don't have time to spy on you, and I doubt anyone else does, either. All we want is for you to successfully complete your studies and go up to Cambridge."

"And what if I don't want to do that? What if I don't want to be Father's reincarnation of Tom?"

Lucy touched his shoulder. "If you hate it that much,

you should talk to him. He will not force you to do something you abhor."

He shrugged her off. "You have no idea what it's like to be a man. To be forced to do your duty, to sacrifice what you want for the sake of your family."

"Do you think I wanted to stay here and bring up my siblings? Don't talk to me about duty, Anthony. I've certainly done mine."

"It's not the same! I've always wanted to go into the army, you know that, and now, because of Tom deciding to be noble and join up himself, I'm not allowed to enlist. No one's asking you to fill a dead man's shoes."

"How about a dead mother's? Does that sound familiar to you?" Lucy gathered the last shreds of her temper and looked up at her brother. "And while we are having this discussion, if all this is simply a tantrum because you are in trouble again, please tell me."

"Trouble with what?"

"Money."

"No! For God's sake, Lucy, I promised I wouldn't get involved in that ever again. Don't you believe *anything* I say?"

"Then where did that porcelain box I found in your pocket come from? Did you win it at play?"

"What box?"

"The one in the pocket of your blue coat. I found it when I was putting on the button."

He flushed. "Firstly, I have no idea what you are talking about, and secondly how dare you go through my personal possessions?"

"I was fixing your coat!"

For a long moment they glared at each other before Lucy stepped back. "If you hate your life so much, Anthony, *be* a man, and tell Papa what you want to do instead of going to Cambridge. He will, at least, listen to you, and even if he doesn't, you can still leave here and make your fortune elsewhere. I have no such choice."

He glared at her and then continued down the stairs with a muttered curse. She wasn't surprised to hear the door slam behind him. She was surprised it hadn't fallen off its hinges by now. It didn't matter how much he blustered and threatened, he was definitely in trouble. All she could hope was that their father was still willing to save him when everything inevitably went wrong.

To Lucy's relief, it was a bright and clear morning. Despite her best efforts to get away quickly, she'd had to deal with Mrs. Fielding at her most sneeringly well-mannered to approve the week's menus, and her father losing the notes for the sermon he expected Edward to write for him. She'd checked that there was neither a burial nor a church service scheduled for that morning and that none of the numerous ladies who aided the rectory would be around to require her help.

Dressed in her oldest gray gown and boots as the graveyard tended to be damp and uneven, she tiptoed down the stairs. There wasn't a perfect solution to the undulations of the ground. At one point, her father had contemplated having goats to keep the grass down, because it was so difficult to swing a scythe without hitting a gravestone. Luckily he had changed his mind, and the graveyard had remained the same.

After a quick look up and down the road in front of the rectory, Lucy marched across to the corner of the church and stood with her back to it looking slowly around. She measured the stain on the wall. It was about five and a half feet from the ground. Was there any more blood visible?

Last night, just before she'd fallen asleep, she wondered at the height of the bloodstains. If they had been left by an animal, surely they would've been lower and not at over five feet high? Unless the creature was a cow or a horse—

but they would scarcely have fitted through the gap between the church and the wall. A person's face or hand could've bled out at that level, or someone being carried. . . .

She pushed that thought away and resolutely resumed her search. On the flint wall of the graveyard, she detected another patch of reddish brown and walked across to it. Yes, it definitely looked like blood, and there was a faint trail of it under the sheltered ridge of the wall with the odd drop falling to the ground. Lucy kept her gaze on the blood and followed it until she reached the gates of the graveyard. They weren't locked, as many villagers liked to come and visit their deceased family members. Lucy often came to place flowers on Tom's grave and tell him what had been happening with their family.

The gate opened with a creak and slowly clanged shut, leaving her in the tranquil, shaded peace of the ancient burial ground. Her father was an enthusiastic amateur archaeologist and before her mother's death had often taken Lucy and Tom to dig for what he insisted were the remains of a pagan place of worship beneath their Norman church. They'd found enough evidence to allow the rector to write a learned paper for a respected scientific journal. After that, his enthusiasm had lapsed.

Lucy felt the ancient inhabitants of the space around her now, as well as the newer ones like Tom. If anything were needed to convince her that death brought peace to many, this would be the place. The silence had a quality all of its own, so thick and layered that it felt like walking through time. When Lucy asked her father about that, he'd looked at her strangely and advised her to pray more often. Her mother had understood and felt the same sensations herself.

She took in a deep breath and smelled freshly turned earth, cut grass, and something more visceral that tugged at her senses and set the hairs on the back of her neck bristling. Death had its own particular smell. Tom had said

that to her once when she'd caught him pacing the hallways of the rectory, too afraid to sleep with his nightmares. Major Kurland would probably understand that,
too. She couldn't imagine how it might feel to face an
enemy of thousands, knowing you might die and that you
must kill, or be killed.

A blackbird cried a warning and she remembered to
breathe, aware that the graveyard breathed with her. If she
wanted to meet secretly with someone, where would she go?
Her gaze traveled to the far left of the space where the older,
mainly abandoned graves and larger mausoleums were situ-
ated. It was also a popular place for village trysts, although
Lucy had often wondered why. But then she supposed life
and death were sometimes more entwined than she wanted
to believe.

She picked up her skirts and threaded her way through
the stones, avoiding tree roots and grave markers crowded
together and broken or discolored with age like a beggar's
teeth. A twig snapped somewhere in front of her, and she
halted. Had Ben Cobbins returned, or was someone
merely visiting a deceased loved one? There were very few
well-tended graves in this area.

Her attention was caught by a vivid smear of red on the
white marble of a mausoleum dedicated to the long-expired
DeVry family. She went closer, her boots crunching on the
fallen acorns from the old oak trees, and saw footprints in
the mud around the base of the tomb. The blackbird cried
out again, momentarily distracting her. She circled the tomb
until she reached the front. The white marble façade was
stained and cracked with age and the inscriptions almost
disappeared.

"Oh my goodness."

Without thought for her gown, Lucy knelt and studied
the scrap of fabric wedged in the door of the vault. It wasn't
exactly the same color as the ribbon she'd found yesterday,
but it was definitely pink. She leaned forward and tugged at

the material, but she couldn't pull it free. She took off her gloves and tried again, her fingers warm against the freezing marble, and still she failed to release it.

With a disgusted sound, she sat back. A flicker of movement to her right made her look up. Before she could do more than open her mouth to scream, she was plunged into darkness and knew no more.

"Devil take it, what time is it?" Robert rubbed his eyes and scowled at Bookman, who stood next to his bed with a worried expression and a tankard of what looked like ale in his hand. Sunlight spilled through the open curtains and the shadows were almost nonexistent, confirming his first dazed impression that it was very late.

"It's about one o'clock in the afternoon, sir."

"Why didn't you wake me earlier?"

Bookman set the tankard down on the nightstand, avoiding Robert's gaze. "I tried to rouse you several times, sir, but you were impossible to revive. In truth, I was beginning to worry and was about to ride for the doctor."

Robert pulled himself up against the pillows and groaned as everything swirled around him. His skin was clammy and his breathing slow. "My mouth tastes like the bottom of a river, and my head is pounding as if I've drunk three bottles of brandy."

"Did you drink to excess last night, Major?"

"Where would I find three bottles of brandy?" Robert demanded. "Do you think I keep them stashed at the bottom of my bed? Foley wouldn't like that at all."

"Foley might choose not to notice." Bookman handed Robert the tankard, and he drained it in one.

"Thank you. Do you have more?"

"I'll bring up a jug from the kitchen." He hesitated. "Do you want me to send for the doctor, sir?"

"No, I damn well do not!"

"As you wish, sir." Bookman left the room and Foley

entered. Robert briefly closed his eyes as his butler approached the bed on tiptoe.

"How are you feeling now, sir?"

"Not at my best, Foley." Robert raked a hand through his hair. The ale settled uneasily in his stomach, and he couldn't seem to stop shaking.

"I was worried when we couldn't rouse you." Foley sniffed. "Bookman insinuated that I had something to do with it. I have no idea why."

"He thinks you conspired with me to leave a cache of brandy in my bed." Foley went to speak and Robert held up his hand. "It's all right. I know that nothing could be further from the truth. You guard that brandy like a preventions officer. I barely had enough for one glass before I went to sleep and that was all dregs and tasted foul."

"Oh, don't worry. I'll tell him, sir. You do look rather pale." Foley leaned closer. "Do you want me to mention the laudanum?"

"What about it?"

Foley coughed. "When I came in this morning, you had the bottle in your hand, sir, clasped to your chest. Is it possible you misjudged the dose?"

"What?" Robert picked up the squat black glass bottle that sat on his nightstand, held it up to the light, and shook it. "Damnation, it's almost empty." He could taste the opiate now, lingering in his throat, clouding and distorting everything. "I don't remember taking any of the vile stuff."

"We all do things in our sleep we don't remember occasionally, sir. For example, last week I was playing cards with Bookman, and I must have imbibed far more than usual because I slept like a drunkard and didn't wake at my usual time at all."

"Don't try to make me feel better, Foley." He put the bottle down. Was that what he'd done? Dosed himself with the opiate, and not even realized it?

"You were under a lot of strain yesterday, sir, what with the recent arrival of Mrs. Armitage and your decision to go downstairs. Perhaps you simply overdid things." Foley patted his hand. "Nothing to worry about at all."

"Apart from the fact that I might never have woken up." Bookman came through the door with more ale. "Do you think I dosed myself with too much laudanum last night in my sleep?"

"Why would you do that, sir?" Bookman glanced at Foley. "Is that what he thinks?"

Foley straightened up. "With all due respect, Mr. Bookman, I found the major this morning with the bottle of laudanum in his hand. I relieved him of it before you, or anyone else, saw it. If the major hadn't decided to apprise you of the fact, you need never have known."

"Well, as to that, Mr. Foley, what were you doing in here at that hour in the morning, when *I* am employed as the major's valet, and it is *my* duty to wake him?"

"You were tardy, Mr. Bookman. I happened to be passing along the corridor when I saw the major's door was open. I stepped in to say good morning to him."

"I wasn't tardy. I'd gone to get his shaving water."

"Excuse me." Robert held up his hand, but neither man backed down. "*Excuse me.* Your bickering is getting us nowhere. If I am swigging laudanum in my sleep, I suggest we keep the bottle away from my bedside, and in a safe place, agreed?"

Both men turned to face him, Foley red with anger, Bookman white, his fists clenched at his sides.

"If that is what you wish, Major," Bookman said. "Perhaps one of us should be in charge of it."

"Are you suggesting it should be you, Bookman?"

"I am, sir. With all due respect, Mr. Foley is too inclined to give way to you."

"That's not true, I—"

"Let Bookman finish, Foley. You think I'd convince Foley to give me whatever I needed?"

"I do, sir."

Robert studied his valet for a long moment. "I reckon you might be right. Lock up the laudanum, Bookman, and keep the key."

Bookman saluted. "Yes, sir, and thank you for your trust." He picked up the bottle and stepped back.

Robert turned to his butler and tried to ignore the increasing thump of his headache. "It's not that I don't trust you, Foley. It's just that you are too kindhearted where I am concerned. If I am drinking too much of the opiate, I need to stop immediately."

Foley bowed, all offended dignity. "Whatever you say, sir. Shall I inform Mrs. Armitage that you are now awake, and would you like some breakfast?"

"Yes, on both counts, Foley. Thank you."

He drank another tankard of the weak ale and contemplated getting out of bed. If he was taking laudanum in his sleep, it was no wonder his staff was worried about him. He thought back over the previous months. Had this happened before? Had he been right to warn Miss Harrington off from believing anything his crazed mind imagined seeing at night? Maybe he hadn't even got out of bed that evening and had imagined the whole thing. . . .

"Do you wish to get up, Major?"

He looked up with a start to see Bookman standing by the bed. "I suppose I should."

"Not if you don't feel up to it. I'm sure Mrs. Armitage and Miss Chingford will understand if you are a bit under the weather."

Bookman's bracing tone was enough to make Robert throw back his covers and swing his legs over the side of the bed. He winced as his feet touched the floorboards and a shard of pain sliced up his leg.

"I'll have my breakfast over by the window, and then you can take me downstairs."

"As you wish, sir."

Robert focused his gaze on his useless legs. "Are you certain you want to stay with me, Bookman? I could give you the names of several prominent military men in London who would be more than grateful for your services." He paused. "I don't want to hold you back."

"From what, sir?" Bookman's smile disappeared. "I'm more than happy to stay here and serve you. You'll be up and about in no time. I'll be so busy keeping your gear straight that I won't have a moment to myself, and I'll be wishing these days back."

"But what if that doesn't happen?" Robert forced himself to ask. "Do you want to be a nursemaid for the rest of your life? What if I never recover?"

"Then I'll keep folding your nightshirts until you die. I'm not going to leave you to Foley's tender mercies, sir. I'm a great believer in loyalty."

Robert held Bookman's dark, unflinching gaze. They'd known each other almost all their lives, learned to swim and shoot together, shared their first woman, their first battle. . . . Their bond went far deeper than the usual one between a man and his valet.

"If you are sure."

"I am, sir. Now, let's get you dressed."

Robert allowed Bookman to shave him and then help him into his clothes. When Foley returned with a covered tray, Robert was sitting in his chair contemplating the overcast skies. Foley placed the tray on his lap.

"Your breakfast, Major Kurland. I took the liberty of bringing up the post, as well."

"Thank you." Robert knew it was pointless trying to talk Foley out of the sullens yet. He was still far too offended.

"You are welcome, sir."

Robert contemplated his plate of scrambled eggs, gammon, beef, potatoes, and toast and swallowed hard. It was imperative that he eat something to settle his stomach, but nothing on the plate appealed to him.

"Could you fetch some plain bread and butter, as well, please?"

His butler disappeared, and Robert forced himself to eat some of the egg and a mouthful of the ham, chewing determinedly to keep it down. He wished he had a dog to feed the rest of the feast to, but his last spaniel had died about three years ago, and he hadn't had time to find another. He missed having a pack of dogs at his heels. When he was up and about again, he'd speak to his gamekeeper and find some suitable pups to train.

After a while, he gave up trying to eat and turned his attention to his mail. There was yet another unfranked letter from his cousin and heir, which he ignored, two letters from his solicitors in London, and one handwritten note.

He opened the unsealed letter and started to read.

> *Dear Major Kurland,*
> *Since we last met, I have discovered why*
> *my best gloves had blood on them. I plan on*
> *following the trail of blood I found near the*
> *church to see if I can discover if it has any*
> *bearing on our investigations. All being well,*
> *I will report back to you by twelve o'clock*
> *tomorrow morning.*
> *Your obedient servant,*
> *Miss Harrington*

Robert checked his pocket watch. It was almost two in the afternoon. He pushed his tray away and turned toward the door his butler was coming through bearing a plate of bread and butter.

"Foley, when was this note delivered?"

"Early this morning, sir."

"While I was asleep? Did Miss Harrington attempt to call on me at twelve?"

"Not that I know of, Major. One of the stable hands brought the note around. I haven't seen Miss Harrington in person today."

Robert shoved at the heavy tray, making everything rattle. "Get this out of my way, and call Bookman immediately!"

"But, Major, you need to eat something, you—"

"Just do as I say! Better still, find Joseph Cobbins."

"If you insist, sir."

"I do, now get on with it!"

He read the letter again, aware of a rising tide of fear. What the devil was Miss Harrington going on about her gloves being bloodied? She hadn't mentioned that to him, and what did it have to do with anything? He clenched his fist and smashed it into the armrest of the chair. What did she think she was doing, wandering off to investigate things without talking to him first? If he'd known her intentions, he could at least have sent someone to protect her. Did she really think she was safe in this village?

Robert took a steadying breath. Why should she not? She'd grown up here, would likely spend the rest of her life here. Why should she see danger everywhere like he did, sense it in his gut like he did? He could only pray to a God he sometimes doubted existed that she was safely back in the rectory immersed in domestic details and had simply forgotten to let him know what had happened.

He glared down at his useless legs. Damnation, he could do nothing except issue orders and hope. As an officer who had always led his troops from the front, being stuck at the rear was an unfamiliar experience and one he was growing to hate.

His door was flung open and Joseph Cobbins appeared, his face flushed. "What can I do for you, Major?"

"Ah, Joe. I hear you are the fastest runner in my stables." Robert tried not to show his anxiety. "I need someone to go down to the rectory and see if Miss Harrington is there."

"Yes, sir." Joe straightened and put his shoulders back. "What do you want me to say to Miss Harrington? Do you want her up here?"

"I want you to see if she is at home. If she isn't, ask where she might be. If no one seems to know, I would like you to check the church and the graveyard."

"Why there?"

"Because she is the rector's daughter and she might be there! Don't overthink this, Joseph. Just run along, find out, and report back to me as soon as possible."

"Yes, sir!" Joe turned sharply and ran off, his boots clumping down the stairs.

Bookman looked in the door. "Did you want me, Major?"

Robert concentrated on concealing his concern. "I'm worried about the whereabouts of Miss Harrington."

"Why's that, sir?"

"She wrote to say she would be here at twelve and, obviously, I overslept."

Bookman brought a pot of coffee over to Robert and poured him a cup. "I wouldn't fret, sir. She's probably just busy doing other things."

"I'm not fretting, she—"

"She what, sir?" Bookman briefly touched Robert's shoulder. "You seem rather agitated. Are you sure you don't want to see Dr. Baker?"

"I'm perfectly fine." He realized he was a breath away from losing his temper. "I'm simply concerned that I have inconvenienced my neighbor."

"Miss Harrington is a good Christian woman and won't

take offense." Bookman left the coffeepot by Robert's elbow. "Would you like me to pop down to the rectory and see if all is well?"

"There's no need. I've already sent young Cobbins." Although he felt like smashing it against the wall, Robert placed his coffee cup onto the table. "I feel so damned useless."

His valet studied him. "With all due respect, sir, don't you think you're taking this rather too hard? You overslept and missed a visit from Miss Harrington. I'm sure she'll return eventually. The woman can't seem to keep away. In truth, I'd imagine you'd be glad to be spared her presence for a day."

"You think I'm overreacting?"

"If you want me to be honest with you, sir, then yes, I do." Bookman hesitated. "Perhaps now if we can keep you away from the laudanum, you'll settle down a bit."

"You believe I'm delusional?"

"Sir, when I checked, half that bottle of laudanum was gone. It was full yesterday."

Robert's flash of temper dissipated and was replaced by a wave of uncertainty that made him want to puke. "That will be all, Bookman. Please make sure I'm informed when Joe returns."

Lucy opened her eyes and quickly closed them again. The smell of decaying leaves and mold surrounded her, and her cheek was crushed up against something cold and hard that definitely wasn't her pillow. With a great effort, she pushed one hand flat on the wet ground and tried to raise her head. She was still in the graveyard. How long had she lain there undiscovered?

She rolled onto her side and managed to sit up. A wave of pain and nausea engulfed her, and she pressed a hand to her aching head. Her fingers came away covered in blood. Had someone come up behind her? She vaguely remembered her cheek connecting with the corner of the DeVry tomb, and nothing else. Her bonnet was askew so she attempted to straighten it and almost cried out. She hadn't just fallen then. Someone had hit her on the back of the head.

She swallowed hard against the desire to be sick, leaned back against the nearest convenient gravestone, and wrapped her arms around her raised knees. The graveyard was silent apart from the sound of the wind sighing through the trees and the occasional call of a bird. Where exactly was she? There was no sign of the DeVry tomb, or any of the larger mausoleums. The peppery scent of chrysanthemums on a nearby grave and the fresh mound of another meant she must be in the newer part of the graveyard.

Had she managed to run away, or had her attacker deliberately moved her? Was he watching her now to see if she would regain consciousness? Panic surged through her, and she stood up in a tangle of damp muddied skirts and unsteady legs, one hand braced on the gravestone. She had to get home. She had to get help!

She picked up her skirts and started back toward the entrance of the graveyard, her breathing as uneven as the ground, fear ruling her. Had someone been waiting for her in the graveyard? Had they watched until she'd knelt down by the tomb and decided she'd seen enough? A low moan escaped her chattering teeth, and she fixed her attention on the gate and the road beyond it. She had to get home.

Without pausing to look behind her, she ran through the gate and toward the rectory. The church clock chimed the quarter hour, but she had no idea what time it was. As she stumbled toward the house, the front door opened and Anthony emerged, talking to their father.

"Lucy! What in God's name happened to you?"

He ran toward her, and within a moment, she was enclosed in his warm embrace. She touched his face and tried to speak.

"I must tell Papa, I must—"

"I'm right here, my dear. Anthony, she looks as if she might swoon. Pick her up and bring her into the house."

"Yes, Father."

Lucy moaned as Anthony manfully tried to carry her in through the open front door. He deposited her on the couch in the small front parlor set aside for the least important visitors, and stood back, visibly puffing.

"Good Lord, you're heavier than you look, Lucy."

"Fetch Anna and Dr. Baker." Her father issued orders with his usual calm air of authority. Lucy didn't think she'd ever been so pleased to hear his voice before. He pulled up a chair and sat beside her. "Now, what happened? We were beginning to wonder where you were."

"What time is it?" Lucy whispered.

"Almost one in the afternoon."

"Oh my goodness." Lucy slumped back against the cushions. "I left the house at about eleven." She struggled to sit back up and grabbed for her father's hand. "Papa, you have to go and look in the graveyard. I think there is a dead body in there."

"Lucy, my dear, you are obviously overwrought. Of course there are dead bodies in there. Now why don't you lie back and wait until Dr. Baker comes to see how you are?"

She clutched the lapel of his coat. "No, you don't understand! You have to go and see for yourself. The DeVry tomb has been opened!"

He gently disengaged her fingers from his coat. "If that is the case, we will go and see for ourselves when you have recovered."

"But you should go now!"

"Please don't distress yourself." He looked up. "Ah,

here is Anna to take care of you. I'll go and ascertain whether the good doctor has arrived."

"Papa . . ." Lucy watched her father hurry away and turned to Anna. "Why won't he listen to me?"

"Possibly because you are behaving quite oddly. I could hear you screeching at him from the hall. Whatever is the matter?"

She struggled to breathe. "I think someone has been murdered! Doesn't anyone care?"

"Of course, we care." Anna motioned at Betty to come forward and help her. "Let's get you out of your bonnet and coat, and make you ready to receive the doctor." She inspected Lucy's dirty hands. "What happened to your gloves?"

"I took them off in the graveyard to try to . . ." She winced as Anna untied her bonnet ribbons and eased it off her head. "I have a terrible headache."

"I'm not surprised." Anna wet a cloth in the basin of warm water Betty held and carefully washed Lucy's hands and then her face. "I think you are going to have a black eye, as well."

"Good afternoon, ladies."

"Dr. Baker. It is so good of you to come so quickly. I think my sister hit her head in the graveyard."

Anna rose and went to exchange pleasantries with Dr. Baker, who stood with her father by the door. When they all lowered their voices, Lucy knew they were whispering about her. Eventually Dr. Baker came over, sat beside her, and possessed himself of her hand and wrist. He was a slight man in his fifties with the wiry build of a terrier and a similarly tenacious temperament.

"My dear, Miss Harrington, how are you feeling? Your pulse is quite tumultuous." He squeezed her fingers. "You should be more careful. The graveyard is a most uneven place to take a walk. I'm not surprised you fell."

He gently examined her cheek, his fingers cool on her

heated flesh. "I'll clean this wound, but I suspect you will have some nasty bruising. Did you hurt yourself anywhere else? Your ankle, your shoulder?"

"My head."

"Yes, as I said, I'll take care of that for you." He chuckled. "Don't worry. I doubt it will mar your beauty for more than a few days."

"That's not what I meant. It's the back of my head that really hurts."

The doctor beckoned to Anna. "Could you assist me in helping Miss Harrington sit up, Miss Anna?"

"Certainly."

She was eased upright and Dr. Baker began to touch her scalp. "Tell me if anything hurts." When his fingers grazed just above the nape of her neck she choked back a cry and he went still. "Ah, there is a definite swelling here, about the size of a hen's egg. You probably hit your head a second time after you collapsed."

"No, I didn't. Someone *hit* me."

"I beg your pardon?"

"I didn't fall and hurt myself. I was already kneeling down. Someone came up behind me and hit me. I must have banged my face when I fell forward, not the other way round."

She was laid back against her pillows and Anna was instructed to continue cleaning her face and to give her willow bark tea for the pain. Dr. Baker withdrew to the other side of the room and spoke to her father, his expression concerned. The odd phrase floated back to her, *"Hysterical . . . overactive imagination . . . damage to the already frail female brain . . . not like her at all."*

"Why won't they listen to me?" Lucy whispered as Anna came to kneel beside her.

"They think you just fell and hit your head." Anna pressed a cold cloth against Lucy's cheek and another at the nape of her neck. "And that you're imagining things."

"I am not!"

"I'm not sure how you are going to convince them of that. And why would anyone want to hit you, Lucy? I hate to say it, but it does sound a little far-fetched."

Lucy glared at her sister. "There are reasons I cannot share with you at present that make it highly likely that someone might want to harm me. Can you send a message to Major Kurland and tell him what happened?"

"To Major Kurland? What on earth does this have to do with him? You can hardly accuse *him* of wanting to knock you unconscious."

"Just do what I ask!" She tried to sit up, and the room swung around most unpleasantly. "Please, Anna, just—"

A small figure appeared in the doorway and stood, mouth agape, surveying the scene. "Cor, look at all that blood, Miss Harrington! What have you been up to?"

Betty approached Joseph Cobbins and flapped her apron at him. "What are you doing here? Get out, you varmint."

Joe held his ground and ducked around Betty to approach Lucy. "Major Kurland wanted to know where you were. Are you all right, miss?"

"I'll be fine." Lucy glanced around at her companions. If she tried to give Joe a message about what she'd found in the graveyard, she'd probably be dosed with laudanum and put straight to bed. "If you could wait a moment, I'll write a note for you to take to the major."

"No, you will not." Anna stood over her, her usually pleasant expression absent, her arms folded over her chest. "You will go to bed. If you are well enough in the morning, you may write as many notes as you please." She turned to Joe. "Tell Major Kurland that my sister is unable to see him today. She will call on him when she has the time."

"All right then, miss. I'll tell him." Joe cast a last commiserating look at Lucy and left before she could utter another word.

Anna glared after him. "How rude of Major Kurland! Just because you didn't visit him for one day, he has to inquire as to where you are! You have spoiled him, Lucy."

"That's not the way it is, he—"

"He is far too used to getting his own way. You were quite right about him all along. Perhaps now he'll have the decency to reflect on his conduct and consider treating you with more respect!"

She didn't have the energy to argue with her sister, and obediently drank the bitter willow bark tea Betty offered her.

Dr. Baker and her father came back into the parlor and stared down at her. Lucy attempted to muster a smile.

"Thank you for your help, Doctor. I'm sure I'll feel much better after a good sleep."

"I'm sure you will, Miss Harrington. I suspect the blow to your head has dissipated your normal good sense." He shared a glance with her father and lowered his voice, turning slightly away. "Let us hope she feels more like herself in the morning. If she persists in believing such delusions, please do not hesitate to send for me again."

"Thank you, Dr. Baker." Her father shook the doctor's hand, and Betty escorted him out of the parlor.

"Now, Lucy, I'll get Harris to carry you upstairs to your bed, and there you will stay until tomorrow morning."

"Papa, I know you think I am imagining things, but can you at least check the graveyard? I lost my gloves by the DeVry tomb."

He bent and kissed her forehead. "Don't worry, I'll buy you another pair."

"But—"

"Lucy, my love, go to bed and stop worrying. You're giving me a headache to rival your own." He gave her his perfunctory rector's smile and she knew he was anxious to get away. She had a strong suspicion that if she kept on insisting things were not as he thought, she'd be the one being sent away for a nice long rest in a madhouse.

"Yes, Papa."

She allowed herself to be picked up and taken upstairs to bed. Anna turned down the covers and Betty put a hot brick at the bottom to warm the sheets. They fussed around her until she was in her nightgown and her hair unpinned, which helped relieve some of the ache in her skull. Her head hurt so badly now that she could barely see. She even took the laudanum the doctor prescribed and tried to find a comfortable place to rest on her pillow. Within moments, she was asleep and free to worry only in her dreams.

"I saw her, sir."

"Where?" Robert sat forward, his hands clenched on the arms of the chair.

"In the rectory."

"So she was just too busy to come up to the manor." Robert couldn't decide if the feeling that swept over him was relief or annoyance.

"She wasn't busy, she was all bloody, sir. It was quite a sight."

Robert's attention snapped back to the boy in front of him. *"What?"*

"Miss Harrington, sir. When I got there, the front door was open, so I went right in. She was lying on the couch in the parlor, and the doctor was there, and her sister, and the rector, and that mean Betty from the kitchen. It was like a death scene from a traveling play, but it wasn't pig's blood in the bowl, I'm thinking."

"Miss Harrington was bleeding?"

"Yes, sir, didn't I just say so?"

"What happened?" Robert raised his voice and Joe winced.

"I'm not quite sure because no one was wanting to tell me nothing, but I *think* Miss Harrington fell down and hit her head in the graveyard, which was why her cheek was bleeding and they was all fussing around her like a bunch of ninnies."

"Did you manage to speak to her?"

"Yes, sir, I did. She wanted to write you a note, but her pretty sister, Miss Anna, said no, and to tell you that Miss Harrington would come and see you when she was ready." Joe scratched his nose. "She didn't sound real friendly-like, if you know what I mean."

"Did you discover why Miss Harrington was in the graveyard?"

"She didn't say, but she did say that she hadn't fallen down. She kept insisting she'd been hit on the head, but the rector and the doctor kept telling her she was being silly." Joe shuffled his feet. "Women are silly sometimes, aren't they? All emotional and crying like a baby."

"Miss Harrington was *crying?*"

"No, but she did look bleeding awful. All pale and muddy apart from that big bloodied bruise on her cheek. She's going to have a right shiner."

"Good God," Robert muttered. "Whatever have I done?"

Chapter 12

"Come along, my dear. There's nothing to worry about."

Lucy took her father's proffered arm and followed him into the graveyard. She still had a terrible headache but found herself unable to stay in bed a moment longer. Her request to revisit the graveyard had been granted somewhat unwillingly, and only after she'd confessed that it might be the only way to set her mind at rest. As she'd hoped, her father had interpreted that to mean she would stop worrying him over nothing if he gave in and agreed to accompany her.

Harris brought up the rear, a stout cudgel in his hand, his gaze scanning the trees for any hidden dangers. For once, Lucy was quite glad to have him with them. She guided her father down to the corner of the graveyard, where the DeVry tomb stood, its pale white walls benign in the early morning sun.

"It was here, Papa. I took off my gloves because I thought there was something stuck in the door of the crypt."

Her father paused in front of the tomb. "I don't see anything now. Do you?"

"No. It all looks remarkably undisturbed." Lucy looked around. Whatever she'd thought she'd seen trapped in the door of the vault had gone, and there were no footprints in the dirt beside the structure except the new imprint of her father's boots.

"Can we open up the tomb and take a look anyway?"

"Lucy, for goodness' sake." Her father frowned. "You cannot go around opening up sacred burial plots on a whim."

"*Somebody* opened it."

He walked over to her and lowered his voice. "Sometimes, my dear, the poor of the parish feel unable to spare the money to have a deceased relative decently laid to rest. They prefer to use their coin to drink themselves into a stupor toasting the dead. Sometimes their solution to the dilemma of wanting the body in sanctified ground, without paying for the privilege, leads to them opening up existing graves and adding a cadaver."

Lucy put a hand to her mouth.

Her father patted her shoulder. "It is possible that someone chose to do that in this case. The DeVry tomb is no longer in use, so there is no one to be offended."

"So no one will mind if we open it up a crack to take a look, either, will they?"

Her father surveyed the tomb. "It looks perfectly fine to me and quite undisturbed. I doubt anyone has opened it in a long while, and I don't intend to be the one to do so. To be perfectly honest, my dear, what probably happened was that you disturbed a local man up to no good, or a band of grave robbers after a corpse."

Lucy shivered and her father put his arm around her. "Don't worry, my love, I doubt they'll be back for a while. You probably scared them more than they scared you."

"But—"

"I'll ask the church warden and Edward to keep an eye on the graveyard over the next few days. If they see anything suspicious, I'm sure they'll let me know." He offered Lucy his arm. "Are you coming? There's nothing more to worry about here."

"Thank you for reassuring me. You go ahead, Papa. I'll be along in a moment. I just want to make sure I can't find those gloves."

"You were always the most thrifty of my children." He chuckled as he headed back toward the gates. "I'll leave Harris here with you. Don't be long."

Lucy's smile faded as she heard the gate shut behind her father. She turned back toward the DeVry tomb. It was truly as if she had imagined the whole thing. . . . There was no blood on the tomb, the scrap of cloth had disappeared, as had her gloves. That was two pairs she needed to replace now.

It was almost too perfect.

She turned and walked a wider circle around the vault, her gaze flicking everywhere. The sun broke through the clouds and threaded its way through the branches of the ancient oak trees that stood guard over the graves. In the scrubby nettles and blackberry bushes that grew around the base of the trees, it touched upon a hint of white.

Trying to avoid both the thorns and the sting of the nettles, she used her booted foot to push aside as much of the foliage as she could and bent down, suddenly all too aware of her vulnerability, the curve of her exposed neck, her lack of vision. . . .

A piece of broken pottery flashed white against the mud, and she carefully picked it up and held it in her open palm. The remnant was porcelain, and fine enough to see her fingers through. From the look of the piece, someone had ground it into the earth beneath his or her boot. Why on earth would anyone do that? Had the object been broken? But why would such a dainty piece be in the middle of a graveyard? She squinted at the piece more carefully. The pastoral pattern seemed somewhat familiar. . . .

A wave of nausea made it almost impossible for her to breathe, and she closed her fingers around the fragment.

"Are you all right, miss?" Harris called.

"I'm fine." Lucy rose to her feet, ignoring the swirl of unsteadiness as she straightened. "Let's go home."

"I think that is a very clever idea, Robert. A movable chair with wheels." Aunt Rose smiled as she passed him a cup of tea. "Don't you, Miss Chingford?"

"Oh, it wasn't my idea." Robert accepted the cup and balanced it on his thigh. "Miss Harrington read something in *Ackermann's* and brought it to my attention."

"Miss Harrington is a remarkably competent young woman."

"Which is just as well, because she scarcely has the looks to become a diamond of the first water." Miss Chingford put her cup down. "She strikes me as the meddling sort."

Robert's smile held an edge. "She does like to manage us lesser mortals, but I owe her a great deal and will not have her spoken of in less than courteous terms."

Miss Chingford hunched her shoulder at him. For the first time, it occurred to him to wonder how it might feel to face her every morning over the breakfast table. Was she just young as his aunt suggested, or was she simply a spoiled beauty who was too used to getting her own way to accept the slightest hint of censure or disapproval?

"By the way, have you heard any more from the rectory about what happened to Miss Harrington?" Aunt Rose poured herself some more tea and took up her embroidery.

"No, I haven't. I thought it best to wait until Miss Harrington wished to communicate with me, rather than bother her if she is indisposed. Blows on the head can be quite unpleasant."

Miss Chingford made a huffing sound and Robert

switched his attention back to her. "Is there something wrong?"

She stood and walked over to Robert. Her blond hair was dressed in a cascade of ringlets that framed her classically beautiful face, and she wore a blue dress that exposed rather a lot of her small bosom. Robert wasn't surprised she complained his house was cold if she insisted on dressing in such skimpy garments.

"Why does everyone talk about Miss Harrington all the time? I realize that this place has no social life to speak of, but there must be something more interesting than her."

Aunt Rose opened her mouth, but Robert quelled her with a look. "Miss Harrington is much respected for her charitable work in the village. I don't understand why you seem so determined to dislike her."

"I don't *dislike* her. She is too far beneath me for that. She is the one who forced herself upon my notice as if *she* is the arbiter of taste and social niceties in this godforsaken place."

"She is considered one of the first ladies of the village."

"But she is so provincial. What this place needs is a woman with taste and sophistication to make it more fashionable."

"You don't like my home?"

She flushed. "It will look much better once I take it in hand, I can promise you that."

"And what if I like it just the way it is?"

"Why would you? The house is old and falling down around your ears."

"But it is my home."

"And it is inconvenient and beneath your status."

He shrugged. "I'm a country gentleman. It suits me rather well."

"But you have the money to make it so much more." For the first time since he'd seen her again, his betrothed looked animated. "And once you have improved the property, I'm sure the crown would be more than willing to grant you a title to go with it. You could probably even afford to buy yourself one if you wished."

Robert couldn't help but smile. "What would I want with a title? I'm quite happy keeping my money for the more important things like improving my lands and supporting my tenants."

"You cannot mean that."

"Why not?"

"Because . . ." Miss Chingford shook her head. "*I* want . . ."

His smile disappeared. "Could you leave us for a moment, Aunt?"

"Of course, my dear."

Robert waited until his aunt shut the door behind her, and then turned back to Miss Chingford, who had remained standing, her hands locked together, her expression mutinous.

"Perhaps it is time for us to speak plainly, my dear." He gestured at the chair opposite his. "Won't you sit down?"

She took the seat, but avoided his gaze. "It is not necessary to discuss anything, Major Kurland. I was perhaps a little presumptuous with my remarks as to what I intend to do with your estate once we are married. I will, of course, consult with you before I instigate any changes."

"That's very kind of you."

Robert studied her averted profile with a great deal of exasperation. She was obviously uncomfortable with him. In truth, he doubted she even liked him anymore, so why couldn't she just say it, and end this charade?

"Miss Chingford, it is no sin to have made a mistake."

"Whatever do you mean?"

He tried to be gentle. "I'm not the same man you met in London three years ago."

"Yes, you are!"

"I didn't mean it literally. Much has changed in the past

three years." He smoothed a hand over his covered legs. "I've been wounded. I'm still not sure if I will be able to take up the reins of my old life or that I even wish to return to the military. I can understand if you find that too much to deal with."

"Are you suggesting I should abandon a man who has fought for his country, a man whom everyone I meet tells me I am lucky to have as a betrothed?"

"It doesn't matter what anyone else thinks."

"Yes, it does!" She glared at him. "You have no idea."

"Obviously not." He made a supreme effort. "But surely, no one would wish you to be unhappy?"

"What is there to be unhappy about? I will be marrying a man my family approves of."

"But what about you? What do you want?"

Her eyes filled with tears and she practically ran out of the room, leaving Robert feeling even more useless than usual. Eventually, his aunt came back in and picked up her embroidery as if nothing had happened.

"She's very young, you know."

"That's blatantly obvious." He sighed. "I feel like a wolf savaging a lamb. She cannot wish to marry me, Aunt. Why can she not just say so?"

"Because it's not that simple for a woman. She's invested three years of her life in you, and she feels she is practically on the shelf. If she breaks her engagement, she'll disappoint her family, and she fears she will be an object of pity and ridicule amongst her contemporaries."

"She told you this?"

"Some of it. The rest I inferred."

"Then why can't she be honest with me? She's only twenty, for God's sake. She's hardly on the shelf."

"Most of her friends are already married and many of them have children. She worries that she has been left behind." Aunt Rose set a stitch in her embroidery. "I also suspect, that having three other daughters to marry off, the Chingford family is eager to hang on to your money and your connections."

Robert contemplated waking up next to the golden beauty of Miss Chingford every morning, of her bearing his children, sharing his life. . . .

"Why did I propose to her? What was I thinking?" He groaned. "I'm not sure how it happened. It seemed to be assumed, and like a fool, I went along with it."

"She is very beautiful, Robert, and she's young enough to be molded into the kind of wife you want."

"I don't want to mold her! She's not a slab of clay and I am not God." He glared at his aunt. "In my present state I'm not fit to be a husband or companion to anyone."

"I'd agree with you on that. Your temper is quite shocking." She smiled at him. "If you wish, I'll talk to Miss Chingford and see if I can find out why she clings to this arrangement when it obviously won't make her happy anymore. I don't think she is a bad person, Robert. She is just confused and scared about the future."

"I know." He stared glumly at his aunt. "There has to be a solution to this. It would help if she didn't run away in the middle of every conversation I attempt to have with her."

The door opened and Foley appeared with a tray of the small cakes his aunt preferred. He still wasn't speaking to Robert, and he lavished all his smiles and attention on Aunt Rose.

"I hope you don't mind, nephew, but I thought it was time to call on your neighbors and renew my acquaintance with them."

"Please, go ahead. Just try not to mention me."

"I can hardly pretend you don't exist. People will want to know how you are getting along."

"Well, tell them what they need to know, but don't encourage them to visit me here."

Aunt Rose topped up his tea and placed three cakes on his plate. He was sick of tea. It was no wonder he yearned for the brandy bottle.

"You will have to face everyone at some point you know, my love."

"Yes, but not yet. I at least want to be able to stand up and greet my guests. Is that too much to ask?"

He hated the thought of being stared at, of being pitied, almost as much as he hated being in pain. But what did that say about his character? Was he really too vain to accept his new reality?

"It isn't too much, Robert, but I think you underestimate your neighbors. Most of them have known you since you were in shortcoats. They're not like the *Ton*. They won't come to stare and spread gossip."

He studied his aunt for a long moment. In her own way, she was as straightforward and honest as he was. "You're probably right. I promise I'll make an effort to be civil to anyone who calls."

"Thank you." Aunt Rose blew him a kiss. "That's all I ask. Your mother would hate to see you like this."

"Barricaded in my bedchamber?" Robert chuckled. "Between you and Miss Harrington, I'm being forced into the open, room by room."

The door opened again and Foley stepped aside to reveal another visitor. Robert automatically tried to rise and then sat down again.

"Good afternoon, Major Kurland, Mrs. Armitage."

"My dear, Miss Harrington. How are you?" Aunt Rose bustled over to take Miss Harrington's arm and seat her on the couch nearest Robert. "We didn't expect to see you today."

"I'm quite recovered, thank you." She touched her bonnet. "Apart from the remnants of a headache, which simply refuses to depart."

Robert scanned her face but could see little of her expression beneath the deep crown of her dull brown bonnet. "Are you quite well?"

Her smile was wry. "It depends who you ask. My father and Dr. Baker think I'm imagining things."

"From the bruising on your face, I find that difficult to believe."

"Oh, they think I fell and hit my face."

Robert glanced at his aunt, who was pouring Miss Harrington a cup of tea. "Aunt Rose, I doubt that tea is hot enough for our guest. Could you ask Foley for a fresh pot? And maybe you might wish to find Miss Chingford and ask her to join us so that she will not miss out on the pleasure of a visitor."

"Certainly, my dear nephew. Why would I want to waste my time sitting down, anyway?" Aunt Rose gave him a speculative glance as she left the room.

He gestured at the cup in Miss Harrington's hand. "If it isn't warm enough, Foley will bring some more."

"It is fine, Major." She sipped at the beverage slowly. "It's a beautiful day. You should consider sitting outside. The leaves are just starting to bud on the trees. I suspect we will have some blossoms soon. The elm trees in your driveway will look magnificent."

"What does the weather have to do with anything?"

"I was merely commenting that with the chill of winter behind us, you would be safe to venture outdoors. Why are you frowning at me?"

"Will you take off your damned bonnet?"

She looked up at him. "I *beg* your pardon?"

"Take off your bonnet. I want to see your face."

She put her cup down so sharply that it rattled in the saucer. He waited as she untied the gray ribbons and placed the bonnet on the seat beside her. For once, her brown hair wasn't braided closely to her head but was arranged in loose curls and waves that softened her appearance considerably. But nothing could cover up the ugly bruise that marred her cheek.

"Good God."

She patted her hair and looked remarkably self-conscious. "I have a bump on the back of my head. I couldn't braid my hair. It pulled too much."

"Come here."

"Major, you don't need to—"

"Please, Miss Harrington, will you at least oblige me in this?"

She rose to her feet and came to stand in front of him, bending down so that he could observe her face at close quarters. He could see the smattering of freckles on the bridge of her nose and the green-gray shards in her brown eyes.

"You will have a black eye."

"So everyone keeps telling me. I'm not sure why they all sound so pleased about it."

He gently touched her cheek. "How did this happen?"

"Have you finished with your inspection? May I sit down? I told you what I intended to do in my note. Didn't you receive it?"

"I received it well after the events had occurred." He glowered at her. "Which I assume was deliberate."

"I didn't want you trying to stop me."

"Because you knew you were in the wrong?"

"No, because it didn't matter what you thought, I knew I was going to do it anyway."

"Didn't *matter?* You could've been killed because of this wild goose chase I started!"

"There's no need to get angry, Major. I agreed to participate in the investigation, and I accept the consequences of that choice." Her eyes flashed a warning. "Just because I'm a woman, doesn't mean I can't look after myself."

"You claim you were hit on the head. Do you consider that looking after yourself?"

"Oh, for goodness' sake, how was I to know that someone would be lurking in the graveyard? You wouldn't have done any better."

"I would've taken the means to defend myself. And if you had told me what you intended to do in good time, I would have insisted you take someone with you, as well."

She had the grace to look a little guilty, but it wasn't enough to assuage his anger. "And what was all that nonsense about your gloves, anyway?"

She told him about the blood on her gloves, and her deductions as to where it had come from and he listened intently.

"... I knelt down in front of the tomb and found a scrap of pink material stuck in the opening. When I tried to pull it free, it wouldn't move. I took my gloves off to get a better grip. The next thing I remember is waking up with my face wedged against the DeVry tomb and a headache of monstrous proportions."

"A bang on the head will do that to a person." He was aware that he wasn't sounding very sympathetic.

"Papa and Dr. Baker decided I was imagining things, and put me to bed with a dose of laudanum. This morning I went back to the graveyard with my father. I told him I wanted to look for my gloves. We found everything just as it should be. No blood on the tomb, no fabric stuck in the door, no signs of any disturbance at all. It was quite uncanny."

Robert smiled. He knew how that felt. "Perhaps you were imagining things."

Her expression turned to ice. "I thought you, of all people, would believe me. Isn't it obvious? Someone didn't want me looking in that tomb."

"I accept that might be the case, but you can't deny that your father also made some very good points."

"About grave robbers, and unsanctioned burials, and the hysterical nature of women?"

"Not the last one, obviously, although you do seem to be getting a little agitated. But there are many reasons why someone might be loitering in that graveyard. You said so yourself. Didn't you see Ben Cobbins in there, too?"

"But none of those reasons concern me quite so intimately as the disappearance of my maid!" She rose to her feet and walked away from him. "You don't believe me, do you?"

"Miss Harrington, if you are angry with me, it is with good cause. I should never have involved you in my stupid schemes. I never intended for you to get hurt. Will you accept my apologies?"

She spun around, her hands fisted. "By that, do you mean that I should go meekly home and sit by the fire, obeying my father's dictates until I am an old maid?"

"That's going rather too far, Miss Harrington. I have no desire to tell you how to live your life."

"Apart from the fact that I should keep out of your current concerns?"

"No. It's not like that. I'm beginning to believe I was mistaken in what I saw."

She sat down quite suddenly and looked at him. "*Why?*"

"My reasons are my own." He had no intention of telling her about his overindulgence in laudanum. "Just let me say that they have nothing to do with you, and your estimable intelligence."

"That's very gallant of you, but are you ordering me to stop looking into this matter?"

"There is no 'matter.' Just two silly girls and some petty theft."

"Silly and petty to you, perhaps, Major, but not to me." She looked right into his eyes. "If nothing had happened at the tomb, why weren't my gloves still there, or any evidence of where I knelt down on the ground? Someone eradicated all traces of my presence."

She reached into her pocket and brought out her handkerchief. For one terrifying moment Robert feared she was going to start sobbing.

"I found this in the bushes near the tomb. Have you ever seen it before?"

She placed the unfolded handkerchief on his palm. He squinted at the piece of broken porcelain and then flipped it over with his finger.

"It reminds me of a snuff box that used to be in my mother's apartment downstairs. She kept it because it was a gift from her father, although she never took snuff. I'll ask Foley if it is still there."

He wrapped the fragment up and gave it back to Miss Harrington. "Even if it is my mother's box, it proves nothing except that we have thieves in our village."

Her shoulders slumped. "You are determined that the disappearances and the thefts are not connected."

"Why should they be? Come now, Miss Harrington. Wouldn't you be pleased to catch these thieves?"

"I'd rather find out what happened to Mary and Daisy."

He heard voices in the hallway and stopped talking as his aunt and betrothed came into the room. Miss Chingford took one look at Miss Harrington and shot him an accusing glare, which Robert ignored. Instead he smiled at his aunt, who had turned to speak to Miss Harrington.

"As you requested, Robert, Foley is bringing a fresh pot of tea and some parkin."

"Your recipe, I hope, Aunt?"

"Of course. No southerner can make good parkin."

"What is parkin, Mrs. Armitage?" Miss Harrington asked.

"It is a kind of gingerbread. Robert always loved it when he was a boy."

"It sounds delightful. Perhaps you could give me the recipe."

"Indeed, I will. It's quite simple to make." His aunt continued to talk and Robert noticed Miss Harrington sway a little and briefly close her eyes. He beckoned to Foley and spoke quietly in his ear.

"Have Granger bring the gig round. He can take Miss Harrington home."

"Yes, sir."

Lucy wasn't sure if the ride in the gig had made her head feel worse or better. At least it was of short duration. Granger handed her down, and set off again back the way he'd come, leaving Lucy to ponder her conversation with Major Kurland.

He'd decided not to pursue the matter, and he expected her to do the same like a well-trained dog dropping a bone on his command. She found herself baring her teeth. How dare he assume she'd just quietly go along with his orders? He wasn't the one who had been hit on the head in a graveyard and left for dead! She slammed the back door and then regretted it as the sound reverberated through her sensitive skull.

And what of the matter of the porcelain box? Feeling like a thief, she'd checked the pockets of all of Anthony's coats and the box she'd seen had disappeared. What if it had been originally stolen from Kurland Hall? Had Anthony taken it? How had it ended up crushed underfoot in the graveyard just where she had been knocked unconscious? All the unanswered questions circled in her mind, making her headache even worse. Anthony had been at home when she'd struggled back from the graveyard. Had he also been there earlier?

A letter awaited her on the hall table, so she took it into the back parlor with her to read. Even when wearing her spectacles the words danced around like hens scattering before a fox. After suffering the indignities of a headache, she was almost beginning to have some sympathy with Major Kurland again. Letter in hand, she went to find Anna, who was in the stillroom at the back of the house making an infusion of witch hazel, probably for Lucy's black eye. They also needed a constant supply of witch hazel for the twins' innumerable bumps and scratches.

"Can you read this for me, please?" Lucy held out the letter.

"Certainly." Anna cleared her throat. "It says, 'Dear Miss Harrington, thank you for your letter. If it is convenient, I will come to the rectory this evening around six o'clock before I return home to Lower Kurland. Yours, William Bowden.' "

Anna lowered the letter. "Who is he, Lucy?"

"Do you remember me telling you that Mary had an admirer who had worked on our new stable block last summer?"

"Yes. Is this him?" Anna folded up the paper into neat squares.

"I believe so."

"I wonder if Mary is with him?" Anna's smile grew hopeful. "Maybe they have got married and she is expecting his child."

For some reason, Lucy found it difficult to smile back. "I hope you are right. I really do."

Anna peered into Lucy's face. "You don't look well. Why don't you go upstairs and have a rest? I'll make sure Mrs. Fielding gets the dinner on the table on time and that the twins eat their food rather than throwing it around the room like that despicable little marmoset monkey Nicholas's grandmother owns. I'll wake you up well before Mr. Bowden arrives, I promise."

"Are you sure, Anna?" For once, she was too overset to argue. It was an unusual sensation. She'd never felt quite so fatigued in her life. Between the horrors of the graveyard, and Major Kurland's unexpected dismissal of her concerns, she was ready to hide under the covers for a month. "I do have a terrible headache."

Anna produced a bottle and a spoon and proceeded to dose Lucy with willow bark tea while ignoring her sister's shudders at the bitterness of the taste.

"Now go to bed. I'll manage."

Lucy tucked the letter into her pocket, made her way back into the house, and wearily climbed the stairs. Her bed had never looked quite so welcoming. With a groan, she stretched out on the sheets and inhaled the scent of lavender and line-dried linen. The usual sounds of the busy household enfolded her. She slept until Anna shook her awake into the darkness of the evening with the reminder that William Bowden would be arriving within the hour.

Despite Mrs. Fielding's obvious disapproval, she ate her dinner in the kitchen, and then helped Betty clear everything away for the night. Her headache had worsened. She was more determined than ever to ignore everyone's advice and find out exactly what was going on in Kurland Village. Major Kurland might have decided they were both inventing things, but she was made of sterner stuff. The ferocity of her headache only reminded her that not everything had been in her imagination.

Betty answered a knock on the back door, and brought William Bowden through to Lucy in the small parlor. She'd decided not to bother her father with news of the young man's presence. It would only irritate him. He was safely ensconced in his study with the latest newspaper from London and a bottle of brandy.

"Miss Harrington." William Bowden took off his hat and bowed. He was a very tall man of about Lucy's age with fair hair and a kind, pleasant face.

"Mr. Bowden. It is good of you to come and see me." She recognized him from his work on the stables during the summer months. "I'm hoping you can assist me with a rather trying matter."

"Mr. Bridges said you was wanting to ask about my Mary."

"That's right." Lucy put a hand to her throat. "She is with you, then? Oh, thank God."

William shifted his feet. "No, miss, she ain't."

"What do you mean?"

"We were sweethearts. She said she wanted to come away and live on the farm as my wife, but she seemed to find it hard to settle."

"Do you mean she broke her promises to you?"

"She broke her promises to everyone, miss."

He looked so miserable, Lucy's heart went out to him. "When was she supposed to come to you?"

"A week or so ago, miss. She swore she'd keep her word, but she never turned up. Left me standing there like a fool. I heard later she'd changed her mind and gone to London."

"To London?"

"Aye, with that Daisy Weeks she was always giggling with."

"You're certain that's what she did?"

"What else could she have done? She's not here, is she?"

"That's true." Lucy bit her lip. "I hesitate to cause you pain, but do you think she might have gone off with anyone else?"

"She did mention another man to me, but she swore it was all in the past. From what I understood, when she met me, she'd broken things off with him, but he hadn't taken it well."

"Was he a local man?"

"I suppose he must've been, seeing as how else would he have known Mary? She never went farther afield than Saffron Walden. I can't say I ever met the man. She was right scared of him, though." He scratched his nose. "I suspect we would've come to blows if we had met."

"So you think Mary went to London with Daisy."

"Aye, I do, and good riddance to the pair of them. If a lass doesn't want a man, she should just tell him to his face rather than muck him around."

"I agree, Mr. Bowden, and I appreciate your help." Lucy rubbed her aching forehead. "I wish Mary had made a better decision and was safe with you."

"Despite everything, I wouldn't wish any harm on the lass, either."

"You are a good man, Mr. Bowden."

"Thank you, miss." He put his hat back on. "If you find out anything more, I'd be grateful if you'd let me know."

"I will, Mr. Bowden, and thank you again."

Betty saw him out, and Lucy remained sitting in her chair as the candle burned down to a stub. Mary had promised William she would leave with him, and then reneged on that promise and left for London with Daisy. Apparently, Mary had also been afraid of a previous lover.

Betty came back in the parlor with a bucket of coal. "Oh, are you still here, miss? Miss Anna was looking for you. Shouldn't you be off to bed?"

"Betty, is Jane still awake?"

"I should imagine so. I heard her shouting at those boys not five minutes ago. I'll go and find her for you, miss."

Lucy waited in the flickering shadows until Jane appeared, her color high and her apron damp from helping the twins to wash.

"Did you want me, Miss Harrington?"

"I'm sorry to interrupt you, Jane, but I remember you mentioning Mary had an old sweetheart?"

"She did, miss. She was worried because she wanted to break things off with him, and he wasn't the sort of man to cross."

"She was afraid of him?"

"I'd say so, miss."

"Did she ever mention his name?"

Jane pleated her damp apron and frowned. "I don't think so."

"And you never met him."

"No, he used to write to her, and then Mary met that young carpenter and fell in love with him and—"

"You think Mary loved William Bowden?"

"I do, miss." Jane met her gaze unflinchingly. "I was right surprised when Betty just told me Mary hadn't gone with him after all."

"It's a real puzzle, isn't it?" Lucy studied the red embers in the fire. "Perhaps Mary decided that neither of the men could compete with the allure of London."

"I suppose that's possible, miss. She was the sort of girl who let herself be talked into things, and Daisy Weeks is a bit of a bossy so-and-so."

Lucy lifted her head. "Thank you, Jane. You've been very helpful."

"Good night then, miss." She rolled up her sleeves. "I've got to go and make sure those young rascals are still in bed and haven't escaped again. I'm thinking of asking the rector if we can have bars put on the windows."

Lucy fought a smile and waited until Jane stomped off up the stairs. It was quiet now, the scent of roast lamb and blackberry crumble from dinner still noticeable in the swirling currents of draughty air. Outside, an owl hooted and was answered by another. She should go to bed. Her head was pounding, but she had a terrible sense of waiting, as if Mary would walk through the door and everything would be the same again.

Why couldn't she let the matter rest? By all accounts, Mary had turned her back on Kurland St. Mary and left for London. Why couldn't she just accept it? It wasn't just because she didn't want Major Kurland to be right. She could even accept that the girls' disappearance might not be connected to the thefts, but something was wrong. . . .

She lit a candle from the embers of the fire and opened her sewing basket. If she was destined to sit up and ponder puzzles, she might as well make herself useful and cut up some squares from the ragbag for a patchwork quilt she was making with Anna. The dull thump of her headache served as a constant reminder that things *weren't* normal, and that she *had* been attacked in the graveyard. Was it time to consider other possibilities?

Had she stumbled across a cache of stolen goods Ben Cobbins had left in the graveyard? She'd heard him arguing with someone there on the previous day. Perhaps the blood had come from another kind of disagreement between thieves. Maybe, finding her meddling, Ben had decided to teach her a lesson. She shivered and narrowly avoided poking herself in the thumb with her needle. If it had been Ben, she was lucky he hadn't carried out his threat to ruin her completely.

But what of the porcelain box? She hadn't told Major Kurland, but she was almost certain that the piece she'd found in the graveyard was part of the box she'd first discovered in Anthony's coat pocket. If the box was from Kurland Hall, how had it gotten into his possession and ended up broken in the ground? Was it possible that Anthony was stealing to finance his gambling? Even worse, was he in cahoots with Ben Cobbins? Had it been Anthony she'd heard arguing with Ben in the graveyard?

Dread flooded her senses, leaving her shaking and cold. She couldn't believe it of her brother. But did she have the courage to confront him and share her suspicions? If he denied everything and went to their father in a rage, she suspected he'd call Dr. Baker to attend to her again. She had no wish to be sent away to recover from her nerves.

*   *   *

Robert opened his eyes and stared out into the darkness. Foley and Bookman had gone to bed and he was finally alone. He still couldn't sleep. Even though he'd claimed not to be interested, his mind was busy sifting through everything Miss Harrington had told him. She wasn't the sort of woman to fall over her own feet. If she said she'd been hit on the head, he'd wager she was telling the truth. So why had he refused to believe her?

He sat up and pushed back the sheets. Because if he did believe her, he had to accept that something was wrong in Kurland St. Mary. And he couldn't do *that* when he was powerless to do anything about it, and afraid he was fantasizing about seeing dead bodies being carted around at night. No wonder she'd looked at him with such disgust and confusion.

She probably thought him a coward.

With great deliberation, he swung his legs over the side of the bed and slowly stood up. Since falling and being unable to get back to bed, he'd been secretly practicing standing and regaining his strength. He was certain Dr. Baker wouldn't approve, but he had a terrible sense that time was running out, and that if he didn't take control of his destiny, he'd end up bedridden and bitter for the rest of his days.

Using the furniture, he made his way toward the bow windows without incident and paused to draw the curtain to one side and stare out at the church. The moon wasn't as bright as it was last time he'd stood there, but his eyes gradually became accustomed to the gloom. He was helped by the sudden gleam of a lantern bobbing along from the direction of the church toward the stile that separated Kurland Hall from the wall of the graveyard.

The light briefly illuminated the anxious face of the curate. What was his name? Edward Calthrope, that was it. He paused at the stile and turned in a circle as if waiting for someone. A dog barked, followed by several others, and

Robert strained to see where the noise was coming from. Ben Cobbins appeared, surrounded by his dogs, and stopped to talk to the curate. At one point he raised his hand and jabbed his finger in the other man's face. Robert wished he could hear what they were saying. What on earth did the curate and the thief have to say to each other?

Robert's left knee gave way, and he clutched at the chair. This time he had enough strength to straighten up and make his way back to bed. He doubted he'd be able to sleep and thought longingly of the brandy decanter Foley had ceremoniously locked up after dinner. His servants seemed determined to stop him from finding his rest. But perhaps that was for the best. He climbed back into bed, stared out into the darkness, and allowed his mind to wander through the conflicting evidence Miss Harrington had provided him with once again.

When the floorboards creaked and a new shadow slid under the door as if someone paused outside, Lucy looked up from her work.

"Who's there?"

She rose to her feet and flung the door open to discover Edward poised for flight, his expression startled.

"Miss Harrington! I didn't expect you to be up so late. I thought someone had left a candle burning. I was considering coming in to make sure it was safely put out."

"Why are you still up, Edward?"

He looked down at his patched shoes. Lucy noticed he had trodden mud into the hallway she'd cleaned just that morning. "I was writing to my mother and didn't notice the time."

She considered asking him why he'd been outside writing in the dark, but didn't want to encourage him to linger. She did, however, have to be civil.

"How is she?"

"Not very well at all." He sighed. "She suffers from a

variety of complaints that keep her tied to her bed almost constantly."

"I'm sorry to hear that. I'm sure your letters are a comfort to her."

His smile was strained. "One would hope so. I suspect, however, that the pitiful amount of money I manage to send her every month is even more welcome. Her pension is very small, and she has my two sisters and younger brother to provide for."

There was a bitter note to Edward's words that made Lucy feel guilty. "I didn't know that you were supporting your family. Have you spoken to my father about increasing your stipend?"

"The rector considers I am adequately paid."

"Does your mother not have any other means of support? Other relatives, perhaps?"

"Unfortunately not. My father was cast out of his family for marrying a woman of lower class. We have always had to make do as best we can."

"If I can help by sending extra clothing or food, please let me know." Lucy shut the lid of her sewing box, blew out the candle, and walked back toward Edward.

"You think my family should accept charity?"

She paused to look up into his face and was shocked by the anger there. "I wouldn't consider it charity. I would be helping another member of the church community."

"It's still alms for the poor, though, isn't it?" His face twisted. "You consider yourself so far above my touch, but my father was as well-born as yours."

"As you rarely mention your family, I have never thought much about the matter, Edward," Lucy said carefully. "I can assure you that I never meant to make you feel inferior."

"Major Kurland's father married a woman from the industrial classes, and he is still received everywhere because he married into money, whereas my mother . . ."

Lucy touched his arm. "Surely we are all the same in God's eyes."

"Of course you would say that, wouldn't you? Always so good and well-behaved and respectable."

"Are you sure that you are feeling well, Edward? You sound quite unlike yourself."

She was beginning to feel a little uneasy, as if she was trapped in a room with a stranger. He took a step away from her and bowed.

"Don't worry about me, Miss Harrington, I'll survive." He took a deep, shuddering breath. "I admit to feeling a little overwrought. I apologize if I said anything to offend you. I am worried about my mother."

"You didn't offend me, sir, but I am concerned about you. If the stress about your mother's financial security is oversetting you, please speak to my father. He knows his duty to the church and to his fellow man. I'm certain he wouldn't want you or your family to be in such a precarious position."

"It's too late for that, Miss Harrington." His smile was ghastly. "I am committed to solving this problem for myself. Thank you for your concern. You are a remarkable woman."

"Are you sure you don't want me to speak to my father for you?"

He'd started to walk away but stopped and looked over his shoulder at her. "No, I thank you." The back door closed softly behind them, and Edward cocked his head at the sound. "Perhaps you might worry less about me, and more about what your brother is getting up to at Red Lion. Good night, Miss Harrington."

Chapter 13

"Major, let me just wrap this scarf around your neck to protect you from the wind."

As his butler bore down upon him with a purposeful expression, Robert snatched the scarf out of his hands.

"Thank you, I'll do it myself. I'm not a goose being trussed up for roasting."

"As you wish, sir." Foley relinquished the thick wool scarf and stepped back. "I believe I see Miss Harrington and her sister on the driveway. Shall I ask her to call back later?"

"Ask them if they'd like to accompany us on our outing. I'm sure Miss Harrington will be delighted to see me outside."

"Yes, sir." Foley bowed and walked off at a decorous pace down toward the visitors who were approaching the front of the house on the driveway. Robert glanced at Bookman, who was deep in conversation with the estate carpenter who had fashioned the wheeled chair out of a variety of objects from his workshop. The wheels were quite large and probably from a carriage, and the chair was a padded one he remembered from his father's study.

"Mr. Walker?"

214   *Catherine Lloyd*

"Yes, Major?"

The carpenter came toward him, his interested gaze moving between Robert and the chair.

"Why did you choose such large wheels? The ones in the illustration were much smaller."

"I tried out several sizes, sir, and I found that the larger the wheel, the more comfortable the ride." He wiped his hands on his apron. "Once you've tried the contraption out, we can tinker with it until we get it right."

"I appreciate your efforts, Mr. Walker."

"That's all right, sir. I always appreciate a challenge." He walked forward and knelt to adjust one of the screws. "Now, you let me know how you do, and try to stay on the path. I don't think it will ride smoothly on the rougher parts of the estate."

"Don't worry, I don't intend to go far today. This is just an experiment." Robert saw the Harrington sisters change course and ascend the hill toward him, accompanied by Foley. His aunt and Miss Chingford stepped out of the house and he waved at them. "Aunt Rose, how do you like my mighty chariot?"

"It is remarkable, Robert!" She turned to Mr. Walker. "Did you make this? How extraordinary."

Miss Chingford came over, her gaze fixed on the chair. She wore a blue pelisse edged with white fur and a bonnet to match. Her hands were thrust into a large swansdown muff. "You don't intend to go *out* in that, do you?"

"Why not? It is better than being stuck inside."

"But people might *see* you."

"On my own lands? I doubt it." He looked up into her face. "Do I embarrass you?"

She averted her gaze. "You will not be using this, this *thing* for long, will you? You'll soon be back on your feet."

"But what if I'm not?" Robert forced himself to say the

words. "What if this is the best I can manage for the rest of my life?"

"I cannot accept that."

"What if you have no choice?" Of course, she did have a choice. Perhaps she would finally acknowledge that. Before she could reply, another voice intruded on the conversation.

"Major Kurland, how lovely to see you outside!"

Robert turned to find Miss Anna Harrington smiling at him. Her older sister had paused to speak to Mrs. Armitage, and seemed disinclined to approach him. Miss Anna looked remarkably lovely in an old printed muslin dress and gray coat that probably cost a tenth of what Miss Chingford was wearing but still made her look stylish.

"Miss Anna, have you met my guest, Miss Chingford?"

She curtsied. "I haven't, but Lucy told me all about her." She turned to smile at the other woman, who was eyeing her suspiciously. "Are you enjoying your visit, Miss Chingford?"

The two girls moved off together, leaving Robert alone in his chair. There was a slight chill to the breeze slicing across the terrace, but it was nothing compared to the weather he'd endured on the continent as a soldier. It was good to be outside. He felt almost like his old self, his spirits lifted, his resolve renewed. He put on his gloves and ran an experimental hand along the rim of the large wheel on the side of his chair. With a wheel on each side and someone to push the chair and steer it, he reckoned he would manage rather well.

Miss Harrington was still talking to his aunt and made no effort to come and speak to him. The rigid set of her shoulders reminded him that she was probably annoyed with his dismissal of her claims. If he got the opportunity on their walk, he would attempt to redeem himself.

"Are you ready to go, then, sir?" Bookman inquired,

and took up his position behind Robert's chair. "I suggest we stay on the path and make our way down to the home farm and the stables. If that's all right with you, sir."

"That sounds like an excellent idea."

The women grouped themselves around him, and followed at a discreet distance by Foley, they set off. Despite the brightness of the sun, the wind stung Robert's exposed face. It reminded him of the snowy French Alps and marching his troops through dangerous hostile territory. Was there anything to fear on his lands? Why did he have the same sense of wariness? Perhaps old habits died harder than he'd thought.

"Can we stop?"

Bookman obediently paused, and Robert stared out over the barren fields to the hills and took a deep, uncomplicated breath. Home. He'd forgotten that smell. Miss Harrington came to stand beside him and he looked up at her. The bruise on her cheek was still dark purple and edged with the jagged slash of broken skin.

"What do you think?"

"Of what, Major?"

"Of this chair! It was your idea."

"It seems to be working quite well."

Ah, there was no animation in her voice. She was still offended.

"I'd like to apologize."

"For what?"

"For doubting you." Robert glanced back at Bookman, but his valet appeared to be looking the other way. "I checked with Foley this morning. That porcelain box I mentioned has gone missing from my mother's rooms."

"Oh."

"I wonder how it got to the graveyard? Perhaps the thief is storing his stolen goods in one of the tombs."

"I thought of that possibility, too." She sighed. "It might be why I was hit on the head."

"You have decided the thefts are not connected to the disappearance of the two girls?"

"I suspect the thefts are connected with someone much closer to home."

The chair jerked forward and Robert jumped as Bookman started pushing him again. Miss Harrington marched alongside him. It was harder to hear her over the reverberations of the chair.

"Do you know who it is?"

"Not yet, but I have my suspicions."

"Which you cannot share with me?"

She gave him a pointed look. "You said you didn't believe anything was wrong and that we were just imagining things."

"And I've thought better of that." Robert held up his hand. "Bookman, will you please stop again? I want to look at the maze and the rose garden."

"Yes, sir."

"Will you also go and check that my aunt and Miss Chingford are warm enough? Miss Harrington can keep an eye on me while you are gone."

"Certainly."

Robert waited until Bookman was out of earshot. He didn't want his valet thinking he was imagining things again. "Have you heard from Mary's admirer?"

"He visited me last night. Mary isn't with him after all. He wanted to marry her and she seemed quite keen, but she was also worried about an old suitor who hadn't taken his dismissal lightly."

"Devil take it." Robert stared out over the tranquil pastoral scene. "Do we need to find *another* man?"

"The carpenter did tell me that Mary had agreed to meet him the other night, but she didn't turn up. He heard later that she'd gone to London."

"Then that's that." Robert sighed. "Perhaps we should

focus our attention on the petty thefts instead. I suspect Ben Cobbins is involved right up to his thick neck."

"But what if Mary didn't go? What if her old lover stopped her?"

Robert angled his head so that he could look up into his companion's face. "Miss Harrington, I am prepared to go along with most of your interesting lines of thinking, but this one veers off into the scandal sheets. Why can't you simply admit that Mary went off with Daisy?"

Bookman's shadow fell over him, and Miss Harrington walked away without bothering to reply. Had he offended her again? It seemed likely. His patience, never his strong point, had been stretched to the breaking point over the last hellish months. He needed to mind his tongue.

"The garden needs some work, Robert."

He smiled at his aunt, who had come up beside him. At least she was a fount of normality and practical good sense.

"I believe it does. I intend to speak to my head gardener this week. My mother would be most unhappy if she could see her rose garden now."

"Aye, she would be." His aunt nodded. "Now, let's get on before you take a chill. Are we going down as far as the stables?"

"I think we should. Do you think the chair will make it?" He glanced back at Bookman, who was staring into space. "Bookman?"

"Oh yes, sir."

Bookman turned the chair around and started off down the slight slope that led to the gray slate roofs of the home farm and the stables. The smell of warm hay and manure rose to greet them, and Robert filled his lungs with it. As a cavalry officer, he'd spent more time with his horse than any other being in the king's army. Despite his frequent absences from home, he'd devoted a considerable sum to updating the stables from their Tudor origins to the well-managed, well-drained stone-and-brick structures of today.

As they came nearer, a shrill whinny split the air and Robert grinned.

"Is that Rogue?"

"Yes, sir. After we'd got you home, I went back to France and brought him and the rest of your kit back to Kurland Hall."

"Was Rogue difficult on the voyage?"

"Why do you ask, sir?"

"Because you are scowling."

Bookman's expression went blank. "Do you want me to get the horse out for you, sir?"

"If you can find Sutton or young Joe, I'm sure they can do it." He pointed at a nearby mounting block. "Leave the chair here and go and find out."

His aunt was busy pointing out the features of the new stable block to Miss Chingford and Miss Anna. Miss Harrington stood to one side with Foley, both of them apparently occupied with their own thoughts. He waited for Miss Harrington to look up and then beckoned her closer. For a moment, he thought she was going to ignore him, but eventually she came over.

"How can I help you, Major?"

"You can stop treating me like a pariah. I said that I was wrong. Why isn't that ever enough for a woman?"

"Because we don't get over things as quickly as a man? If my conversation is so inadequate, why don't you speak to your betrothed instead? I'm sure she has to agree with every word you say."

He eyed her narrowly. "Miss Chingford is none of your concern."

"Obviously not, but she doesn't seem very at ease here. What did you do?"

"What did *I* do? Perhaps the fault lies with her."

She sniffed. "Spoken like a true man."

He opened his mouth to reply when the sound of horse-shoes ringing on the cobblestones brought his attention back to the galley between the stalls. Joe Cobbins was leading Rogue by a halter. The boy looked tiny compared to the horse and Robert swallowed hard.

As the horse drew nearer, he couldn't take his eyes off the huge hooves that he'd seen crush fallen soldiers' skulls with the ease of a sledgehammer. Distantly, he became aware that his whole body was shaking and that he was sweating as if he had a fever. The closer the horse came, the more trapped he felt, the more desperate to get away, to breathe, to—

"Major?"

The horse stopped and reared up on his hind legs. He was too big, too damned big. Robert flung himself out of the chair onto the ground covering his head with his arms and curled up into a ball.

The ring of hooves striking back onto the cobbles made him grit his teeth and close his eyes. He was vaguely aware of shocked sounds, of someone shouting, of the horse being taken away.

"Major Kurland." A woman's calm voice, the touch of her bare fingers at his throat on his thundering pulse. "There is nothing to fear. The horse has gone now. You are not in any danger."

He couldn't move as a blinding hot rush of shame and humiliation washed over him. He forced himself to open his eyes. Miss Harrington knelt beside him, her slight fig-ure shutting out his view of everything, blocking anyone else from seeing his terror. . . .

She stroked his cheek. "It's all right."

He wrapped his shaking fingers around her wrist and held on tight.

"Mr. Bookman, can you and Sutton help the major

back into his chair? I believe he lost consciousness, but I don't think he harmed himself."

She gently pried his fingers from her wrist, holding his gaze, as if silently trying to tell him that everything would be all right. Bookman and Sutton picked him up and placed him in the chair.

"Did you hurt yourself anywhere when you fell, Major?" He shook his head, words as yet still beyond him. "Are you quite sure?" She turned to Bookman, who was standing right beside her. "Perhaps you should take the major home."

"Yes, Miss Harrington."

Bookman fell in behind the chair and turned Robert away from the stables and back toward the house. As they rotated, Robert caught a glimpse of Miss Chingford's expression. Her horrified disgust and revulsion were plain to see. What had he looked like on the ground curled up and whimpering like a scared child? Fear had engulfed him out of nowhere and thrown him back into those nightmarish moments when his horse had fallen on him during the battle. Moments he hadn't even realized he remembered . . .

Aunt Rose blew him a kiss but he couldn't respond. Nausea clawed at his stomach, and for the first time in his life he understood what made a man turn tail in a battle and run for his life. He was no better than any other coward. And the threat he'd run from didn't even exist anymore. Rogue wasn't the horse responsible for his injuries. So why had he panicked so badly?

"Here we are, sir."

He was surprised at how quickly they reached the house. Bookman and James lifted him out of the chair and carried him up to his bed. He managed to thank James, but even that was an effort. Bookman took his time undressing Robert down to his shirt and breeches and then drew the covers up over him.

"Close your eyes for a little while, sir."

"Thank you, Bookman."

"You don't need to thank me. I'm just doing my job." He hesitated. "Perhaps you tried to do too much. Maybe you're not ready to go out yet."

Robert let out his breath. "Maybe I'm not."

"Especially with all those women coddling you, sir. It's enough to make any man bilious when he ain't." He poured Robert a glass of water from the jug and set it beside his bed. "Between Miss Chingford and her sulking, and Miss Harrington with her overactive imagination, it's a miracle you didn't pass out days ago."

Robert knew he should reprimand Bookman for his comments about his betters but he couldn't find the strength. In fact, the man's loyalty was reassuring.

"You keep away from those two, sir, and you'll feel a lot stronger. Miss Harrington should know better than to keep agitating you."

"She didn't. I asked her—"

"And more fool you, sir, if you'll excuse me for saying so. I heard what she said." He produced a black bottle from his pocket and a spoon. "Women lie and meddle. You can't trust a word they say. Now open your mouth, sir."

"I don't want any laudanum. I thought we'd agreed—"

He stopped speaking as Bookman tipped a spoonful of the noxious draught into his mouth and then another.

"This is an emergency, sir. You need your rest. Stay in bed and stop worrying about other people's problems."

Robert blinked as the opiate hit his stomach. His eyes started to close. "But I'm the lord of the manor. I should be involved, shouldn't I?"

"Not with this, sir. Trust me. Leave it alone, and let Miss Harrington work it out for herself. She doesn't need your help."

"But I forgot to tell her about the curate and Ben Cobbins. . . ."

"Don't you worry about that. I'll tell her myself."

Bookman's tone was implacable, and Robert allowed himself to fall asleep.

"Poor Major Kurland!" Anna exclaimed as they followed Mrs. Armitage into the parlor. "How horrible for him."

"Indeed," said Mrs. Armitage. "And he was so looking forward to getting out in that ingenious contraption you suggested, Miss Harrington. What a pity the strain was too much for him. I'll ring for some tea so that we can all get warm again."

Lucy took a seat next to her sister and briefly squeezed her hand. "I'm sure Major Kurland will be fine."

It seemed that she'd managed to conceal the major's moment of terror from the other members of the party. She knew he'd be mortified if everyone knew he'd panicked at the sight of his horse. What had he seen when the horse came toward him? For a horrible moment, he'd looked like a woodcut of a Christian martyr being burned at the stake.

Miss Chingford hadn't taken a seat and was pacing in front of the window. After a moment, Lucy went to join her.

"Are you all right, Miss Chingford? It was something of a shock to us all."

She shuddered. "He looked so dreadful lying there, so *deformed* and unnatural. I told him not to expose himself to ridicule by sitting in that ridiculous chair you recommended."

"And what did he say to that?"

"He dared to suggest I might have to get used to it!"

Lucy regarded her companion. "He does have a point. After such terrible injuries, there is no guarantee he will ever walk again."

That was the worst possible outcome, but Lucy realized she had a burning desire not to see Major Kurland married to the sort of woman who cared more about what people *thought* than about the health and happiness of her intended bridegroom.

Lucy studied Miss Chingford's discontented face. "Would you object to marrying a man who was confined to a chair?"

She walked away from Lucy, her hands twisted in front of her. "As you are unlikely ever to get married and would probably grasp at any offer, you wouldn't understand. I don't have much choice in the matter."

"You could break off the engagement."

"And waste all this time? Major Kurland is an excellent catch, as I'm sure you are aware."

"I suppose he is, in his way."

"He's rich!"

"So I've heard. I've known the major all my life, and I'm quite immune to any claims as to his wealth, prospects, or attractiveness. He will always be the annoying boy who threw me in the fish pond fully clothed one summer, and got me into terrible trouble with my nurse."

"I don't believe you."

"I can't make you believe me. All I can say is that because he is my friend, it would make me sad if you married him and weren't prepared to accept that he might never walk again."

"My family insists I marry him."

There was a note of hysteria in Miss Chingford's voice that made Lucy feel more sympathetic. She of all people knew how the chains of family duty could constrain a woman's ambitions.

"Your family doesn't have to live with him. You do. If you can't honor him and support him, you will both be terribly miserable, you know that. He has a dreadful temper, which has not been improved by his current condition." She touched Miss Chingford's rigid arm. "Surely one uncomfortable conversation with your parents and the opportunity to find another husband you can love is worth more than a lifetime of regret?"

Miss Chingford's chin came up. "You want him for yourself, don't you?"

"No, I do not." Lucy held her gaze, her own full of wry amusement. "I would probably murder him on our wedding night. He is not an easy man."

"He is quite horrible to me." Miss Chingford shuddered.

"Then don't marry him. Release him from his promise and then write and tell your parents what you have done. By the time you return to London, the worst of their anger will be over, and they will be busy making other plans for you. I'm sure Mrs. Armitage would help you, as well. She wouldn't want either of you to be unhappy."

Miss Chingford bit her lip. "You make it sound so simple."

"It is simple. You just have to be brave." Lucy smiled. "You are so beautiful that I'll wager all your parents' threats about you being left to die an old maid will be proved wrong in an instant."

"I did have a large number of suitors."

"And I am sure that several of them are still wearing the willow for you. At least think about what I've said."

Miss Chingford curtsied. For the first time, she looked a little more hopeful. "Perhaps I will."

"I know how difficult it is to stand against your parents' wishes, but you need to be strong." Unwilling to belabor the point and raise any more suspicions as to her motives, Lucy turned back to her sister. "I think our tea is ready, and then Anna and I really must be getting on our way. It has been rather an exciting morning."

Chapter 14

With a quick prayer to the heavens, Lucy knocked on Anthony's bedchamber door and stood back to listen. It was mid-afternoon, and if she was correct, he had finished with his tutor and was about to embark on another of his mysterious expeditions. To her relief, there was the sound of movement and the door opened.

"Lucy? What is it? Have you seen any more ruffians in the churchyard?"

She fixed him with her best sisterly glare. "That isn't amusing. In truth, I wanted to talk to you about something else."

The good humor died from his face. "What am I supposed to have done now?"

With ill grace, he stood back and she preceded him into his room. She looked for a place to sit amongst the piles of books, clothes, and riding equipment that littered the surfaces. Eventually, she removed a hefty folio of Shakespeare's plays that she knew her father had been looking for from the chair beside the fire, and sat down.

She studied her hands in her lap and took a deep breath. "I don't want to quarrel with you, but I need to know something."

"Is this about me gambling away Father's fortune?"

"Not exactly." His expression darkened and she hastened to continue. "If you will just let me explain. As I mentioned before, I found a porcelain snuffbox in your blue coat when I was mending it. You denied all knowledge of the item."

"I still do."

She looked up at his uncompromising face. "The thing is, I found a piece of the box in the graveyard crushed in the mud. I asked Major Kurland if he recognized the fragment, and he confirmed it had belonged to his mother and that it had disappeared along with several other items from Kurland Hall."

"And now you think I stole from him as well as Father?"

"*No,* but if you won't tell me why you are sneaking out at night and acting so suspiciously, I fear others might believe you are involved in the thefts."

"Because I took money before."

"Yes."

Silence fell between them and Lucy continued to stare at her clasped hands. Eventually, Anthony sighed.

"And if I give you my word that I have never seen the damned box, or stolen anything from Kurland Hall, will that not suffice?"

"For me, yes, but I am not the only person seeking this thief. Others might wish to press charges or make accusations." She drew an unsteady breath. "If I am asked to tell what I know, I will not lie, even for you."

"And what do you think you know?" He got up and walked over to the window, his hands clasped behind his back.

"That I found stolen property in your pocket and that you spend an inordinate amount of time dodging your tutor and loitering at the Red Lion."

"Who told you about the Red Lion?"

"It doesn't matter who it was. What matters is *why*."

He sat down on the window seat and shoved a hand through his thick hair. "I'll wager it was Edward. He'll do anything to get into your good graces."

Lucy ignored that. "What draws you to the Red Lion?"

He looked away from her. "It's a rather delicate matter, not fit for your ears."

Lucy quickly sorted through the possibilities. "Then I assume there is a woman involved?"

His head shot up. "What makes you think that?"

"If you aren't gambling, it is the only thing that makes sense." She raised her gaze to the heavens. "Why didn't I think about that before?"

"Because you are a young lady who shouldn't know about such things."

"Now you sound like Papa. I'm older than you, and I'm a rector's daughter. I know everything." She held his gaze. "Who is she?"

"Not someone you would know. She isn't of our social class. Not that I care for such matters." His brown eyes softened. "She is worth a thousand of most of the young ladies I've met."

Lucy held up her hand. "Unless you are treading on highly dangerous ground and courting Mrs. Dobbs, there are only two unmarried women at the Red Lion young enough to interest you. The landlord's daughter, Chrissie, or the new barmaid, Dorcas. Which one is it?"

Hot color flooded his cheeks. "You are the devil."

"Which one?"

"If you must know, it's Dorcas. She is an angel."

Lucy studied her brother's enrapt face. "May I ask if you have considered marrying her?"

"What?"

"I just wondered why there is all this secrecy."

He started to fidget, his color high. "Lucy, you are incorrigible! Do you think I'd ask her here? I'm not quite that stupid. Father would have my head, and poor Dorcas would be so overawed that she'd be unable to speak!"

"Then you don't see her as a permanent fixture in your life?"

"I'm off to Cambridge in the autumn, you know that." Gloom descended over his features. "I can hardly ask her to go with me."

"It wouldn't be fair on her, either, would it? She'd lose her job. Does she have family around here?"

"Yes." Anthony looked out of the window. "That's one of the reasons we've been keeping things quiet. They wouldn't approve of me at all."

"Whom exactly is she related to?"

He hunched a shoulder. "Her mother was sister to Ben Cobbins's wife."

"*Ben Cobbins?* Now I understand why you have been creeping around at night." Lucy shook her head. "I hope to God that you have been careful and Ben doesn't have cause to seek you out and force you to marry this girl. He'd love to bring our family low." A thought struck her. "Ben hasn't spoken to you recently about her, has he? I thought I heard him shouting at someone in the graveyard the other day."

"That wasn't me. As far as I know, Ben doesn't suspect a thing. At least I hope that's the case." Anthony groaned. "The only person from this household I've seen Ben talking to recently is Edward, and I somehow doubt he is chasing Dorcas. She isn't that kind of girl."

That wasn't what Lucy had heard, but she wasn't going to say that to her obviously infatuated brother. Why hadn't she suspected he was at the perfect age to fall in love with someone unsuitable? She remembered Tom's infatuation with the dairymaid at the Kurland Hall home farm, how he'd constantly smelled of the cowshed and they'd suffered from a surfeit of milk. . . .

"So you don't intend to see Dorcas when you move to Cambridge?"

"At first I thought I would, but it wouldn't be fair on her, would it?" He met Lucy's gaze for the first time. "She'd be better off finding a nice local man who wants to wed her."

"She probably would be better off," Lucy said gently. "If she gets a reputation for being above herself, she might suffer for it."

He sighed. "I know, but I do care about her. She is so sweet and understanding and her brother was in the army and—" He paused. "And I need to talk to Father about my future, don't I?"

"If you know what you want to do."

He stood up. "I've always wanted to be a soldier. I just don't see myself at Cambridge."

She rose, too, and smiled at him. "Do you want me to come with you?"

"No. I need to do this myself." He hesitated. "He's going to be very angry, isn't he?"

"Maybe at first, but I'm sure he'll come around."

He grabbed her hand and brought it to his lips. "Thank you, dear sister."

"For what?"

"For believing me when I said I hadn't stolen a thing."

"I wonder who *is* stealing things." Lucy disengaged her fingers and headed for the door.

"If you want to catch the thief, I'd try to discover who put that box in my pocket."

Lucy stopped, her hand on the latch. "That is a very good thought. Thank you."

Anthony bowed. "You are welcome." He came up alongside her. "And you won't breathe a word to anyone about Dorcas, will you?"

"Not unless I have to, and even then I will be terribly discreet."

"I depend on it." He headed off down the stairs. "Now wish me luck."

She watched him from the landing as he headed confidently toward their father's study, knocked on the door, and was swiftly admitted.

Lucy walked slowly down the stairs to the back parlor. If he had the confidence to confront their father, her little brother was growing up in more ways than one. She wasn't sure if that pleased or horrified her. Why was she the only one who was expected to accept her lot and not complain? Everyone else would be moving on with their lives, and she would be left behind. It wasn't fair.

She pushed such pointless, rebellious thoughts aside and considered her conversation with Anthony. Who had put the box in his coat? The most obvious answer was Mary, and it tied in nicely with her original theory that the girl had stolen some small items to finance her journey to London. But how had the box ended up smashed underfoot in the graveyard? And how had it gotten out of Anthony's coat pocket if he hadn't seen or touched it? Either Mary or Daisy were robbed before they left Kurland St. Mary, or they'd sold the items beforehand to someone else.

The room was so gloomy that she lit a working candle and sat down. Was it possible that Ben Cobbins had bought their purloined treasures? He had a reputation for handling stolen goods in the village. Had the box accidentally smashed during the exchange and been left behind as worthless? Lucy shook her head. It still didn't make sense. She'd found the box in Anthony's pocket *after* Mary and Daisy had left. Perhaps in her haste, Mary had forgotten it, but it still didn't explain how the box ended up in the graveyard.

Lucy rubbed at her temples. It was all too confusing. If only Mary or Daisy would write from London to say that they were settled and all was well, at least they might discover the truth. At the moment, all she had was half the puzzle and it was infuriating. The clock struck four, and she rose to her feet and picked up the candle, knowing she was too restless to sit for much longer. Even the thought of Ben Cobbins lurking in the oncoming darkness couldn't keep her trapped inside. Anna was reading to the twins, and Lucy would join her later for dinner and then prayers. Before that, she would put on her bonnet and make her way to the Hathaways' house to consult with her friend Sophia.

Robert opened his eyes to candlelight and the crackling and hissing of fresh damp wood being placed on the fire. He carefully turned his head and found Bookman crouched on his haunches in front of the hearth, feeding the flames with new logs and balled-up pieces of parchment. He watched for a while, enjoying the flickering light and the hint of wood smoke that reminded him of many campfires.

"I hope you are burning the letters from my cousin Paul."

Bookman jumped and swiveled to face Robert. "I didn't realize you were awake, sir. The opiate must have worn off quicker than I thought." He tossed the last piece on the fire and stood up, dusting his breeches. "I read once that the more laudanum you take, the more you need."

"Which is why I am supposed to be avoiding it. What are you burning? Love letters?" His voice sounded thin, weary, and most unlike himself.

"Nothing important, sir." Bookman stared into the flames, his face half-hidden in the shadows. "I didn't mean to bother you. The chimney in my room was smoking too badly to risk a fire."

"I remember in France that you would use anything to make a fire as long as you didn't have to burn those precious letters from your sweetheart."

Bookman kicked the grate so hard that sparks flew out onto the rug. "More fool me, sir."

"Is all not well between you?"

"You could say that, sir." Bookman swung around. "Is there anything I can get you?"

"Could you fetch me something to drink?"

"There's water right by your bed, sir, don't you remember?" Bookman walked over to him. "Shall I help you sit up?"

"I think you'll have to. I feel as weak as a newborn foal."

He hoisted him upright and placed his pillows behind him. "There you are, sir."

Robert eyed him consideringly. "There's no need to talk to me as if I were five, and for God's sake, don't start feeling sorry for me again. I thought we were done with that. I concede I overreached myself today, and suffered the consequences, but I'm not despairing quite yet."

"Nor should you be, sir." Bookman refilled his glass. "Miss Harrington might have the best intentions in the world, but she doesn't know when to stop, does she?" He snorted. "Worrying you with all this talk of theft, forcing you to rush ahead and take command again. And now look where it's left you."

Robert let Bookman lecture him. It was easier than defending himself. He doubted his valet would be the last of his acquaintances to advise him to stop getting overexcited and to concentrate on getting well. The only person who treated him like a responsible, intelligent human being was Miss Harrington, and he sensed that since the last debacle with the chair, Foley and Bookman might try to exclude the rector's daughter from the house altogether.

He wouldn't allow that, although he had to admit his life had been more peaceful before she'd turned up and bullied him into taking on his responsibilities. She wasn't, however, responsible for this latest crisis. That had been entirely of his own making. . . .

Bookman mentioned something about dinner, and Robert nodded, his attention focused inward as he replayed that moment when Rogue had reared in front of him. He'd never felt such cold, sickening, unreasonable fear in his life. And for a horse! How was he ever supposed to go charging into battle if he was too afraid to even look at his mount? Despair swept over him as he envisioned his future. He'd be better off dead.

"Major Kurland?"

He opened his eyes to see Miss Chingford standing by his bed. Could his day get any worse? She was swathed in a large paisley shawl that he knew belonged to his aunt.

"Miss Chingford."

She clutched the shawl tightly to her chest and averted her gaze from his. "There is something I want you to know. I've written to my parents to tell them our betrothal is at an end."

"It is?"

"You must have guessed I was unhappy."

"I had begun to suspect as much. If that is what you want, I will not try to dissuade you." He studied her woe-begone face. "I realize I am no longer the man you envisioned marrying."

"My parents will try to make me change my mind." She hesitated. "They have other daughters to marry off, and they will see my refusal to wed you as a rejection of my duty."

"But you should not sacrifice yourself for them."

"That's what Mrs. Armitage said." Her words came in a rush. "I cannot imagine my life tied to an invalid. It wouldn't be fair. I deserve *so* much better. I'm sure you can understand that."

"Perfectly, Miss Chingford." Even though her words slashed at his already tottering self-respect, he held out his hand. "May we part as friends? I promise never to speak ill of you to any of our acquaintances, and I accept all the blame for the failure of our relationship. In fact, if you wish, I will write to your parents and tell them that."

She took his hand, her fingers warm against his. "Thank you. Perhaps you will find another woman grateful enough to accept your deformities and ill temper for the opportunity to be your wife. Miss Anna Harrington is pleasant enough to look at, and she seems to have a more willing disposition than her sister."

Her self-absorption continued to both fascinate and repel him. Had he been that selfish at twenty? He suspected he might have been. "Thank you for the suggestion. Do you know if my aunt is at home?"

"She is the one who sent me up to speak to you." Miss Chingford stepped away from him. "She seemed to think I needed to tell you my decision in person."

"That was very brave of you."

Oblivious to his sarcasm, she smiled for the first time. "I thought so, too. But if I plan on facing my parents, this can only be good practice for such an ordeal—although you are far more frightening than they are." She curtsied and turned to the door. "I'll send Mrs. Armitage up to you."

Robert allowed his head to fall back on his pillows and stared up at the embroidered hangings of his four-poster bed. An ancestor of his—no doubt in an effort to inspire future generations—had embroidered the family crest above his head.

"Fight until breath and blood have fled and fight again."

He didn't feel like fighting anymore.

Bookman came through the door balancing a tray on his hip. "Mrs. Armitage says to tell you she will be here in a moment. She is just finishing writing a letter."

"Thank you. I suppose she is writing to the Chingford family. Miss Chingford has decided we will not suit."

Bookman put down the tray. "That's a shame, sir."

"Not really. She is quite right. We would not suit each other at all." Robert sighed. "It seems we are both unlucky in love, Bookman."

"At least Miss Chingford had the guts to tell you to your face, sir." With a snap, Bookman placed Robert's napkin on his lap. "Do you want to start with the soup or the lamb?"

"The soup, I think, although my hands are still shaking."

"I can feed you if you like, sir."

"No, thank you, Bookman. I'd rather manage for myself." He took the spoon and concentrated on getting the fragrant broth from the bowl to his mouth. It seemed all he was capable of at the moment as his body trembled and threatened to betray him. What a fool he'd been to venture outside. He should have stayed in bed where he obviously belonged.

"Mr. Hodges was after you earlier today, sir."

"Who is that?"

"Your head gardener, sir."

There was that tone again, as if Robert were an invalid who needed pandering to. But he was abnormal, wasn't he? Miss Chingford had very kindly pointed it out to him while repudiating his proposal of marriage. Of course, she'd also had the pleasure of seeing him rolling on the ground in terror over nothing. If only she knew his physical deformities were only the most obvious of his problems. . . .

"Major?"

He looked up. "Yes?"

"Have you finished with the soup?"

He stared at his empty bowl. "I suppose I have. It was delicious."

"Would you care for some lamb?"

"The soup was quite sufficient."

"You should try and keep up your strength, sir."

"For what? So that I can lie in bed and grow fat?"

Bookman took the tray. "You'll come about, sir. You always do. Just stick with me and Foley and we'll see you right. Keep away from women. They always complicate matters."

Robert slid down under the covers again. "I'm beginning to think you have a point."

"What point is that, dear?"

"Aunt Rose." Robert opened his eyes and struggled to sit up again. "Thank you for persuading Miss Chingford to change her mind, and make us both much happier."

"Oh, it wasn't me, dear. It was Miss Harrington."

"Miss Harrington? But Miss Chingford despises her."

"I'm sure she does, but she at least had the sense to listen to her. I've written a letter to the Chingfords. I'm sure you will want to add a note of your own. I will take her back to Town in a few days and help her navigate the wrath of her parents."

"That's kind of you."

"I'm not doing it for her. I'm doing it for you. She would've made you a terrible wife."

"No, you have that wrong. I was informed that *I* would make her a terrible husband, and that she deserved far more than an elderly invalid."

"She didn't actually say that to you, did she?"

Robert's smile was wry. "She came pretty damn close. But I have to respect her honesty. She knows what she wants from life, and she is determined to get it."

Aunt Rose took his hand. "I'm sorry, love. You deserve so much better. When you are on your feet, we will look around and make a list of all of the eligible young ladies. Then you can have your pick."

"I don't think so, Aunt. I'm hardly much of a catch."

"Don't be so modest, my lad. You still have your wealth and position."

"Ah, how kind of you to remind me that if all else fails, I might always be married for my money."

She patted his cheek and left him alone with his thoughts.

* * *

Lucy walked back from the Hathaways' through the deepening gloom, her thoughts troubled, her steps slow. Wisps of fog from the deep-water ditches alongside the road floated across the path, muffling the sounds of nature and obscuring Lucy's vision. Despite her objections, Sophia had reiterated her invitation and Mrs. Hathaway had seconded the proposal so firmly that it seemed it might be *made* to happen. If only her father could be persuaded. The Hathaways didn't know that Anthony was about to disturb his father's plans for the future, and that he might retaliate by clinging more fiercely to his other children.

The plan was for Mr. Hathaway to invite the Harringtons to dinner and to take her papa aside and broach the idea of Lucy accompanying Sophia to London next spring. Lucy knew that her father would take more note of the idea if a gentleman he respected proposed it.

A horse neighed behind her on the path and Lucy looked over her shoulder, suddenly aware that she was very much alone. Did Ben Cobbins own a horse?

"Good evening, Miss Harrington."

The smell of warm saddle leather and horse surrounded her, and she looked up at the rider who touched his hat.

"Mr. Jenkins."

His smile was warm. "I hear that you visited my grandmother this week. I'm sorry I missed you."

"It was of no matter, sir. We only talked of the most domestic things. You would probably have been bored to tears."

"Probably. But I always enjoy your company." He indicated the path ahead. "You shouldn't be standing around in the cold. May I walk my horse alongside you?"

"If you wish." She could feel the heat coming off his horse in waves and was grateful for the shelter it provided from the stiff breeze. "I am heading home."

He glanced behind. "Ah, you were visiting the Hathaways. Are they well?"

"Yes, indeed."

"And your family, Miss Harrington? Your sister?"

Lucy concealed a smile. The honorable Nicholas Jenkins, whose grandfather was a viscount, was definitely rather fond of Anna. "She is in great beauty. My father is considering sending her to London next year to stay with his brother, the earl, and make her curtsy to the queen."

"To London?"

She marked his frown and kept smiling. "Yes. It is about time, don't you think?"

"I suppose it is. Will you be accompanying her?"

"I'm not quite certain. Our plans are not yet fixed."

"I'm considering going up to London myself next year. My grandfather says all young men need a little town polish."

His parents had perished of the smallpox and his grandparents had brought him up at Farleigh Manor. He was an amiable young man and a friend of Anthony's, whom Lucy liked very much. "Then you might certainly encounter Anna. It will be nice for her to see a familiar face."

"Indeed."

They continued in silence until Lucy spied the approaching crossroads that designated the parting of their ways. "It was nice to see you, Mr. Jenkins. Please give your grandmother my best wishes."

"I'll do that, Miss Harrington, and please tell Miss Anna I was asking after her." He tipped his hat again and then paused. "I just remembered something my grandmother said to tell you if I saw you. She said that she'd lost two figurines and two small candlesticks from her morning room. Does that make any sense to you?"

"Unfortunately, it does. It seems several of the houses in Kurland St. Mary have been suffering from theft."

"That's a bad business." He frowned and his horse shifted its feet. "Do you have any idea who it might be?"

"Not quite yet, but I'm determined to discover the culprit."

"She also said that the only people who have been in that room recently are her servants, you, the curate, and Mrs. Hathaway." He turned his horse's head. "Well. I mustn't keep you chatting in the cold, Miss Harrington. I'd best be on my way."

Lucy smiled up at him. "Thank you for your company."

He nodded, wheeled his horse around, and trotted down the lane. Lucy kept walking until she could see the tower of the church clearly in her sight. The welcoming lights of the rectory cheered her and made her increase her pace. Anna met her at the front door.

"How was your walk?"

Lucy divested herself of her bonnet and gloves. "It was most productive. I spent some time with Sophia and her mother. I met the Honorable Mr. Jenkins on the way home. He asked after you."

Anna smiled the complacent smile of the acknowledged local beauty. "He always does."

"He is a very nice man."

"I know."

"He told me that his grandmother had some pieces stolen, as well."

Anna held on to Lucy's coat. "Was it that awful monkey? I bet he steals things."

Lucy followed Anna into the back parlor. It was almost time for dinner, and she didn't want to get in Mrs. Fielding's way in the kitchen. "I don't think it was Claude. In fact, if you discount her servants, it could only be one of a very small number of people. . . ." Her gaze fell on her sewing box, which was open, the contents spilling onto the floor. "Were you looking for something?"

"It wasn't me." Anna frowned at the mess. "I wonder who did that? It was probably the twins."

"I have to go and see Major Kurland."

"At this hour?"

"I have to go. If Father asks, will you tell him I've gone to bed with a headache?"

Lucy ran past the church, squeezed herself through the gap between the cornerstone and the wall, and hurried across the expansive lawn to the side door of Kurland Hall. She didn't bother to knock, just lifted the latch and made her way through the narrow winding passageways into the cavernous kitchen. Foley sat at the table with a tankard at his elbow and the newspaper in front of his nose. He went to rise but Lucy held up her hand.

"Is Major Kurland still awake?"

"I don't know, Miss Harrington." He glanced at the kitchen clock. "Do you wish me to inquire?"

"Don't trouble yourself, Mr. Foley, I'll go and see for myself."

"But—" Foley was half-rising to his feet.

Lucy had already left the kitchen and started up the main stairs. She paused at the major's door, but there was no sound from within. She gently raised the latch and peered inside. The major was in bed, but he was sitting up and staring pensively at the fire. His gaze fastened on hers and he frowned.

"Will this day never end? What do you want?"

"That's hardly a polite way to greet a guest, Major."

"Guests wait downstairs and are announced by my butler. Then I decide whether I wish to see them or not."

"I told Foley I'd see myself up the stairs." She studied his averted profile, noticed the harsh lines of strain around his mouth and eyes. "Don't you want to talk to me?"

"It doesn't seem as if I have any choice, do I? I can hardly leap out of bed and run away."

She took a step closer. "Are you angry with me because of what happened earlier today?"

"Why would I be angry? Humiliated beyond measure,

perhaps, but hardly in a position to be annoyed." He finally looked at her. "In truth, I should be thanking you for concealing the real reason why I threw myself to the ground like a coward in the stable yard."

"I'm still not quite sure why you did it. Was it something to do with the horse?"

He glared at her, his blue eyes glinting in the candlelight. "You know damn well it had to do with the horse! I was terrified of the creature."

"Well, that is hardly surprising seeing as the last time you were on one it fell on top of you and broke both your legs."

"Stop being so damned reasonable." A muscle flicked in his cheek. "I have no reason to be scared of a horse. I'm a major in the Prince of Wales's Tenth Hussars."

"Well, you were." She advanced another step. "I doubt you'll ever be again."

Pain flinched across his face as if she had slapped him. "Don't you think I know that?"

"You cannot allow one facet of your personality to define you. You are far more than a soldier."

"Yes, I'm an invalid and a coward. Let's not forget those fine attributes."

For one moment, she wanted to walk over and hold him in her arms, and tell him that everything would be all right, but she sensed he wasn't ready to accept her sympathy yet. Perhaps he never would be. Male pride was a peculiar beast. She had to reach him another way.

"You might be an invalid, but you are certainly not a coward. It takes more courage to get out of bed and try to improve your condition than lie around bemoaning it."

"Stop nagging me." He rubbed a hand over his unshaven cheek. "Perhaps I'm tired of trying."

She took three more hasty steps until she was right next to him. "Don't be so stupid. This is a minor setback. Next time—"

He cut her off. "There won't be a next time. I'm not leaving this house unless I can damn well ride a horse, or call on my neighbors on foot!"

She stuck out her hand. "Do you want to make a wager on that?"

"What?"

"I'll wager you five pounds that you will do both of those things."

"You can't wager on what I'll do! That's ridiculous!"

"Oh yes, I can, because I will do anything to make sure it happens! I refuse to let you slide back into a morass of self-pity and invalidish behavior."

"You are the devil. All I have to do is have Foley bar you from the house, and you'll never get near me again."

"I'm here, aren't I? Foley didn't stop me this time."

She was so close to him now that they were nose to nose and she could stare right into his eyes. It wasn't a reassuring sight, rather like she imagined looking over the rim of a volcano. It was time to employ her last stratagem.

"If you won't get better to help yourself, will you please consider helping me?"

His gaze instantly turned to one of concern. "What's wrong?"

She perched on the side of his bed, which was most improper. "My sewing box was ransacked."

"So?"

"And I realized something important. Mary sewed the button on Anthony's coat."

"What the devil does that have to do with anything, and why are you bothering me with it now?"

"I also think you are right. The thefts aren't connected to the disappearance of the girls." She gazed at him expectantly.

"Well, thank you for finally agreeing with me for once. I'm still not sure how you reached that conclusion from the scattered facts you've given me so far."

"Mary sewed the button on so badly that Anthony couldn't wear the coat. In truth, at first he couldn't even *find* his coat because she had put it in Edward's closet."

"So what?"

"I had to sew the button on again. I found a porcelain snuffbox in the pocket, and asked Anthony where he'd acquired it. He denied all knowledge of the piece, which led to us arguing about his previous troubles with gambling. He got quite angry when I asked him if he was in financial trouble again."

"Why are you surprised about that? No man enjoys being questioned by a woman, especially about money."

She cast him an austere look. "The box disappeared again. The next time I saw it was in the graveyard in pieces."

"And you are sure it was the same one?"

"I believe so. The painting was particularly fine and unique."

"This is the box you asked me to identify? The one from my mother's rooms?"

"Yes."

"Then how did it end up in the graveyard?"

"That's exactly what I've been wondering. At first I was worried that Anthony had indeed been stealing things to cover his gambling debts."

"Which is why you didn't mention any of this to me before now."

She felt her cheeks heat. "I found it hard to believe the thief was my brother."

"And now?"

"I know that his furtive behavior is because he is carrying on an unsuitable alliance with the barmaid at the Red Lion." She shrugged as the major's eyebrows lifted. "He is of the age to have his head turned by the fairer sex, and Dorcas is very pretty and very generous with her favors by all accounts."

"You continue to surprise me, Miss Harrington. Please go on."

"And then it occurred to me that Mary sewed the button on Anthony's coat."

"So you think she took the box to sell it? But you just said the two events were unrelated."

"Major, you are missing the point!"

"There doesn't seem to be one."

"Mary sewed the button on, and mistakenly put the coat in Edward's cupboard instead of Anthony's."

"So she hid it in the wrong place and forgot to go back for it?"

"No! Edward hid the box in there, thinking it was his coat."

He stared at her for a long moment and then shook his head. "And my staff think I am the one in danger of losing my wits."

She smacked his hand, which was resting on the quilt. "Just listen. Edward is supporting his entire family on his small salary. He seems to take the responsibility very seriously."

"Which is admirable, but hardly makes him a thief."

Lucy ignored him. "Having talked with you, the Potters, and the Hathaways, it occurred to me that the thief had to be either a servant who visited the big houses and had access to all the rooms, which seemed unlikely, or someone from the gentry. That's why I originally thought the culprit was Anthony. Just when I realized it couldn't be him, Mr. Jenkins informed me that his grandmother had also had some items stolen. She was positive that only her staff, Mrs. Hathaway, the curate, and I had visited her in that particular room. And that's when I saw my sewing box and remembered the mix-up with the coat."

She sat back. "What if Edward is stealing things to finance his family's survival? He has access to all the big houses, and the Potters' shop. No one would question him."

"But how would he sell the items?" Robert asked. "He can hardly send them off to his family and claim they are part of his salary, can he?"

"That's the other thing." Lucy clasped her hands together. "One of the reasons why I ended up in the church graveyard looking for traces of blood was because I heard Ben Cobbins arguing with someone in there. What if *he* was selling the goods for Edward? I doubt he'd treat him very well."

"If I know Cobbins, he was probably threatening to tell your father what Edward was doing and charging him twice." He paused. "I saw your curate talking to Ben the other night, did Bookman tell you?"

"No, he didn't."

"I wonder why not?"

"Poor Edward."

He gave her a scathing glance. "Poor Edward? It was probably him or Ben Cobbins who hit you on the back of the head. They obviously caught you prying into their business."

Lucy started to disagree, and then thought better of it. At least he seemed to be in accord with her about the identity of the thief. "So what should I do now?"

"You will do nothing. I will speak to your father, and we will decide how to proceed."

"No, you will not!"

"I beg your pardon?"

"You will not brush me aside when I am the one who has discovered everything!"

"Miss Harrington—"

She scrambled off the bed and pointed her finger at him. "You told me how much you hated being treated like a child. Now, do not do it to me!"

He stared at her for a long moment and then nodded. "All right. Would you prefer it if we confronted him here together, and then made sure he confessed the whole to your father?"

She regarded him suspiciously. "Are you being serious?"

"I am. You made a good point. I am trying to be conciliatory for a change."

"Thank you."

"You are welcome. Perhaps you could ask Edward to accompany you here tomorrow, and we can discuss the matter with him then."

"I will, Major."

"Now will you go home?"

She smiled at him. "Yes. Thank you for listening to me."

"As I said, you gave me little choice."

She picked up the bell that sat beside his bed. "You could've rung this at any time and your loyal servants would have come through that door and taken me away in an instant."

"Would you believe me if I said I'd forgotten it was there?"

"No, I wouldn't. You've already made a choice to keep living whether you choose to admit it or not." She curtsied. "Good night, Major Kurland."

"Good night, Miss Harrington."

She was still smiling when she closed the door and started along the corridor toward the stairs. A figure stepped out from the shadows and barred her way.

She clasped a hand to her throat. "Mr. Bookman, I didn't see you there. Is something wrong?"

He didn't smile. "It depends, Miss Harrington. What I want to know is what gives you the right to think you can just barge in and see my master whenever you feel like it."

"I beg your pardon?"

"You heard me, miss. The major is sick and getting worse. The last thing he needs is you setting him off, and getting him all excited over nothing."

"I've merely tried to keep his spirits up and encourage him to believe in himself again."

"And wrecked his health in the meantime. He's not doing well at all. He drinks laudanum like water, downs brandy much the same, and can't remember half of what he's done or said or seen. He couldn't even remember who his head gardener was this morning."

"I know you are concerned about him, Mr. Bookman, but it can't be good for him to lie in bed and do nothing."

He moved closer.

"It's better than him meddling in what doesn't concern him. I've heard you, Miss Harrington, stirring him up with wild tales of disappearing women and stolen goods. He needs peace and quiet to get well again. That's all he needs. Me and Foley can do that well enough without your help."

He exhaled and rubbed a hand over the back of his neck. "I apologize if I sound angry, miss, but I don't want the major to suffer anymore."

"I understand, Mr. Bookman. I promise I will do my best not to overexcite him in the future."

"Thank you, miss." Bookman stepped back to allow her to pass. "Do you need someone to see you safely home?"

"I'll be fine, thank you." She sped past him down the stairs and out toward the kitchens, more shaken by his interference than she wanted to be. His concern for Major Kurland seemed a mite excessive.

With a shiver, she left the house and ran to the safety of the rectory.

Chapter 15

"I'm not quite sure why Major Kurland wants to see *me*, Miss Harrington. In the past he's made it abundantly clear that my very presence annoys him."

Lucy linked her arm more firmly through Edward's and knocked on the front entrance of Kurland Hall. Foley opened the door and ushered them inside.

"Good morning, Miss Harrington, Mr. Calthrope. Major Kurland awaits you in his study."

She waited until Edward handed Foley his hat and gloves and then followed the butler down a hallway lined with intricate Elizabethan paneling to the back of the house. The door to the study was open, and Major Kurland sat behind the desk. Despite her fears as to the outcome of the meeting, it was the first time she'd seen him doing something that didn't immediately draw attention to his condition. It gladdened her heart considerably.

The sight of Bookman standing to attention in front of the desk made her pause. But as soon as he saw them approach, he saluted the major, turned sharply on his heel, and walked out to take up a position in the corridor outside. He winked at her as he passed, but she couldn't quite forget the cold enmity of his words on the previous night or the hard lines of his face.

Major Kurland nodded at Edward. "Good morning, Mr. Calthrope. I apologize that I am unable to rise to greet you."

"Good morning, sir. It is a pleasure to see you so recovered." Edward cast a glowing look at Lucy. "Miss Harrington is an exceptional nurse."

"She is, indeed. I don't know how I would've survived without her."

Lucy studied the major carefully but his expression didn't change. She had to concede from his tone that he actually meant to compliment her. It was a novel sensation. She took a seat in front of the desk and waited for Edward to follow suit. Foley lingered by the door, but Edward seemed unaware of him.

Major Kurland cleared his throat. "I wished to ask your opinion as to a rather delicate matter, Mr. Calthrope."

"My opinion, sir? Surely you would do better to speak to the rector himself?"

"I intend to do that if it becomes necessary, but my first business is with you."

Edward fidgeted with the cuff of his frayed shirt. "I would be delighted to be of service to you. How may I assist you?"

"I'm not sure if you are aware of it, but there has been a series of small thefts from local businesses and the big houses in the neighborhood."

"I was not aware of that, sir."

"Are you quite sure?" The major nodded at Lucy. "Miss Harrington and I have been racking our brains trying to work out who might have the opportunity to steal such small trifles unobserved."

"There are many thieves around us, sir."

"That's true, but most of them aren't welcome in the drawing rooms of the local gentry."

Edward tugged at his stock. "I'm still not quite sure what this has to do with me, Major."

"Miss Harrington might care to enlighten you."

Lucy turned to face Edward, who looked rather pale. "I found the snuffbox you put in Anthony's coat pocket."

"I beg your pardon?"

"Don't you remember? Mary accidentally put Anthony's coat in your room and you left a snuffbox that belonged to Major Kurland's mother in the pocket."

"I have no idea what you are talking about, Miss Harrington." Edward's mouth opened and then closed like a fish gasping for air. "Where is this 'box' I am supposed to have stolen?"

"I found the remnants of it in the graveyard the other day." Lucy paused. "You must have panicked when you realized you'd left it in the wrong coat. Did Ben Cobbins become annoyed with you when you failed to bring it to him when promised? Did he refuse to take it when you finally retrieved it?"

Edward's head swiveled toward Major Kurland. "Sir, you cannot believe this nonsense. Miss Harrington is still clearly afflicted by that blow on her head. She is talking in riddles."

"I don't believe she is, Mr. Calthrope. Shall I ask Ben Cobbins to come in here and tell me the truth of what's been going on? Trust me, if I pay him enough, he'd betray his own mother."

With a groan, Edward buried his face in his hands and his shoulders started to shake.

Lucy met the major's gaze and he shrugged. "Let the man compose himself, Miss Harrington, and then, perhaps, he'll tell us the truth."

Eventually Edward looked up, his expression ravaged. "Are you going to tell the rector what I've done?"

"You admit it, then?"

"That I am the thief?" He swallowed. "Yes. But I wasn't stealing for myself."

"So, I understand. Miss Harrington told me that you support your whole family."

"That is true. My brother's school fees alone are crippling, and my sister has no chance of making a good marriage. In fact, she is considering going into service simply to relieve my mother of her care."

Lucy waited quietly as the major studied Edward, his gaze keen. "I can't see how a man in your profession can avoid confessing such a sin to his superior, but I am more than willing to speak in your defense." Edward lifted his head. "If you stay here, I am also willing to aid the rector in increasing your salary to avoid you having to resort to stealing again."

"You would do that for a thief?"

Major Kurland's smile was crooked. "No man can be faulted for trying to feed his family, Mr. Calthrope. I suspect you will have to change parishes. My aunt is acquainted with several bishops in the north who might be more than willing to find you a vacant position with a house and security for your family. I'll consult with her before she leaves for London."

"Thank you, Major Kurland." Edward shook his head. "I don't deserve such consideration. I felt like a rat caught in a trap. The more I struggled, the harder Ben Cobbins made it for me to break free. He threatened to blackmail me and started buying the goods at such low prices that I had to steal twice as much."

He turned to Lucy. "In truth, after he destroyed the snuffbox, and threatened me with discovery, I decided it had to end. I intended to tell Ben this week that I could no longer steal for him." He shuddered. "If I were dead, at least someone might take pity on my family and help them better than I could."

Lucy reached out to pat his shaking hand. "I'm sorry,

Edward. I wish you'd told us what your situation was. We could've helped you so much more quickly."

He covered her hand with his own. "I didn't want your father to know my true situation when he seemed inclined to favor a match between us. I reckoned if we married, I could bring my family to live with us."

Too aware of the major's sardonic gaze, Lucy removed her hand from under his. "I don't want to marry you, Edward. I thought I'd made that quite clear."

"I hoped your father would persuade you, but it was not to be." Edward heaved a gusty sigh. "I suppose I should go and confess to the rector now."

Major Kurland held up a letter. "I've written to the rector. Perhaps you would give him this."

"I will, sir." Edward took the letter and stowed it in his coat pocket. "Thank you." He glanced at Lucy. "Are you coming, Miss Harrington?"

"I think you'd do better without me being there, don't you?"

"I agree." Major Kurland nodded. "I've asked Bookman to accompany you back to the rectory, Mr. Calthrope, just in case Ben Cobbins is lurking anywhere."

Edward opened the door and Bookman nodded in greeting. "Good morning, sir."

Lucy watched as the two men set off down the hall and let out her breath. "Thank goodness that's over."

"It went remarkably well," Major Kurland commented. "I think he was ready to confess, don't you? He isn't the sort of man who steals because he enjoys it. He stole because he had to." He paused. "Why are you looking so glum, Miss Harrington?"

"Because now everything will be back to normal."

"You've enjoyed investigating this matter, haven't you?"

"If your life was as predictable as mine, you would enjoy such moments, too."

"But my life has been predictable. I've spent the last

nine months in bed and in pain." He straightened the papers on his desk. "Have you decided the girls are safely in London now?"

"I suppose they must be."

"And you believe I saw nothing that night to convince you otherwise?"

Lucy sat bolt upright. "Major, now you are being contrary. Both you and your staff have tried to convince me that you are not in your right mind and that you have taken enough laudanum to pickle your brain. What would you like me to believe?"

He frowned. "Who told you about the laudanum?"

"Bookman, but don't tell him I told you so. I'm already in disgrace for disturbing your peace."

"I apologize for that. Bookman is not happy with the fairer sex at the moment. He has been unlucky in love. If it helps, he was most uncomplimentary about Miss Chingford, as well."

"That I can understand."

He raised his eyebrows, but she refused to say any more. He'd already told her Miss Chingford was none of her concern.

"I suppose I should be getting home." Her shoulders slumped. "I'll go and see your aunt and Miss Chingford and then I'll be on my way. Hopefully my father will have dealt with Edward by then. Did you say they were leaving soon?"

"Yes, but my aunt intends to return quite regularly. She has decided that she would rather stay here and visit her daughter in London than deal with the snobbery of that household."

"Her daughter should be ashamed of herself. If it wasn't for your aunt Rose, she wouldn't have such a lifestyle."

"I agree."

She stood and Major Kurland looked up at her. To her

surprise, he very slowly rose to his feet. Propped up against the desk was a stout walking stick.

"Thank you for your help, Miss Harrington."

She curtsied. "You are welcome, sir."

"I apologize for not escorting you to the door, but that is still beyond me at present." He glanced down at the cane and shrugged. "I decided that if I couldn't yet ride a horse, I should concentrate on learning how to stand on my own two feet."

"An admirable decision." Lucy tried not to smile, but he saw it anyway and scowled in return.

"My head gardener is coming to see me at eleven, so I shall await him here. I'm sure Foley will see you out."

"Be careful, Major, or I will soon be owing you five pounds."

His answering smile was slow, but worth waiting for. "I'm counting on it, Miss Harrington. How else am I going to afford that increase in Mr. Calthrope's wages?"

Lucy took the long way back to the rectory, and despite the wind, dawdled along the elm-lined driveway. Sharp green buds covered the surfaces of the silver branches bringing the promise of leafy shade and color on a summer's day, but she couldn't even embrace the thought. She should feel proud of having unmasked a thief, but she dreaded the return to normality. The complex matters of getting the twins outfitted for school and Anna's potential season in London would soon engulf her, leaving her needs to be put aside yet again.

In her own way, she supposed she was just as selfish as Major Kurland and her father. The difference being that they all had the ability to determine their own fate whilst she did not. She eyed the approaching front of the rectory with some trepidation. Between Anthony's revelations as to his future plans, and Edward's confession of theft, her father's composure would be severely disturbed.

She decided to go around the back of the house and saw Anthony emerging from the stables, his dark hair wind-blown and his cheeks reddened from the cold.

"Lucy! I was looking for you earlier." He grinned. "As you can see, Papa didn't shoot me on sight. He certainly wasn't pleased, but I think he'll come around." His expression sobered. "I tried to reassure him that with Napoleon's defeat my chances of being killed were significantly lower. But I don't think he can quite forget about Tom."

Neither could Lucy, but she didn't want to spoil Anthony's good humor. He linked arms with her and walked toward the house. "Do you think Major Kurland would put in a good word for me with his old regiment?"

"I'm sure he would. Why don't you go and ask him?"

"I thought he wasn't receiving visitors."

"If you tell him your plans, I'm sure he'd make an exception for you."

"I'll write him a note now and ride up and see him tomorrow." He heaved a sigh. "After I've taken leave of Dorcas."

She squeezed his arm. "If you're going to London to seek a commission, that's probably for the best."

"She's going to be very sad. She says I'm irreplaceable."

Wisely, Lucy said nothing and walked through from the hallway into the kitchen. Mrs. Fielding was stirring something on the stove.

"Mrs. Weeks was looking for you, Miss Harrington."

There was an ominous note in the cook's voice that had Lucy searching her memory. "What did she want?"

"I can't say. She refused to tell me." She sniffed. "Although the rector's birthday is fast approaching. The sly minx probably thinks to beg you to make his cake."

"Thank you, Mrs. Fielding. I'll speak to Mrs. Weeks when I go into the village tomorrow," Lucy promised. "Is the rector still in his study?"

"I believe he is, miss."

"Perhaps Betty could bring me some tea."

There was no answer to that. Lucy made her escape into the hallway and knocked on the door of her father's study. He was sitting at his desk, staring down at a letter written in a distinctive slashing hand, his expression careworn.

"Papa?"

He looked up. "Ah, Lucy. Do come in. I've just had an extraordinary interview with Edward."

"I know." She took a seat. "Did you read Major Kurland's letter?"

"I just finished it." He shook his head. "The major is being exceptionally generous considering the circumstances. My first thought was to turn Edward off without a character, but luckily for him, my Christian charity reasserted itself. It will also help tremendously if Major Kurland can find a new living for Edward. If word gets out as to his activities in this neighborhood, I doubt anyone would welcome him into their houses again."

"I'm quite confident that Major Kurland will find a new place for him. He can be quite determined when he sets his mind to something."

"So I've heard, although we've hardly seen any sign of it since his return from the continent."

"I truly believe he is on the mend now, and more than ready to take up his responsibilities."

"Well, thank goodness for that. It hasn't been easy being the sole arbiter of authority in this district. Quite fatiguing, in fact." He sighed. "And now we will have to go to the bother of finding a new curate."

"I'll help you with that, Papa."

He put on his spectacles. "I'm afraid I'll need your help for a lot of things in the near future, my dear. In fact, I won't be able to do without you."

"I know, Papa." Lucy forced a smile. "I'll do my best."

"As you should, my dear." He smiled at her fondly. "You, of all my children, know your duty."

She stood up, walked over to the desk, and kissed her father on the cheek. "I must go and see about dinner."

"That's my girl." He patted her hand. "And make sure Mrs. Fielding doesn't offer me mutton again, will you?"

"Of course, Papa."

Lucy closed the door to the study and stood for a moment in the darkened hallway, leaning against it and listening to the stifling silence. After a deep breath, she squared her shoulders and went to do battle in the kitchen.

Anna selected a square of fabric from the ragbag and inspected it in the candlelight. "This will do for a border, but won't make a full square." She dug her hand in again and pulled out another piece. "Are you worried about having so many different colors in this quilt, or is that the intention? Whom is it for?"

Lucy started and looked down at her sister, who sat by her feet. It was quiet in the house. The twins were in bed, and Anthony had gone to see his tutor to explain why he would no longer need his services.

"The quilt is for one of the Coles' family. It doesn't have to be perfect."

Anna laid her hand on Lucy's knee. "What's wrong?"

"Why should you think anything is wrong?"

"Because you look so sad this evening."

"I'm sorry, love. I was just wondering what would become of Edward."

"Have you come to care for him, Lucy?"

"Not in that way. But I do feel sorry for him. We might not have everything we want here, but at least we are always well fed and not in fear of losing our home."

"We have much to be thankful for." Anna picked out another piece of material. "Do you think the Cole boys will mind some pink?" Anna unfolded the square and smoothed it out.

Lucy stared at the pattern until it seemed to have burned into her brain. "Whose dress was that from?"

"This pink?" Anna asked. "I have no idea. Why, is it important?"

Lucy ran toward the stairs, the scrap of fabric clutched in her fingers. She burst into the nursery, surprising Jane, who was settled at the nursery table darning socks.

"Jane, have you seen this material before?"

"I think so. I helped Mary hem a summer dress she'd made in that color last year."

Lucy clutched the fabric to her breast and briefly closed her eyes.

"Are you all right, Miss Harrington?"

Lucy nodded and walked back down the stairs. She was absolutely certain that the material she held was identical to the swatch of fabric jammed into the doorway of the DeVry vault. Her thoughts circled as she tried to decide what to do. If she went to her father in his present mood, she was certain he would refuse to accommodate her wish to open the tomb. But whom could she ask for help?

Before she realized what she was doing, she walked toward the back door. Major Kurland was the local magistrate. Surely he would have the power to overrule her father and order him to open the vault? She paused with her hand on the latch. Was she willing to take such an outrageous step? Her father would think her mad. But would the overprotective Bookman let her anywhere near the major at this time of night? Somehow she doubted it.

"Lucy?"

She glanced up the stairs and saw Luke standing on the landing in his nightgown, one hand cupping his cheek.

"What is it, love?"

"It's my tooth. It's hurting like the devil."

"Don't use that word, dear. Did you tell Jane?"

"I wanted you."

She tucked the material into her pocket and went up the stairs toward him. She frowned at his obviously swollen jaw. He looked like one of the field mice that clung to the heads of corn, all wide eyes and chubby cheeks. "Let me see."

He reluctantly opened his mouth to disclose a small back tooth that was badly decayed and swollen around the gum.

"That does look painful. I suspect you'll have to have the tooth drawn. I'll take you to Dr. Baker first thing in the morning."

"Oh, goody, will there be blood?" Luke's twin, Michael, appeared beside her, his eyes bright with anticipation.

"There will not. Dr. Baker is very skilled. Come along, boys." She put an arm around both of them and steered them back to the nursery. "I'll get you some laudanum, Luke, so that you can at least get some sleep."

He pressed up against her, his small, strong body hot to the touch. "Thank you, Lucy. Will you stay with me until I fall asleep?"

"Of course, I will."

Lucy patted his tousled blond head and helped him into bed while Jane fetched the laudanum. After Luke was settled, she would take a moment to pen a note to Major Kurland and have it delivered first thing in the morning.

Chapter 16

Dr. Baker's house was at the opposite end of the village to the rectory, and quite a long walk. Despite Michael's strong objections, Lucy had left him with Jane, and taken Luke by himself. To her relief, the good doctor had not only been home, but dispensed with the tooth in a matter of seconds, leaving Luke sniveling and clutching a bloodied handkerchief to his cheek, but otherwise unharmed. Dr. Baker informed her that it had been a baby tooth, without much of a root. He told Luke to take better care of the new tooth that was pushing up underneath.

As they entered the high street, Lucy glanced down at the woebegone face beside her. "I have to speak to Mrs. Weeks at the bakery. Perhaps you might choose a cake to take home for your tea?"

"Just for me?"

"Well, it might be nice if you shared it with Michael."

He considered the enticing display in the steamed-up window. "It depends how big it is, doesn't it?"

Concealing a smile at his logic, Lucy pushed open the door and walked up to the counter. The smell of yeast and sugar billowed around her, and she realized it was early and the Weeks family was still baking.

"Can I help you, miss?"

"Yes, I wanted to talk to Mrs. Weeks about my father's . . ." Lucy stared at the apparition who had appeared from the back of the shop. *"Daisy?"*

The girl's mouth turned down at the corners. "Yes, Miss Harrington." She gestured at Luke, who had his face pressed against the glass separating the cakes from the buyers. "Does he want something?"

"I'd like a Chelsea bun, please," Luke said clearly. "That big one at the back because I have to share it with my brother."

Lucy waited as Daisy put the bun in a paper bag and handed it to Luke. She touched her brother's shoulder. "Do you want to start for home? Tell Anna I'll be there as soon as I can. If your face pains you, ask Jane to give you some more laudanum."

Luke happily departed clutching his bun, and Lucy turned to Daisy.

"When did you come back?"

"The day before yesterday."

"Was London not to your liking?"

She scowled. "It was horrible. The only work that was offered to me was in a brothel. I didn't want that. When my money ran out, I decided it was better to come home."

"A wise decision." Lucy paused. "Did Mary come back with you?"

A flush covered Daisy's cheeks. "Mary who?"

"Mary Smith, who was in service at the rectory. I understand that you planned to leave for London together."

"Mary changed her mind, miss. She was like that, always agreeing with everyone and then letting people down."

Lucy gripped her reticule so hard her fingers hurt. "Then where is she?"

"How should I know?"

"You're saying that she didn't come away with you?"

"She said she was coming, and then at the last minute, when I met her at the rectory, she said she couldn't go, that she'd rather stay here."

"Why?"

Daisy bit her lip. "She said she had some man trouble, an old flame and a new one. She was afraid of the first, and eager to marry the second. That's why she didn't come with me to London. She said she was going to meet William Bowden instead. I was right cross with her, miss. I wasn't counting on going to London all by myself."

"Did you see her with William?"

"No, we had a bit of a fight and I left her standing by the church. That's the last time I saw her face-to-face, like."

"She didn't meet William. He was left waiting in vain for her, too."

"Then where is she, miss?"

"I don't know. Will you come with me to Major Kurland and tell him what you've told me?"

"Why would you want me to do that?" Daisy glanced over her shoulder, her fingers pleating her apron. "I don't want any more trouble, my mam will kill me."

"I'll ask her if you can go with me, so that she knows that you are safe." Lucy gathered up her skirts. "Is she inside? May I come in and speak with her?"

Five minutes later, Lucy and Daisy were walking up the driveway of Kurland Hall. Lucy entered through the back door and sought out Foley.

"Is the major awake?"

"I believe so, Miss Harrington. He's in his study. He is expecting you."

"Can you take us to him?" She nodded at Daisy to follow her. "Is Mr. Bookman here?"

"No, he's out at his mother's this morning. There was a hole in her thatch roof that needed patching. The major gave him leave to attend to it."

"That was good of him." Lucy smiled reassuringly at Daisy, who was looking around rather apprehensively. "Thank you, Mr. Foley."

Major Kurland looked up as she entered. For the first time, he was formally dressed in a brown coat, cravat, and waistcoat.

"Good morning, Miss Harrington. Foley, would you bring us some refreshments? My aunt and Miss Chingford are out saying their good-byes to the local families. They won't be back for some time." He turned to Daisy. "And who is this?"

She dropped an awkward curtsy. "I'm Daisy Weeks, Major. How do you do?"

"Daisy *Weeks*?" He stared at Lucy. "But I thought Miss Weeks left for London with your Mary Smith."

"Apparently not." Lucy gestured for her companion to take a seat. "Daisy did go to London, but she had the good sense to see that she wasn't yet qualified to obtain the position she wanted, and she came home."

"But what about Mary?"

"She didn't go with her." Lucy held the major's appalled gaze. "She didn't go with William Bowden, either, so where is she?" She turned to Daisy. "Can you tell Major Kurland what happened the night you left?"

As Daisy continued her tale, Robert sat forward, his hands gripped in front of him on his blotter. "So when you met Mary at the church, she refused to come with you?"

"Aye. She said she was supposed to meet William, but that something bad had happened."

"Did she say what that was?"

"No, but she was shaking and pale. I thought she was

lying to get out of going with me, so I didn't give her much chance to explain things."

"And you didn't see her meet up with William Bowden, either?"

Daisy hesitated. "When I looked back along the path, I saw her with someone. I thought she'd been fibbing again, and it had to be William, but maybe I was wrong. He didn't look quite the same."

"You've met William before?"

"Yes, he's as tall as a haystack. We used to laugh at him when we were younger, but he grew into himself if you know what I mean."

"So it could've been another man."

"I suppose so. Maybe that was why she was scared. Maybe the other one was after her." She looked troubled. "Now I feel badly for not listening. I thought she was making things up."

"It's all right, Daisy. You had no way of knowing what was really going on."

"But I did know she was scared of John, sir. She'd hoped he wouldn't come back."

"John was the name of her former lover? Do you know his last name?"

"I don't remember it, sir. He was an older man, I think, about your age. She was only thirteen when he took up with her." She shivered.

"Did you meet him?"

"I'm not sure, sir. He was away with the army for many years and only recently came back home. Daisy tried to break things off with him in a letter before he came back, but from all accounts, he didn't take it very well. Maybe he was angry at her for finding another man."

Robert let out his breath. "You have been very helpful, Daisy. May I suggest that James, my footman, walk you home? Perhaps you might wait in the kitchen while I write a note for your parents."

Miss Harrington rang the bell and Robert wrote a short note to the Weeks family, asking them to keep Daisy safe inside for a few days. When James arrived, he handed the note to him, then told him to collect Miss Weeks from the kitchen and see her safely home. A reply to his note would also be appreciated.

Miss Harrington poured them both a cup of coffee from the pot Foley had brought in. "What do you think of her story?"

He lifted his gaze to hers. "John is Bookman's first name."

"What?" She put her cup down with a satisfying clatter. "What are you suggesting?"

He raked both his hands through his short hair. "It makes a horrible kind of sense. Bookman wrote to a sweetheart here for years. It's possible it was your Mary. She came here when she was twelve, didn't she? Who else could it be? How many other local men named John have recently returned from service in the army?"

"Probably quite a few."

"But the possibility that it is Bookman has to be high. He's been warning me off involving myself in your inquiries ever since you started them." He groaned. "He's also been in charge of administering laudanum to me! I'd begun to think I was going mad. . . ."

Miss Harrington patted his shoulder. "It's all right. I was beginning to think I was quite deranged, too." She took something out of her reticule. "I found this last night in our ragbag. That's why I wrote to you."

He studied the piece of cheap pink fabric. "What of it?"

"This is the same pattern as the fabric I saw stuck in the tomb." She paused. "It's a remnant from a dress Mary made for herself last summer. Her *best* dress. I suspect if I was running away thinking I'd be getting married, I'd wear my best gown, too."

"Good Lord. Did you tell your father about this?"

"No, I didn't think he'd believe me. I thought I'd ask you to use your powers of persuasion as the local magistrate to order him to open the DeVry tomb."

"That's certainly possible." Robert shook his head. "I still can't believe that Bookman would—"

"Kill someone? Major, you and he are trained to kill. What could be more natural?"

"You don't understand. It's different in a battle. I could no more murder anyone here than you could."

But Bookman could. The thought took over before he could stop it. His valet had always been prepared to kill.

"Before we open the tomb, I want to give him a chance to defend himself. We could be wrong."

"Major—"

He held up his hand. "Let me finish. You said it yourself: There are many ex-soldiers who have come back to these parts recently. And John is a common name."

"But what if he turns on you?"

"We've been friends all our lives. I doubt he'd do anything to hurt me."

"Apart from try and convince you that you are going mad, and are addicted to laudanum? For goodness' sake, Major, he tried to convince *me* that was the truth!"

"Then we must think of a way to get him to confess and then stop him either from running away or silencing me." He held her gaze. "I'm sure we can come up with something."

Lucy made her way out of Kurland Hall and cut across the lawn in front of Major Kurland's windows, heading for the shortcut beside the church. She had to admit the major's plan was straightforward, but provoking a man with the ability to kill so easily struck her as dangerous. Bookman was due back from his mother's house before dinner, and Major Kurland intended to confront him that very night.

She almost wished she could be there. But if word got out that she was loitering in an unmarried man's bedchamber after dark, her reputation would be ruined, and poor Major Kurland might be obliged to offer for her. It was probably better if she stayed at home and waited for Foley to come down in the morning and tell her what had happened. She heaved a sigh. It was, however, frustrating not to be involved. She stepped into the shadow of the church tower and immediately felt chilled. After a quick glance along the path, she squeezed through the narrow gap between the wall and the cornerstone and started toward the welcoming lights of the rectory.

Fingers closed around her upper arm and yanked her backward, slamming her hard against the stone. Before she could do more than squeak, her mouth was covered with a large hand.

"I told you to leave the major alone."

She stared into Bookman's cold brown eyes and swallowed hard.

"What did you find that made you write to him this morning?" His hand tightened on her arm. "Didn't you know that I read all the major's correspondence? Especially letters from interfering women. Tell me what you found."

He removed his hand from her mouth and wrapped it around her neck. She stared at him, refusing to drop her gaze or give in to the fear. His fingers tightened, and she suddenly couldn't breathe.

"Tell me."

"That Daisy Weeks had returned," she choked out.

"And why did you think he needed to know that?"

"Because I thought she'd gone to London."

He stared at her and then slapped her cheek. "Don't lie to me."

She tasted her own blood where she'd inadvertently bitten her lip. "It's the truth. I wanted to know if Daisy had seen Mary in London."

Would that be enough to keep him from killing her, or ruining Major Kurland's attempts to extract a confession from him?

"And had she?"

Lucy shook her head.

"I know where she is. Do you want to see?" Bookman smiled and she wanted to vomit. "Come with me."

He pulled her along with him, her arm twisted up against her spine, his hand again over her mouth, and headed for the graveyard. When they arrived at the DeVry tomb, he pushed her down onto her knees, and she saw the gleam of a knife. She jerked away from him, but he only pulled at her skirts and cut off a swath of fabric.

While his attention was momentarily distracted, she tried to crawl away, but he'd planted his boot firmly on the rest of her skirts and she couldn't move.

"You did me something of a favor with all your poking around. I didn't realize the tomb wasn't secure and thanks to you, I was able to fix that." He bound her hands together and then gagged her. "Can't have you screaming, can we? Don't want anyone to hear."

He was smiling as he retrieved a crowbar from the bushes and set to levering open the door of the tomb. "It's a shame that you didn't use that intelligence in a different way, Miss Harrington. Like all women, you just had to keep meddling. But no more."

The door of the tomb yawned open, and she smelled the sweet awfulness of decay. In the gloom, she could just make out a hint of a pink skirt and pale pearlescent skin. Bookman grabbed her around the waist, and she started to shake her head and kick out but he was far too strong. She screamed behind her gag as he tossed her into the tomb and she scrambled to get up, to turn around to—

The vault door closed behind her with a grating rumble, and she was left alone in complete darkness. She slammed her bound hands against the door, but it was useless, the stone was immovable. With a sob, she rested her forehead against the unforgiving stone and tried to quiet her frantic breathing. She had to get the gag off, or she would faint.

Luckily, he'd tied her hands in front of her, so she was able to use them against the material of the gag and force it down inch by painful inch. Her breath exploded outward as her mouth was suddenly freed. She turned around until her back was aligned with the door of the tomb and she faced inward. It was so dark that she could see almost nothing, only the dark shapes of shelves with coffins on them. She reached out until her bound hands brushed cotton and she instantly recoiled.

Mary was here. Her choices cut short by a man who had refused to allow her to love another. What had driven Bookman to kill his longtime sweetheart? What would it take for him to turn on his longtime employer, as well?

Lucy settled down to endure. If Major Kurland managed to convince Bookman to confess, perhaps she would be rescued. If Bookman outwitted the major and managed to get away, her chances of being found were almost nonexistent. Coldness seeped through her thin gown and she started to shiver. This might be her final resting place. With all her strength, she closed her eyes and began to pray.

Robert folded the newspaper and took off his reading spectacles. "Has Foley gone to bed, Bookman?"

"I believe so, sir. Why, do you want something?"

"Not particularly. I just haven't seen him for a while." The old clock on the mantelpiece struck eleven times and then wheezed to a halt. "I suppose he might have been helping Miss Chingford and my aunt to pack. They are due to leave tomorrow."

"Is Mrs. Armitage coming back?" Bookman looked up from tidying Robert's linen.

"I believe she is. Her intention is to restore Miss Chingford to her parents, attempt to deflect their concerns about their daughter's future, and return to spend a few weeks with me."

"I'm glad she's returning, sir. She's a treasure."

"Indeed, she is." Robert contemplated his folded newspaper. "I wonder what will happen to Miss Chingford now?"

"No doubt she'll take up with some new man as soon as she can find one." Bookman slammed the drawer shut.

"Is that what happened to you?"

"What do you mean, sir?"

"You seem disenchanted with the fairer sex, Bookman. Did your sweetheart find another man too quickly?"

Bookman turned slowly around and leaned against the chest of drawers. "What makes you think that?"

"As I said, you seem bitter."

"Women are faithless, lying creatures who rip out a man's soul and trample it in the dirt while they laugh and move on to another. I thought my girl loved me. I cherished her letters, read them and reread them until they were nigh worn through."

"I remember," Robert said gently.

"And what did she do when I returned to claim her?" Bookman slapped his hand down on the wooden surface, making the sideboard rock. "She swore she'd written to say all was finished between us. She said I'd changed, I was too hard, and that I frightened her. What she really meant was that she'd taken up with another man."

"And what did you do about that?" Robert tensed as his valet sauntered over to the bed.

"What did I do? What do we do to traitors in the army, Major? We teach them a lesson."

"But she was a young girl."

Bookman shrugged. "So? Shouldn't she be held to the same standards of loyalty and decency as the rest of us?"

"Not if she isn't a soldier."

"She was my woman. She betrayed me. I had a right to demand justice."

Robert held his gaze. "And what exactly did that entail?"

"Why does it matter to you? You've killed with the best of them and never asked questions."

"In a theater of war, yes, but not here in Kurland St. Mary. I repeat, what did you do?"

Bookman's smile was chilling. "I think you know, Major. That bloody Miss Harrington must've told you more than I realized."

A stab of unease caught Robert in the gut. "What's this got to do with Miss Harrington?"

"Oh, come on, Major, do you think I was born yesterday? She's the one who's been getting you to poke your nose in where it's not wanted. If it weren't for her, you wouldn't be asking all these questions. You'd just let things lie."

"Why would you think that?"

Bookman's contemptuous gaze swept over him. "Because you've become a coward lying here, letting me and Foley take care of you. You've shown no interest in anything."

"I'm interested now. I certainly cannot allow you to impose military rules on my village. When did you last see Miss Harrington?"

"What does it matter? She's not going to come telling tales to you tonight, I can assure you of that."

Robert slid one hand beneath the covers. Despite his growing concern for Miss Harrington, he had to carry through with his plan.

"Where is Mary Smith?"

"She's safe enough." He grabbed hold of the bedpost

and looked down at Robert. "Major, it's me, Bookman, the man who saved your life on more than one occasion. What do you care about one stupid servant girl?"

"I care that you might have harmed an innocent."

"She wasn't innocent. She was a lying, faithless slut."

"Who had the decency to write to you to say she had a change of heart. Who expected you to respect her decision and not destroy her for wanting another man? I cannot condone such behavior, Bookman."

Bookman smiled and brought the laudanum bottle out of his pocket. "You disappoint me, Major. Where's your much-vaunted loyalty to me? Why shouldn't Mary feel a little of the pain I've endured being shot at, bayoneted, and stabbed? She told me she was going to marry another man. Why should I have to come home to *nothing*?"

"We've all endured such things. It doesn't give us the right to inflict them on innocent civilians."

"Why not? We inflicted them on the damned French! We slaughtered innocents by the hundreds over there, and you damn well know it!" Bookman was sweating, his skin pale, his nightmarish gaze back in the past with the horrors he'd endured. "I fought for the likes of her to live a peaceful life, and she betrayed me."

"So you killed her."

"Damn right I did, Major. Strangled her with my bare hands." Bookman stared at him. "And I'd do it again if I had to."

Robert studied his longtime friend and valet, and it was like looking at a stranger. He'd seen it before. Some soldiers never came home from the terrors of war; they could never settle down in peace.

"Bookman, I can't let you get away with this, but I swear I will stand by you. I'll note your exemplary war record, your mentions in dispatches, your—"

"You'll do no such thing, Major." Bookman studied the black glass bottle. "You'll drink this down like a good boy, and you'll go to sleep and never wake up. No one will be surprised. I've told enough stories about how worried I am about your addiction to the stuff."

He uncorked the bottle and stared down at it. "I'll be mortified when I realize how you took advantage of me and swiped the bottle when my back was turned." He chuckled. "Not mortified enough not to accept the pension your aunt will surely give me, though. Now come on, sir, lie back and let me settle you to sleep. What do you have to live for anyway? You're unlikely to walk again, you're scared of your own shadow, and no woman in her right mind would want to marry a bad-tempered cripple like you."

He put a hand on Robert's shoulder and Robert pushed aside the sheet to expose the gun he held in his hand.

"Step back, Bookman."

His valet laughed. "You think you've got the nerve to shoot me, sir? How many times have I had to save your neck when you were too scared to pull the trigger?" He held up the bottle. "Now come on, sir, lie back."

Chaos erupted as Robert fired and James and Foley ran from the corridor to secure a cursing and bleeding Bookman, his hand clasped to his shoulder.

"Nicely done, Major," Foley puffed, as Bookman slid to the floor in a dead faint. "Enough to incapacitate him, but not kill him outright."

Robert put his smoking pistol on the nightstand. "That's the thing Bookman never understood. You can stop a man quite adequately without killing him."

His insides were churning at the smells of blood and powder mingled, and he swallowed hard. Violent death wasn't meant to happen in the quiet of a man's bedchamber. It defiled him somehow.

"Tie him up, James, and put him in the storage cellar. Send for Dr. Baker and the village constable."

"Yes, sir."

James hoisted Bookman over his shoulder and took him out, leaving Robert and Foley staring at each other. Foley mopped his brow and picked up the fallen bottle of laudanum.

"That was a very close thing, sir. A very close thing indeed."

Robert slowly exhaled. "Get Joseph Cobbins and go down with him to the rectory as fast as you can. Rouse the Reverend Harrington and tell him if he wants to save his daughter, he needs to open the DeVry tomb immediately."

"The tomb, sir? Are you quite sure?"

"Yes, Foley. I've stopped taking laudanum, remember? Go quickly, her life might depend on it."

Were there mice in the tomb? Lucy wiggled her frozen toes and contemplated the faint scratching sounds. She didn't dare contemplate what else the noise could be. It sounded far too like fingernails scraping on the stone, and if it wasn't her fingernails, whose were they? Her teeth started to chatter and she firmly clenched her jaw. At least her lip had stopped bleeding in the freezing cold.

No wonder the gentry built icehouses that looked like mausoleums. This tomb would do a fine job of keeping the coldest of desserts frozen. She tried to ease her wrist in the tight binding, but couldn't slip it free. How long had she been there? It felt like hours, but she had no sense of time at all. She turned her wrist again, glad that she was wearing gloves against the chill.

For goodness' sake, she had *gloves* on. With a squeak of annoyance, she drew her hands up to her mouth and nibbled on the button closure of her glove. If she could loosen that, surely she could get at least one hand free? It seemed to take forever, her chattering teeth slipping and jarring against the unforgiving metal fastening. Eventually she eased it free, and holding her hands between her upright knees, she pulled her fingers free of the tight kid glove and the restraint of the binding around her wrists.

Now at least she could use her fingers to feel around the edge of the door and see if there were any weaknesses or cracks. She turned and her cramped legs folded under her, bringing her down hard on the floor. She managed to catch herself on her hands and knees and stayed there for a moment to regain her breath. It took her a moment to straighten her back, and reach for a handhold on the shelves that bordered both sides of the crypt. Her fingers brushed frozen flesh and she paused.

In the darkness, there was no way of guessing exactly what she'd touched, but the fact that the body wasn't entombed in a coffin, indicated it was a very unusual burial. With great care she traced a freezing cold hand, arm, and shoulder, shuddered as fine hair entangled her fingers like a spider's web. It was definitely a woman and she was quite dead.

Lucy said a quiet prayer over the body and then sank back down again. No one was going to come. She was going to die here alone and without the benefit of a proper burial from her loved ones. She felt like crying, but she had a strong suspicion that her tears would freeze on her cheeks like hail in a winter storm. The cold made it hard to think. She wanted to close her eyes, go to sleep, and forget everything. Would anyone even miss her? How foolish of her to worry about going to London next year when she should simply have told her father about the invitation and left him to deal with his cook by himself. How petty her concerns seemed now . . .

She closed her eyes and rested her head against one of the shelves. Once she'd had a sleep, she'd think of something to help her escape. She just knew she would.

The sudden blast of fresh air and the flickering torches made her shield her eyes and cower away. Had Bookman come back to kill her? If he had, she wasn't sure she had any strength left to stop him.

"Miss Harrington!"

She stared bemused up into Foley's familiar face. He turned and shouted something she couldn't comprehend. Suddenly, Anthony and Harris were there, lifting her out of the tomb and carrying her back to the rectory. She managed to tug on Anthony's sleeve.

"There's someone else in there. Don't leave her."

"It's all right. We know. We'll take care of Mary, don't you worry. Now come inside and let Anna get you to bed."

Chapter 17

Robert stared impatiently at the clock on the mantel-piece and then back at the door. Where *was* she? Was it too much to ask for a woman to be punctual?

Foley knocked and came in, a smile on his face. "Miss Harrington is here, Major. Shall I show her in?"

"She knows the way, Foley. Go and make yourself useful and fetch some tea."

"Yes, Major." Foley stepped aside to reveal Miss Harrington hovering at the doorway.

Robert beckoned to her impatiently. "Come in."

"There's no need to bark at me. I'm coming as fast as I can."

His gaze fastened on her face. "Good Lord. What did Bookman do to you? Take off your bonnet so I can have a proper look at you."

She halted in front of him, her chin raised. "Major, may I remind you that I am neither your chattel nor under your command? I shall remove my bonnet when I choose to." She continued to glare at him as she untied the ribbons and placed the bonnet on the couch beside her. "There, are you satisfied now?"

Robert sucked in a breath. "He hurt you. If I'd known that, I'd have shot him right through his black heart."

She took the seat opposite him and patted the immaculate braids of her hair coiled like a coronet on top of her head. "You did the right thing, Major. You ensured he will come to trial." She hesitated. "That must have been difficult for you."

"It was, but I've come to realize that Bookman hadn't settled into civilian life very well at all. He was still haunted by what had happened on the continent, and was unable to control his violent impulses. It's not uncommon for a soldier to find the transition difficult. Most of us come to terms with it eventually. I don't think Bookman ever could."

He sighed, "And of course, Mary's 'betrayal' gave him the perfect outlet for that violence. He considered it justice for her behavior. When he found out she was planning to marry, his rage exploded. He must have confronted her, strangled her, and left her body in the tomb."

"Which would explain what you thought you saw that night."

"And why Bookman didn't answer my calls for help after I'd fallen on the floor." He grimaced. "I suppose there is some satisfaction in the fact that I am not going mad, even if it does come at some considerable expense."

"If you hadn't seen him, we might never have found out what happened to Mary."

"That's true. The worst of it was that Bookman seemed to think I'd side with him in the matter. I tried to tell him it wasn't the same as killing in a battle, but he decided I was being equally disloyal and deserved to die, too."

"Foley told me what happened." She shivered. "How horrible for you."

"In the end, it was quite simple. I couldn't allow him to get away with murder in Kurland St. Mary."

She nodded and glanced down at her folded hands. "Will he hang?"

"I should imagine so. I did write to the judge and plead for leniency and transportation instead. The mood in the country isn't kind to returned soldiers at present, so I'm not sure if it will have any effect."

"At least you tried."

"Yes. And how have you been faring, Miss Harrington? Being shut up in a tomb with a corpse would be enough to shake even the strongest constitution."

"I can't say it was an experience I would care to repeat. I was so glad to be rescued I've tried to forget about it."

He noted the dark shadows under her eyes. "I suspect you are having nightmares, though."

"I am." She shook her head. "I've lived such a quiet life that being hit on the head and tossed into a tomb are almost fantastical experiences. I find it hard to reconcile them with my current existence."

"In my experience, Miss Harrington, the nightmares will eventually cease and you will be able to put the whole episode behind you."

"I hope so." She looked up, her brown eyes bright with determination. "But it did make me think about my future. When I was trapped in the vault I realized how petty my concerns were, and how I had to stop living my life for everyone else."

"I've had many a similar revelation on the eve of a battle. It can be enlightening." He smiled at her. "What do you plan to do? Escape to Egypt on a camel?"

"Oh, wouldn't that be wonderful? I was thinking more about leaving the rectory for a visit to London."

Foley entered with the tea tray, and Miss Harrington spent a moment pouring them both a cup. She brought his over to him.

"Why on earth would you want to visit London?"

He wondered if he sounded as petulant as he felt. She

put his cup down by his elbow. "Because I haven't been there since I was a child and I've always dreamed of having a Season there."

"But why would you want to do that?"

"Because I want to find a husband and not always be the daughter at home."

He considered that. "I still don't understand why you need to go to London. There are plenty of men looking for wives around here."

"And they all look at my sister Anna."

"She is rather beautiful."

"I know." With a twitch of her skirts, she went to move away from him. He caught her hand.

"I haven't thanked you for everything you've done for me yet."

"Oh, for goodness' sake, it was nothing." He was amused to see she was blushing.

"It was far more than that. In his way, Bookman was right. You forced me to open my eyes, and pay attention to what was going on around me."

"More fool me." She gently tried to ease out of his grip, but he held on. "I should have left you lying there in your bed in great state and saved myself an adventure."

He smiled. "Come now, Miss Harrington. You must have enjoyed some of it. Deciphering clues, getting rid of my fiancée, matching your wits against a killer?"

"Some of it was quite interesting." She paused. "Miss Chingford is no longer engaged to you?"

He nodded. She glared down rather pointedly at her hand. "Now will you let me go?"

He brought her hand to his lips and kissed it. "Thank you, Miss Harrington. Thank you for everything. Perhaps you might consider staying in Kurland St. Mary for my sake."

She wrenched her hand free and stepped away from him. "What on earth do you mean?"

"I was rather hoping you'd take on the position of my secretary."

"Your *secretary?* You—"

She twirled around, picked up her bonnet, and headed for the door. Foley, who was coming the other way with a plate of scones, just managed to step out of the way. He frowned at Robert.

"What did you say to set Miss Harrington all a flutter?"

"I have absolutely no idea."

He picked up his tea and finished the cup before asking Foley to pour him another. He had a lot to do. A new valet to find, an estate manager and, judging from Miss Harrington's reaction to his proposal, a new secretary, too.

His proposal . . .

What on earth had she been expecting him to say? He recalled the look of absolute horror on her face. For the first time in months, Robert found himself laughing out loud.